VIGILANTE

Also by Kady Cross
and Harlequin TEEN:

Sisters of Blood and Spirit (in reading order):

Sisters of Blood and Spirit
Sisters of Salt and Iron

The Steampunk Chronicles (in reading order):

The Strange Case of Finley Jayne (ebook prequel)
The Girl in the Steel Corset
The Girl in the Clockwork Collar
The Dark Discovery of Jack Dandy (ebook novella)
The Girl with the Iron Touch
The Wild Adventure of Jasper Renn (ebook novella)
The Girl with the Windup Heart

H HARLEQUIN®TEEN

VIGILANTE

JUSTICE. REVENGE. SAME
REVENGE. JUSTIC
SAME THING, RIGHT? JUSTI
RIGHT? JUS
KADY CROSS

ISBN-13: 978-0-373-21177-7

Vigilante

This book is dedicated to all the girls who have survived.
You are strength incarnate, and I hope you continue to heal, grow and thrive.

Also, this book is for Amy Lukavics and Gena Showalter, my signing sisters.
Love and miss you both so much! I will always treasure
that drive from Houston to Austin where our friendship took root.
The two of you are shining examples of light, beauty and strength,
and I'm honored to call you my friends.

And for Steve, because they're all for you, babe.

CHAPTER 1

Before

Someone had written *slut* on Magda's locker again. I watched her try to scrape it off with the zipper of her makeup bag.

Last time she'd cried, but there weren't any tears in her dark eyes this time, and instead of being flushed, her cheeks were actually pale. They were getting to her, I realized. Wearing her down.

I pulled a Sharpie from my bag, walked up beside her and changed the *u* to an *a* and added an *e* at the end.

"Slate?" she asked.

"Sure," I said, my mind frantically reaching for an explanation that might please her. "As in clean."

Her face darkened. "I'm not the one who got a clean slate. They did." But she didn't go back to scraping.

I didn't know what to do. It seemed like I couldn't do anything right lately. I hadn't since the night my best friend was raped and images of it uploaded to the internet. Besides me, and Magda's family, no one really seemed to believe she'd been raped at all. In fact, the boys who did it said she'd wanted to have sex with all four of them, and the entire school believed them, even though Magda hadn't so much as gone out on a date with a guy before that night. It was easier to believe a teenage girl would want her first time to be with multiple partners than it was to believe four popular boys were capable of rape.

I looked at my friend; her expression was blank. The fact that Magda didn't look too upset was good, right? At least, I thought it was. I'd never say anything to her, but I'd been starting to get impatient with her. I knew what happened to her had been terrible—but they hadn't hurt her so badly that she hadn't healed properly. She'd survived what they'd done. No, it wasn't fair that they got to walk around free while people called her a slut, but when was she going to start defending herself? I kept waiting for her to get mad—maybe punch somebody. Tell them off. But she didn't—she just took what they said and tucked it away inside herself. She hardly smiled anymore, and I was so tired of it. I just wanted my friend back—and I had no idea how to make that happen.

We walked home together, like we always did. It was a gorgeous spring day—sunny and warm. A block from Magda's house, a car pulled up beside us. In it were three boys from the senior class.

"Hey, Magda," one said, leaning out the passenger window. "We're having a party this weekend. Want to come? We need entertainment."

Her face turned scarlet, but she didn't say anything. Why didn't she tell them off?

"Fuck off," I said to them, putting myself between her and them. "Just fuck off."

He grinned at me. "You can come too, baby. No need to get jealous. There's enough of us to go around."

I had a can of grape soda in my hand, and before I could think about it, I'd dumped what was left over his stupid head. It ran down his surprised face in purple rivers, staining his white shirt. His friends stared at me, mouths hanging open.

"You stupid bitch!" he cried. He started to open his door, but I kicked it shut, and held it like that with the strength of my leg. I didn't know what I was going to do if the other two decided to get involved.

"Cops!" the one in the back shouted. I turned my head and saw the cruiser approaching. The car took off so fast I fell on my ass. Shit. It hurt.

By the time the police car pulled up, Magda had already helped me to my feet. I recognized the woman behind the wheel as Diane Davies. She'd worked Magda's case before it became a joke.

"You girls okay?" she asked, but she was looking at Magda.

"Yeah," my friend said. "We're fine, Detective Davies. Thanks."

The cop didn't look like she believed us. "You want a lift home?"

Magda shook her head.

"Okay, then. Be careful." She didn't look happy about leaving us, but short of forcing Magda into the car, what could she do?

We watched her drive away before we started walking again.

"You don't always have to defend me." Magda sounded

pissed. "They would have driven away. You didn't need to start a fight."

"Yes, I did. Those pricks deserved it. You shouldn't have to keep paying for a stupid mistake."

Magda stopped suddenly, under the shade of a huge tree. "What mistake?"

I stared at her. Was she medicated? "Going off with Drew Carson at that party."

"You've never gone off with a guy before?"

She knew I had. "You know what I mean. You just picked the wrong guy."

"Was I supposed to know that?" Her voice had gotten louder, and her eyes were wide as she looked at me. "And I didn't pick him, he picked me, but that doesn't matter, because I thought he liked me. I never thought his friends would be waiting for us. I never wanted that, Hadley. And that wasn't my fault!"

"Calm down." I'd never seen her like this before. "I didn't mean it was your fault."

"Yeah, you did. Just like everyone else in this shit-hole town. I haven't heard anyone ask Drew, Brody, Jason or Adam why they raped me, but everyone has questions for me. Why did you wear that skirt? Why did you go with Drew? Why didn't you scream louder? What did you expect to happen? Here's a question for you, Had—why don't you just fuck off?"

She ran away from me then, leaving me standing on the sidewalk like an asshole, staring after her in openmouthed shock. What the hell? I hadn't meant to upset her. I was on her side for crying out loud!

I continued walking home. I could have gone to her house, but I didn't want to fight, and she needed time to cool off. And so did I. After all I'd done, all the times I'd defended her, this was what I got in return? If she thought I appreciated being lumped in with the rest of the people who blamed her, she was stupid and wrong. I'd believed her when no one else would.

Yes, it had been stupid of her to go off with Drew. Most of us knew he was a dog, but he and his friends had never done anything like that before. They were all from fairly decent families, and were good-looking. They didn't need to rape in order to get sex. But Magda wouldn't lie. I'd seen her afterward, and I knew something horrible had happened. I wished I had been able to stop it.

My parents weren't home when I got there. Mom was still at work, and Dad was away on business. I heard them fight once in a while. They didn't know I knew, but our house wasn't that big.

I did my homework and helped Mom with dinner when she came home. Then I walked over to Magda's to apologize and talk. Her older brother Gabriel answered the door. He smiled when he saw me, and my heart did this little flip in my chest. When had he gotten so hot? Those dark eyes of his and long dark hair killed me—made me feel like I couldn't think straight.

"Hi, Had. Mags is in her room. She's been listening to some sad-bastard music. Maybe you can cheer her up."

I smiled, my insides still dancing around like lunatics. "I'll try."

His gaze narrowed. "Everything okay with you two?"

"We had a bit of a fight earlier. I said something stupid." I looked him in the eye. "Sometimes I don't know the right thing to say to her."

He nodded, his expression somber. "None of us do." Then he hugged me, and I let myself enjoy it a little longer than I should.

When I knocked on Magda's door, she didn't say anything. She probably couldn't hear me over the music. I turned the knob and pushed the door open. She was going to scream when she saw me—she scared so freaking easy.

She was on her bed. For a moment, I thought she was sleeping—and then I saw the pill bottle, and I realized she wasn't breathing.

CHAPTER 2

Magda and I were supposed to go into senior year together, but on the first day of school, I was alone and Mags was dead.

I arrived ten minutes before the bell for homeroom. It was a nice day, warm and sunny, and there were kids all over the front lawn of Carter High School. A year ago, Magda and I had been among them, excited to be back, but dreading the daily grind.

I walked up the concrete path to the main doors and walked inside. The halls teemed with kids—tall, short, fat, skinny, nervous or bored. There was every hair and skin color imaginable represented. I saw a girl with pink hair, a guy with a mohawk and a kid with a septum piercing clustered together, talking animatedly by a classroom. The three of them would probably get hassled at some point during that day. Would anyone stand up for them?

No one had stood up for Magda. No one but Magda's brother Gabriel and me. I hadn't always been the friend I should have been to her. I hadn't understood what she was going through. I had to live with that—and without my best friend.

There was a shadow box on the wall by the principal's office that had photos of kids who had been killed during the school year. They'd started it back in the eighties. There were a lot of pictures in it. Magda's wasn't there. They justified her exclusion by calling it a suicide. But Magda's life had been over months before she took those pills. She'd been murdered, and her killers had been allowed to walk free. Their names were even protected by the press because they were underage. We were all going to be under the same roof that day, the four of them and me. It seemed more ominous after a summer of missing Magda, like her absence had intensified the gravity of what they'd done.

I looked for them as I roamed the halls, but I didn't see them. They traveled as a pack, usually followed by sycophants and foolish girls who believed that cute boys couldn't possibly be monsters. I hoped none of those girls discovered how wrong they were.

Gabriel had graduated last year, and would be starting classes at a local college in a couple of days. I missed having him with me. After Magda died, the two of us had become each other's support—it was the only way we could get through the day at school. We kept each other from falling apart, and when the charges against Magda's rapists were dropped, we raged and cried together.

"Hadley?"

I turned at the sound of the familiar voice. Standing beside a row of lockers was Zoe Kotler, who I'd known since first grade. We weren't close friends, but we'd hung out a bit over the years. I remember she cried at Magda's funeral, something I hadn't been able to do.

"Hey, Zoe." A guy wearing a huge backpack practically hip checked me into the wall.

"Watch it," I snarled.

He shot me a dirty look. "Fuck you."

There were meaner things he could've said. By the time you get to senior year the F word has lost much of its gravity and ability to offend. It's almost a regular part of the lexicon of teenage language, like texting, or soda.

I watched him walk away. Normally I would've had a good comeback, but I couldn't summon one. What I wanted to do was kick him in the back of his stupid head. I could do it.

Zoe scowled after him. "Douche," she said to his retreating back.

I shrugged. "The school's full of them."

She laughed. "You've got that right." When I met her gaze, I saw concern and wariness in her brown eyes, like I was a wounded animal she wanted to pet but was afraid would take her hand off if she did.

"I know this might sound weird, but a few of us have started a petition." She pulled a stapled stack of paper from her binder and handed it to me. I looked at the pages; the petition was to have Magda's picture added to the shadow box.

I stared at all the signatures. There had to be at least forty there already.

"It's not fair that she's not there," Zoe said. "Three other people whose pictures are there died the same way."

I looked at her, tempted to ask if those people had been

raped, but I knew that wasn't what she meant. She meant they'd killed themselves. "Do you have a pen?" I asked.

She smiled and handed me the pen she had clipped to her binder. I signed my name.

"I miss her, you know?"

I handed the petition and pen back to her. I wanted to tell her that she knew nothing. That she was a stupid cow who had no idea what it was like to lose your best friend, someone you knew so well they felt like a part of you. Wanted to tell her she should be glad that she had never seen someone she loved suffer like Magda had. I wanted to tell her that I hoped she never walked into a friend's room and found them on their bed after they'd taken a handful of sleeping pills—enough to kill them, but not enough to do it quickly.

I remembered holding Magda in my arms, screaming for help. My brain latched on to that memory of her, so pale and unresponsive, and rolled it around in my head until my lungs felt as though they were being squeezed by a giant hand, each breath more strangled and difficult than the last.

Mostly, I hoped Zoe never knew what it was like to feel responsible, to know that the last thing you'd said to your best friend had broken her heart and her spirit. I'd let Magda feel alone, and she'd killed herself.

"Yeah," I rasped. "I know. I have to go." I pivoted on my heel and walked away as fast as I could without running. I dived into the nearest girls' bathroom and ducked into a stall. I closed the door and locked it before pressing my forehead against the cool metal.

I breathed in through my nose, out through my mouth until the panic faded. My mother thought I had PTSD. Maybe I did, but calling it that felt like I was trying to excuse my grief. It felt like a lie. Because what I had was not a disorder, but a sadness that ran so deep I could feel it in my bones. Sometimes I felt like Magda had taken my own life with hers that day.

I tried to push thoughts of her away. My parents and my therapist had been concerned about how returning to school would affect me. I thought they were the crazy ones, but it seemed they understood me better than I did. I should have taken a Xanax before I left the house. At least that would have taken the edge off.

The bell rang. I made my way to the auditorium with the rest of the throng. Magda and I always sat as far back as we could. I couldn't bring myself to climb the stairs to the back of the room, so I sat four rows back from the front. The seat to my right remained empty as the auditorium filled up. I could almost pretend my friend was there beside me.

They divided freshmen into their classes first, calling out names and then telling them where their classroom was located. Next was the sophomores, then the juniors and finally the seniors.

I sat there, numb and disinterested, until four familiar names were called: Jason Bentley, Drew Carson, Brody Henry and Adam Weeks. People actually cheered them. Those raised voices set my teeth on edge. Then, the universe decided to be cruel.

"Hadley White."

No one cheered for me or applauded. I doubted many of them even knew who I was. It didn't make me feel any better, though. Because I had been Magda's best friend, and those four boys had destroyed her. They should know who I was, but they didn't. I could probably walk right up to all four of them and spit in their faces, and they would have no idea why I had done it.

My name was the last one called for that class. I stood up with the others and filed out of the auditorium. Like all the other sheep, I followed the four of them to our homeroom class. I was the only one who didn't seem to want their attention.

I was probably also the only one who wanted to kill them all.

Last Year

"I don't understand what you see in him," I said as Magda and I walked to our lockers. It was only the second week of school, and she couldn't stop staring at Drew Carson. "He creeps me out."

She frowned at me. She looked like an angry deer, her dark eyes were so big. "I think he's cute. He grinned at me in class this morning."

"That's not a grin, it's a leer." We stopped at my locker, and I turned the dial on the combination lock. "Seriously, I've heard stories about him, Mags. He's not a good guy."

"Take a pill. It's not like I want to marry him." Her eyes sparkled now. "I just want to see if he's as good a kisser as I think he is."

I grimaced. Gross. There was only one way to stop this conversation. "You know who *I* think would be a great kisser?"

She leaned forward, eagerly, as though I was about to tell her the secrets of the universe. "Who?"

"Your brother."

"Ugh!" She looked like she'd bit into something rotten. "Don't even go there!"

I laughed as I grabbed my books. "But he's so pretty, and his lips look like they'd be really soft, y'know? But firm." I'd never admit that I wasn't joking with her. My crush on Gabriel was my little secret.

"Stop it! Okay, fine, you win. Let's talk about something else. Are you still sleeping over Saturday night?"

"Sure." I shut the locker door and we walked the short distance to hers. "Are you going to cancel on me if you get a better offer? 'Cause I can always just hang out with Gabe if you have other plans."

She rolled her wide, dark eyes. She was so pretty. "Please. Like I'd ever choose a guy over my best friend."

I grinned. "Nothing will ever come between us. Ever."

I was wrong.

I had only one class that none of them were in. AP English literature and composition would be my refuge. I was tempted to see if I could transfer out of some of the other classes, but then someone might want to know why.

If Mags hadn't died, she would be right there with me. She'd spent months in the same classroom with those assholes after they hurt and humiliated her. She suffered through it until she couldn't anymore. Changing classes would seem like an insult to her memory. Besides, there was part of me that liked sitting a few seats behind Drew Carson, staring at his back as rage bubbled inside me. Maybe it was the fact that I felt *something* that made me like it, or maybe I was just broken.

Jason Bentley sat next to me. I started to shake so bad I

could barely hold my pen. I picked up my stuff and moved two rows over. There was no way I could spend the rest of the year next to him.

After my last class I went to my locker, gathered up what I needed and left. How was I going to do this for the next eight months? One day had felt like a year.

Halfway home I heard someone shout, "Hey!" behind me. When they did it again, I realized they were talking to me. I stopped and turned around.

It was Jason.

I wanted to run—away from him and *at* him. Every instinct I had screamed for me to escape while my heart urged me to pick up a rock and throw it at his face. Instead, I just stood there, unable to tell if it was defiance or stupidity that kept me still.

He approached me with a confused and wary look on his face, sort of like the one Zoe had worn that morning. "Hey," he said. "You're Hadley, right?"

I just stared, unable to speak for fear that all that would come out of my mouth was a scream, not of fear, but something primal and filled with rage. God, was I having a heart attack? My chest was so tight.

At one time—before he and his friends ruined my best friend—I'd found him cute. He was smart too, and out of the four he was the only one who ever paid any attention to me. Whenever Magda was around, I was always surprised when a boy looked at me. I wasn't ugly—in fact I've always thought of myself as passably pretty—but Magda was gorgeous, and she'd had no idea just how beautiful she was.

"Can I ask you something?" he asked.

I continued to stare.

"Why did you move when I sat next to you in class today?"

Did he really have to ask? Yes, apparently he did, because there didn't seem to be any malice in his tone or expression at all. He truly had no idea why I despised him.

"Magda Torres was my best friend," I whispered, staring into those blue eyes. Disgust rolled in my stomach, rose in the back of my throat until I thought I might puke. Hate was a vile-tasting thing I wanted to spit onto his expensive sneakers.

Jason's eyes widened as the color drained from his face. He took a step backward. "Oh."

I took a step toward him, unwilling to allow him to escape so quickly. My chest wasn't so tight now. Instead, it burned with rage. "Is that all you have to say?" I smiled, but it felt more like a twisting of my lips. I mean, he'd followed me all this way. It wasn't just to ask me why I moved, was it?

What was I doing? He was bigger than me, and even though I'd been taking martial arts ever since I was a kid, I'd never actually fought someone outside the dojo.

He held up his hands. "I don't want any trouble."

"No, and you didn't get any, did you?" I glared at him, took another step forward. "You didn't even go to trial. How does it feel to have gotten away with it? Did you and your buddies celebrate when she killed herself?"

Jason looked horrified. Good. He just stared at me, shaking his head.

A car pulled up beside us. Drew Carson was driving, and Brody was in the passenger seat. Adam was in the back. For a second I was terrified that they were going to throw me in the car, take me somewhere secluded, and do to me what they'd done to my friend.

Brody's window came down. "Dude, we've been looking for you. Get in."

I didn't look at them. I couldn't. I was already shaking so badly my teeth chattered. If I looked at them, they'd see my fear. They'd see my rage. And I didn't want to give them the satisfaction.

Jason glanced at me before opening the car door and jumping into the backseat. I stared at the ground and heard them laugh as they drove away.

When I finally felt like I could walk without falling down, I didn't head straight home. My legs shook for most of the walk, but eventually they became strong again and they carried me up the hill to the local cemetery. I didn't have to look at the headstones to find the one I was looking for. I knew exactly where it was. It was the newer one at the end of the row with so many roses on it. Magda had loved roses. It didn't matter what color so long as they smelled like they should. Usually I brought her one when I came to visit, but I hadn't planned on visiting her until Friday.

I set my book bag on the grass left of her headstone and sat right on top of the mound that covered the hole where she'd been buried. I pulled a weed from the base of the heart-shaped stone her mother had erected that simply had her name, her birthday and the date she died engraved upon it.

Usually when I visited, I talked to her and told her what was going on in my life. I would tell her about our favorite TV shows, the books I'd read, local gossip, but today I didn't feel much like talking. I just wanted to be near her, so I sat there, on the grass, and let the sun warm me.

A little while later, I heard footsteps behind me. I didn't have to turn around to see who it was. I already knew.

"I thought you weren't coming until Friday," he said.

I didn't look up, but moved a little to the left so he could sit down beside me. We always shared the mound and never made the other sit on the flat grass.

Gabriel and I came here a lot. We never planned to be here at the same time, and sometimes we weren't, but when we were it was okay. Once you cried on someone, it wasn't such a big deal if they saw your grief again.

Magda's older brother was tall and lean with long dark hair and even darker eyes. Like his sister he was gorgeous, and seemed naively unaware of it. He was more cynical, though. Magda had seen good in everybody; Gabe knew it wasn't true.

"Rough day?" he asked.

"Yeah."

I'd known Gabriel since I was five years old, so when he put his arm around my shoulders I leaned into him, my cheek resting on his chest. I could hear his heartbeat, and for some reason that made me incredibly sad and happy at the same time.

That's when the tears finally came, because I hadn't felt happy since before my best friend had her rape smeared across the internet. I didn't feel like I deserved to be happy now, when I should have been the one to save her, and had failed.

CHAPTER 3

I had Aikido class that night, in a strip mall located on West Main Street. The instructor was a great big guy named José, who was very strong, and surprisingly light on his feet. He smiled a lot, which made him look completely unthreatening. I liked him. I'd started taking his class a couple of years ago. It was one of the few things Magda and I hadn't done together. She tried it, but just didn't like it. She didn't like hurting people—or getting hurt.

"We have a special guest tonight," José said. "Detective Diane Davies from our local police station. She's going to talk to you all about how you can use aikido to protect yourself from an attacker."

Detective Davies was tall. She wore a T-shirt and sweatpants, and I could see muscle definition in her arms. She'd seemed nice at the time, like she really wanted to help. But in the end, she'd let Magda down too.

"I need someone to help me demonstrate these moves," Detective Davies said. "Would anyone like to volunteer?"

I put up my hand before I could stop myself. It wasn't that I wanted to be helpful, but that I was hoping to have the chance to punch her in the face. Not a particularly sane thought, but I was just so angry. Angry that Magda was gone. Angry that Jason Bentley hadn't known who I was. Angry that everybody was just going about their regular lives like nothing terrible had happened. My best friend was dead, and she had been for months. My life hadn't been the same since she was attacked, and it never would be. I was always going to wonder what Magda could've been, what she could've achieved, and about the fact that four assholes had made certain she'd never do any of it.

So yeah, the chance to unload a little violence—with no ramifications—on one of the people who had let Magda down was too tempting to pass up.

And maybe she'd land a couple of strikes on me, and I could let the pain inside me go somewhere else. Take the punishment I deserved.

Detective Davies met my gaze as I approached the front of the dojo. When we stood face-to-face she smiled at me, and said, "I know you. It's Hadley, right?"

So she did remember. "Yes."

Her smile faded a little. Good. I hope she remembered Magda, and that she felt at least a little guilt standing there with me.

"First I want you to come at me," she instructed. "I'll defend myself against you, then we'll break down the moves, and then you'll use them on me."

I shrugged. "Sure."

She moved a few feet away from me. "Whenever you're ready."

I didn't run toward her, or lunge. But I quickly closed the distance between us and aimed a kick I had learned in tae kwon do at her sternum. She was fast, way faster than I anticipated. She grabbed my leg, using my momentum to throw me off balance and facedown on the floor.

I sucked in a deep breath to replace what had been knocked out of me, and pushed myself to my feet. She was good. And I was pissed at myself for not being at least as good.

The detective addressed the class. "You all know that aikido is about displacing the energy of an attack. I didn't have to strike out, and I avoided being hit simply by using Hadley's momentum to my own advantage and against her. Now, Hadley, would you mind helping me break the moves down so that everyone can see before you use it against me?"

I walked back to the center of the mat with her. We went through the movements again, this time in slow motion. I paid close attention to how she grabbed my leg and twisted her own body. This time when I hit the mat it was with barely any force at all, and I was able to catch myself.

"Now," Diane said. "I will attack you."

Obviously she knew other martial arts as well, because she came at me fast with a confident kick aimed at my midsection. Remembering her moves, I grabbed her leg and with a sharp pivot of my body, brought her crashing to the mat. I hoped she found it as hard to breathe as I had.

I offered her my hand to help her to her feet. She took it. As she rose to her feet she gave me an odd look, like she knew what was going on in my head. It made me uncomfortable.

"Very good," she told me. "Why don't the rest of you pair off and take turns practicing on your partners?"

Not everyone had shown up for class that night, so I was left without a partner. Normally I wouldn't have cared, because it would've meant I got to spar with José. This time, however, it left me with the cop.

"You're very good," she told me. "Though I don't believe aikido is meant to be used with such anger." She actually smiled when she said it.

I wanted to tell her off, but even I wasn't that ballsy. "Sorry."

She laughed. "Don't apologize. If you're ever attacked, I want you to be angry about it."

I looked her in the eyes. "I'm angry if any woman gets attacked."

Her smile slid from her face. "That's where I know you from. You were Magda Torres's friend."

"I still am her friend. The fact that she's dead doesn't change that."

"No," she agreed. "I wouldn't think that it did." She watched me like I was something potentially dangerous, as though she wasn't quite sure that I was safe to be around.

"Sorry," I said, even though I didn't mean it. "Today was the first day of senior year. Magda and I had a lot of plans, and today I realized that none of them were ever going to happen." Saying that out loud made my throat tight and my eyes burn. I blinked fast to clear them. This woman was not going to see me cry.

"I wish I could say I don't know what you're going through. But unfortunately I have too good an idea. When I was in college, a good friend of mine was raped on campus. She didn't take her own life, but she carried the trauma with her for years afterward. She still does. They never caught the guy who did it. She's the reason I became a cop."

"Do you know who he was?"

She shook her head. "No."

"Everyone knows who raped Magda." Maybe I was just stupid, or maybe I just didn't care what the consequences were, but I stepped close to her and stared directly into her eyes. "And you weren't able to catch them, either. Maybe you should consider another career choice."

She didn't even blink. "Believe me, I considered it. But I have to believe that I can make more of a difference as a police officer than I could outside the law."

"Good luck with that." I turned away from her and walked over to where José stood going over some paperwork. "Will you spar with me?" I asked.

He looked up, his friendly face looking bewildered. "I thought you'd want to learn from Detective Davies."

"I don't think she can teach me anything helpful."

I used to think that some girl rolling her eyes at me, or sneering at me, was the worst expression in the world. Contempt—even hatred—those are things I don't mind seeing in somebody's face anymore. What I hate is pity—that moment when someone looks at you and you can see it in their eyes, that they feel so badly for you, like you're a puppy that just got kicked.

"Give her a chance," he suggested. "I think the two of you might be able to help each other."

I knew better than to argue. José didn't get angry; he never raised his voice. Once you were in his class for a couple of sessions, you realized that he meant whatever came out of his mouth, and no amount of urging, begging or even threats could persuade him otherwise.

I stepped back to where Diane Davies stood. She was checking her phone.

"José made you come back, did he?" She didn't even glance up from her screen.

"Yes." I said it through clenched teeth.

She looked me in the eye. "I'm very aware of how much I let Magda Torres and her loved ones down. How much the system let them down. I would give just about anything to go back and change that, but I think you and I both know you can't go back."

"No, you can't. If we could, I would have never let her out of my sight at that party. I would've stopped her from taking those pills."

"But you can't do either of those things. No one can. I know something you *can* do."

"What?" I could practically taste the bitterness and mockery in my tone.

"José and I have been talking about starting a self-defense course for girls. I would like for you to be a part of it if you're interested. Help us teach other girls to protect themselves, so that what happened to Magda maybe won't happen to one of them."

I stared at her. Was she serious? She did know that Magda had been drugged, right? Being able to throw a punch wouldn't have helped her. "Why me?"

"Because I think helping other girls might give you a place to channel all that anger."

"I'm not angry."

Instead of laughing like I expected her to, she gave me an understanding look. "No, you're heartbroken."

Maybe she understood a little better than I thought. "This class, are you going to teach them to actually fight, or will it just be things like blowing whistles and sticking people with keys?" Because Magda had taken one of those classes, and it had done her absolutely no fucking good.

"There might be a little bit of whistles and keys. But we'll be teaching them to fight, and to fight dirty. We're talking forcing testicles to retract, that kind of fighting."

For the first time in months, a genuine smile curved my lips. "I'm in."

"You should eat something."

Sitting at the kitchen table, I looked up at my mother. She had that pinched expression on her face that I'd seen a lot since Magda died. It was an expression I understood to mean that while she was worried about me, she was also annoyed with me. I think she thought that I should be over it by now.

But did we ever get over losing someone we cared about? I mean, it wasn't like Magda had moved to another city, or had gone away to school. She was gone. Forever. Three-quarters of my life had been spent with her and then, during the space of a few hours, she'd stopped being. How did you just "get over" that?"

"I'm not all that hungry."

Mom spooned some scrambled eggs onto my plate. "At least eat these. You need the protein."

She was right. I wasn't one of those kids who thought my parents were wrong all the time. Usually they were right. Well,

Mom usually was. My father pretty much just pissed me off whenever I saw him.

Then again, it didn't take much to upset me these days.

I didn't argue about the eggs. I ate them on autopilot, not really tasting them. I couldn't live the rest of my life like this— numb except for bouts of rage. I knew it was part of the grieving process, but it was also exhausting.

"You've gotten so thin."

I ate another mouthful of eggs as a response. I hadn't really lost much weight. After the funeral I did lose about ten pounds, but some of those had come back. The difference was that I had been working out like mad. Aikido was the third martial arts class I had taken since I was thirteen. It hadn't started out as me just wanting to hit or kick something. I signed up for martial arts because I wanted to be fit, and it was really the only thing I found fun enough to stick with. And now it was the only thing that calmed me down.

Magda hadn't been into the kicking and punching. She liked to run and had been on the school track team. The muscles in her legs had been like granite. I ran with her once in a while, but I could never keep up.

Regardless, I was working out more, turning the soft parts of my body into something hard and strong.

"The police officer that was at class last night asked me to help her with a self-defense class for girls."

Mom look surprised at this. "Really? Why would she do that?"

I shrugged. "She thinks I'm good. And she knew Magda."

There was that pinched look again. "I don't know if that's a good idea, Hadley."

"I do." And it wasn't until that moment when she opposed it that I realized I had already made up my mind about it. "I'm good at it, Mom. And if I can help even one girl escape what happened to Magda, it will be worth it."

She sighed. "I suppose if I say no you'll only do it anyway."

"Why are you making it sound like I want to go out and do something reckless? Or something that might get me hurt or in trouble? *Jesus*, Mom." I shook my head. "I just want to do *something* good."

She looked pained, like I was doing this deliberately to hurt her. I had no idea why she was so opposed to this. I had no idea what was going through her head. It was almost like she blamed Magda for my emotional state. It didn't make sense, but I was sure it was true.

"Fine. Help at the class. If your grades start to suffer, you will quit."

I nodded. "Sure." But I only made the promise so she'd stop talking about it.

Mom wasn't done. "Your father isn't going to like this."

It was so tempting to say that I didn't care if Dad liked it or not. I wanted to ask why she was so worried about his opinion anyway. It wasn't like he was ever around. He was always working or... Whatever.

"I'll tell him," I said. "He'll be okay with it when I tell him that I think it would be good for me—help me work out the guilt I feel for Magda being raped."

My mother winced. The R word always made her intensely uncomfortable. "It wasn't your fault. You know how much I liked Magda, but she ought to have known better than to be drinking at a party with that many boys around."

My fingers tightened around my fork. Her words—so stupid and careless—made me remember what I'd said to Magda that day about being punished for making a mistake. She hadn't done anything wrong. "No, those boys ought to have known better than to drug and rape a girl."

"Hadley…"

"Don't you say it. Don't you *dare* say it." I didn't understand how she could think it, let alone believe it. I knew, however, that my mother wasn't the only woman to think that Magda had asked for what happened to her. Hell, even I had thought it once or twice. God, I wish I could take it back, because that guilt was a weight I'd carry the rest of my life. "Even if I walked into school stark naked with a box of condoms and a bottle of lube, I would not be asking to be raped."

"Oh, Hadley!" She made a face. "Don't be so crude."

"What if it had been me, Mom? Would you blame me? Would you say those things about me?"

"Of course not!" She looked offended that I'd even suggest it. God, she really didn't have a clue. "I hope I raised you well enough that you wouldn't get yourself into such a situation."

I'd had enough. There was a very real possibility that I was going to stab my mother with my fork if I didn't leave the house at that moment. I pushed back my chair—it screeched against the floor—and practically jumped to my feet.

"I have to go. I'll be late for school." I grabbed my bag and stomped from the kitchen, throwing open the door so hard that it banged against the wall.

"Hey!" my mother yelled. "There's no need for that!"

I ignored her and kept walking. I was halfway to school before I realized that I still had the fork in my hand.

CHAPTER 4

I ran into Zoe at lunch that day. Actually, I was outside sitting on the grass, letting the sun beat down on me in the hope that it might thaw the coldness inside, when she plopped down beside me.

"So," she began, "are you going to the party Saturday night?"

I turned my head toward her, looking at her through the dark lenses of my sunglasses. "What party?"

"Jason Bentley is having a party Saturday night."

I laughed—it was not a happy sound. "No."

"He asked me to tell you about it."

I peered at her over the top of my sunglasses. She was shitting me, right? "Seriously? Why would he do that?" Was he trying to mess with me?

She pulled a pair of pink cat-eye sunglasses from her bag and put them on. "He didn't say. He just asked me to tell my 'pretty blonde friend' about the party."

"And you thought he meant me?"

Zoe smiled. "He saw us talking in class."

He must have asked her to do this before he came after me yesterday. "I'm not sure why he would think I'd want to go. Zoe, you know he's one of the guys who raped Magda."

She glanced away. "He was never charged."

Was I the only person who had a grip on reality around there? "That doesn't mean he didn't do it."

Her shoulders slumped. "I know. I'm sorry, Hadley. I've known Jason for years. I just don't want to believe he could do such a thing."

And I never believed Magda would kill herself. I never thought my father would turn out to be an asshole. "Yeah, but that doesn't mean he didn't do it, either."

"So what, you're just going to avoid all social gatherings your last year of high school?"

"No. Just the ones Bentley and his friends are involved with."

"They're going to be at all of them. They're the most popular guys in school."

"I know. That's how they managed to get away with it. They're rich and popular. They're also rapists. If you go to that party, don't let Drew Carson get you a drink."

"I don't let anyone get me a drink."

So maybe she wasn't as gullible as I thought.

Zoe pulled her knees up to her chest and wrapped her arms around them. "Has it occurred to you that maybe if you go to the party, people will see you and remember what happened to Magda? Maybe another girl will think twice before going off with one of them."

I stared at her. I didn't know why it was so important to her that I go to this damn party, but she had a point. "I'll think about it."

She smiled. "I can pick you up."

If she'd wanted me to go to the party with her why hadn't she just said so? I wanted to warn her that I wasn't much of a wing man, but I couldn't make the words come out. I wasn't in the market for a new best friend, either. Still, I kept that to myself.

Instead, I said to her, "We're starting a self-defense course for girls at my dojo. Diane Davies—she's a cop—is putting it together. She's asked me to help. Are you interested?"

Zoe's pretty face brightened. "You mean like teaching us to fight?"

I nodded. "It would be about protecting yourself from an attack, but yes, we teach you to fight." Maybe I shouldn't make that promise, but if Detective Davies wasn't going to do it, I would.

She grinned. "Cool. I always wanted to learn how to fight. When does it start?"

"Thursday night. I know that's soon, but we wanted to get going as quickly as possible. It's at seven. Here's the address." I gave her one of José's cards.

"Thanks." She glanced at it before putting it in her bag.

"If you know anybody else who'd be interested, feel free to spread the word." The more girls we got, the less chance there was of Drew Carson and his friends being able to continue hurting people. Warning girls that their drinks might be spiked only did so much.

"I will."

We sat there for a while, not saying much. It was nice to

hang out with someone. I hadn't done that since Magda died. Lunch was almost over when I heard laughter. I turned my head toward it and saw Drew, Jason, Brody and Adam standing together farther down the lawn. They were talking to a group of girls, all of whom looked at them like they were special. I didn't understand it. We all knew what they had done. Everyone in that school knew what had happened that night. For fuck's sake, everyone in the goddamn town knew what had happened that night. Why, then, did the four of them get to continue on with their lives as if nothing had ever happened? Why did people treat them as though they were innocent, even though they had taken pictures of what they'd done to my friend?

And why did Magda, the best person I've ever known, get treated like she had done something wrong? I could almost understand why guys wouldn't care, but I would never understand why the girls didn't.

I stared at them, that familiar burn of anger and helplessness churning in my stomach, spreading up into my chest and throat until I thought my ribs might cave in from the heaviness of it, and I might choke to death.

They would all be at the party at Jason's. They would be there, and so would those girls. And one of those girls would get Drew's attention. Maybe he already had her picked out. He would get her a drink, and he would put something in it that made it difficult for her to fight back or even move. And he would take her to a bedroom, where he and his three best friends would take turns violating her while one of them took video and photographs. And if anybody found out about it, they would say she was willing. That she *wanted* it. That she was a slut. And they would get away with it, because they always got away with it. I knew of three other girls who had been assaulted by one or more of those assholes, and nothing had been done about it.

The edges of my vision were black, as I gasped for breath. Was this a panic attack? Or was I finally being suffocated by my grief, guilt and rage? My anger was not a bad thing. My anger was righteous. Teaching girls to defend themselves was only a small part of what needed to be done. Someone had to show those boys that they would not be allowed to hurt people, that there was a price. They owed Magda her life, and that was a debt they could never repay. But as I sat there watching them, caught between imploding and breaking down, I realized something with absolute clarity. The four of them had to pay.

And it was at that moment that I realized I was going to make sure they did.

I arrived at the dojo early Thursday night. Detective Davies was already there setting up. José was with her. They smiled when I walked in.

"Thanks for helping get this off the ground," Detective Davies said to me. "I hope we get a good turnout."

I shrugged. "We probably won't. A lot of the girls from school don't think anything bad could ever happen to them."

Her smile faded. "Until it does."

"Yeah." How much violence against women had she seen since becoming a cop?

By the time class started we had five girls, including me. To be honest, it was a better turnout than I expected. Zoe was one of the girls. She had her auburn hair in a ponytail and was wearing leggings and an oversize T-shirt.

"I have a couple of friends who will come next week," Zoe said. "They both had band meeting tonight."

"Great," I said. The more the better.

Detective Davies started the class by talking about non-violent ways for girls to protect themselves. She talked about not leaving your drink unattended at a party, and not drinking anything that you hadn't poured yourself.

"You know," one of the girls said, "it would be a lot easier if boys didn't act like assholes."

The detective nodded. "It would be. No matter what happens, you're not to blame for any of it. Unfortunately, the unfairness of the situation is that there are boys, and men, out there who will hurt you if they can. And until society stops allowing that, women have to look out for themselves and each other. That's one of the most important things—you girls looking out for each other."

I swallowed the bitterness that rose in the back of my throat. Guilt tasted like shit. I should've taken better care of Magda. I should've watched out for her and protected her instead of turning my back. The reality of it was that I'd been jealous. Jealous of the fact that boys seemed to find her so desirable and barely looked at me. I tried to tell her Drew was a jerk, but she didn't believe me. I had wanted her to find out for herself, but not like that. Never like that.

Detective Davies went on to talk about things like pepper spray and using keys as a weapon. She talked about having safety words with your friends, so that if you thought a guy was a threat you could warn each other.

Half an hour passed before she got to the actual physical part of the class. The five of us sat on the mats in front of her chair.

"How many of you have heard of Krav Maga?" she asked.

I put my hand up. So did Zoe.

"Krav Maga is a form of fighting developed for the Israeli military. It combines several kinds of martial arts and street fighting. Like a lot of disciplines, it promotes avoiding violence, but if that is unavoidable the idea is to terminate the conflict as quickly and efficiently as possible by using attacks aimed at vulnerable parts of the body and designed to do as much damage as necessary."

"By vulnerable do you mean the balls?" a girl named Jenna asked. A couple of the other girls giggled.

Detective Davies smiled. "That's one place. But a lot of times men expect that to be the first point of attack, and they're good at protecting what's between their legs. Also, what if your attacker's not a guy?"

We all exchanged glances. None of us expected a threat from one another. But I'd seen girls fight before, and they were nasty.

The older woman continued. "It is rare for women to perpetrate sexual assault against each other, but we can be just as violent as men. If you are attacked by someone who doesn't have testicles, you need to know other areas to strike. Of course, these areas are also vulnerable on men. The eyes, the throat, the solar plexus, which is the area right here—" she gestured to an area in the center of her chest "—the knees, the face, the fingers... All of these areas are vulnerable. And I will show you ways to hurt all of them."

I smiled, and so did the other girls. I guess she was right

when she said we could be just as bloodthirsty as guys. But I don't think any of us were gleeful at the idea of being able to hurt somebody—well, except for me. It wasn't about inflicting pain. It was the idea of not having to be afraid. Sure, you still had to be smart, but there was power in the idea of being able to fight back.

We started with practicing how to fend off an attacker while on our feet. Detective Davies showed us how effective a shove could be, but then also turned it around and showed us how to use momentum against our attacker if they tried to shove us.

I don't think most of us would even have thought of using what she showed us on our own.

"As women, we are taught that physicality is masculine, and any woman who fights is vulgar. I'm telling you, as a physically strong, older woman, that it is okay for you to do whatever necessary to save yourself." Detective Davies's face was slightly flushed from demonstrating defensive moves. "If you can grab your attacker's finger and bend it, or break it, *do* it. If you can gouge his eye, knee him in the groin or stomach, do it. Smash your head into his nose or mouth. Punch him in the throat. Hit him with anything you can get your hands on.

"You've been told all your life not to hurt people, and now I want you to forget that. If someone is trying to hurt you, I want each and every one of you to do whatever necessary to escape. I want you to hurt back."

I wanted to applaud. I won't lie. I wanted to hug her, even if she had let Mags down. I wish Magda hadn't had to die for her to teach this class. If she had learned how to protect herself, maybe it would've helped. Then again, Drew Carson had drugged her, so she hadn't had much fight in her anyway.

I raised my hand.

"Yes, Hadley?"

"Can you show us how to get out of a pin? What if someone bigger than us has us pinned to the ground?" Or a bed?

The older woman looked at me for a moment. She seemed… thoughtful. "I had planned on doing that in another class, but I can show you now, and we can work on it more later. Why don't you come up here and help me?"

I stood up. She'd used me for a lot of the class already, getting me to help her demonstrate different techniques as I was the only one there with a martial arts background.

"Lie down on the floor on your back," she instructed.

I did. The mat was cool beneath my back. We may not have gotten into anything too vigorous, but I had still managed to work up a bit of a sweat. Detective Davies knelt in front of me and then braced her hands on either side of my head so that her hips were between my thighs and her torso had me pinned.

One of the girls giggled. I rolled my eyes, a gesture that made my "attacker" smile. "Okay, you can see that I am bigger than Hadley. I'm taller and heavier, and I have gravity on my side. All I have to do is push or press down. To move me, Hadley has to exert force upward, so not only is she fighting my body weight and my strength, but she is also fighting gravity. Her shoulder blades are flat on the floor, which makes it even more difficult for her to escape. Now, what are things she can do to get out of this hold?"

Her question was met with silence. I turned my head to the side and saw the four girls looking at each other, as though waiting for one of them to speak first.

"Hey," I said. "I'm your best friend, and we're at a party together. You walk into a room and you see a guy trying to get my clothes off and rape me. You can't attack him physically, but you can tell me how to hurt him. What do I do?"

The girls had gone pale. They weren't looking at each other anymore, they were looking at me.

"See if you can work your legs under his," Zoe suggested. "Then he can't rape you, and you're in a better position to knee him in the balls."

I did as she suggested, miming trying to knee Detective Davies between the legs. But as I did so, the woman quickly snapped her leg shut and shoved her knee between mine again. She was strong, and for a moment I was filled with an irrational fear of what she was going to do to me.

The girls must've seen my fear because suddenly they jumped to life.

"Bash his nose with your forehead!" Jenna yelled.

"Punch him in the solar plexus!" another shouted. Anna, that was her name.

"Gouge his eyes!" That was Zoe again.

"Push your forearm into his neck so you're shoving his head back, and then punch him in the throat with your other fist." This was calmly delivered by the fourth girl, whose name I didn't know, but whose face I would never forget. It was the face of a girl who'd been in this position herself and was only now realizing that she could've fought.

Hers was the advice I took, pushing Detective Davies's head back and mock punching her. She jerked backward, and I seized the opportunity to get my legs around her, lift up and flip her so that she was the one on her back and I was the one on top. Then, I pretended to punch her repeatedly in the face until she was unconscious.

I met the gaze of that girl. "Thank you. You saved me."

I wasn't prepared for the tears that suddenly appeared in her eyes. She nodded, blinking furiously to stop herself from crying. The other girls did a funny thing—instead of comforting her, they applauded—turning her from victim to hero. Her tears evaporated into a smile. It was a shaky smile, but it was still a smile.

I climbed to my feet and offered Detective Davies my hand to help her up. She took it and gracefully rolled up onto her feet.

"Well done," she said. "You knew exactly what to say to them."

"I wish I hadn't." Our gazes met. "Known what to say to them, I mean."

She patted my shoulder. "Me too." Then, she turned to the class. "I think that's a good place to leave it for this week. We'll meet again next Thursday at the same time. Feel free to bring a friend with you. Until then, feel free to practice what we went over. Although try not to actually hurt anyone who doesn't deserve it." She smiled.

The girls stood up. I approached the girl whose name I didn't know. The one who had told me how to get out of Detective Davies's hold. She had brown hair, and blue eyes that seemed to look right through me. "Hey," I said. "I'm Hadley."

She nodded. "I know. I'm Caitlin. Thanks for setting this up."

I shrugged. "I didn't really. Detective Davies did. It was her idea."

"Well, thanks anyway." She turned to walk away.

"Hey," I called. She turned around. "Are you coming next week?"

"Yeah," she said. "You?"

"Yeah, I'll be here." This had to be the most awkward conversation I've ever had. I felt so stupid. What had I expected? That we would be instant friends?

Her smile was lopsided, and I think maybe a little sarcastic. "Well, see you then." And then she walked away.

"Hadley?"

I turned. Zoe stood there with her friend Anna. "Did you like it?" I asked.

The two of them grinned. "Yeah," they chorused.

"We're going over to the frozen yogurt place," Zoe said. "Do you want to come with us?"

I meant to say no. No was what I'd said ever since Magda's funeral. No, I didn't want to hang out. No, I didn't want to go to the dance. No, I didn't want anything to eat. And no, I did *not* want to talk about it.

"Sure. Are you going right now?"

Zoe nodded. "Yeah. You can come with us, or you can meet us there if you have something to do." She sounded almost as awkward and uncertain as I felt, which was strangely comforting. It struck me as odd that we seemed even more vulnerable *after* learning how to kick the shit out of somebody than we had before. Why was that?

"I just have to grab my jacket."

"We'll wait," Anna blurted. She blushed. "If you want us to, that is."

At this rate, by next class we wouldn't even be able to make eye contact. I felt myself smile, and not just because I wanted to put her at ease, but because I actually *wanted* to smile. I felt a strange tickle in my chest, like when your foot falls asleep and gets all prickly when the blood starts to circulate again. I hadn't hung out with another girl since Magda. Since her suicide I'd been pretty antisocial. The only person I saw on a regular basis that wasn't family was Gabe. Which reminded me I needed to go by the cemetery tomorrow after school.

"I'll just be a second," I said. "We can walk over together."

Anna actually clapped her hands. "Yay!"

I laughed as I walked away. I thought this class would just be about violence. My experience with other girls was that once you put a group of them together they got all bitchy with one another. Maybe this class was going to be different. Maybe instead of fighting with each other we'd start fighting *for* each other.

And God help any guy who got in our way.

CHAPTER 5

Gabriel was already at Magda's grave when I got there on Friday. Like me, he must've come straight from class, because there was a backpack on the grass by her tombstone.

He sat cross-legged on the grass, leaning back on his forearms as the afternoon sun shone down on his face. It was warm—even for September—and he'd taken off his jacket. His eyes were closed, so I just stood there for a moment and looked at him.

I didn't remember when my feelings for him had become something more than just friendship, but I know it had been at least a couple of years. I'd never told Magda that I had a crush on her brother. She would've found it weird. I found it weird.

I don't think there were many girls who would blame me for having a thing for him. He was gorgeous. But more than his looks, he was a good person. Strong and honorable. He could make me laugh—even after all that had happened.

Finally, I decided to approach. If he opened his eyes and saw me standing there gawking at him, he'd think I'd gone nuts.

"Hi."

He opened his eyes, squinting at me. "Hey. I was beginning to wonder if you were going to show."

"School only let out twenty minutes ago," I told him. I put my bag beside his before plopping down on the grass on the opposite side of the tombstone. We both faced the same direction as the stone. It made it easier to pretend that Magda was between us rather than beneath.

"Right." He slipped on a pair of sunglasses that had been lying on the grass by his hip. "I forgot. How's it going?"

I shrugged. "Okay. It doesn't seem right without her."

Gabriel stared straight ahead. "Nothing does. It's getting a little easier, but that just makes it all the more painful when I remember she's gone."

I didn't say anything. I didn't have to. He knew I felt the same way.

"Diane Davies has started a self-defense course for girls."

He turned his head to look at me, but I couldn't see his eyes behind the dark lenses. "The cop?"

"Yeah. We had the first one Thursday night. She's doing it at the dojo." Gabriel had been the one to get me into aikido in the first place, but he hadn't been there in a while.

"You're taking it?"

"You sound surprised."

"I am. I thought you hated her. And you already know how to kick ass."

"I was mad that she couldn't make the four of them pay for what they did. I guess now I know it wasn't her fault—like you said."

"It's good that she's doing something. Did many girls show up?"

"A few. Hopefully we'll get more." I plucked a blade of grass and shredded it between my fingers. "Jason Bentley's having a party on Saturday night."

His back stiffened. The tightened muscles in his arms were like smooth stone beneath his skin. "Are you going?"

"I don't know."

This time when he turned his head his gaze lingered on me. "Yes, you do."

I don't know how he did it, but he always seemed to know when I was lying. "Okay then, fine. I'm going."

"Why?"

"Because if Drew Carson tries to drug and rape another girl, I want to be there to stop it."

"And just how do you think you can do that? Are you going to stand guard outside the bedrooms?"

"If I have to." My voice was sharp and belligerent.

"What if he takes that as an invitation? What if the girl he targets is you?"

"That won't happen. I'm not going to let him get anywhere near me."

"That won't matter if the four of them gang up on you. Even you're not capable of fighting off four guys."

He was right, and I knew it. I also hated him for it. "I'm not going alone. I'm going with another girl."

"I'm coming with you."

My heart jumped in fear. "No. You can't do that. If you walk in there, the four of them and all their friends will jump you."

"My odds of not being raped are significantly higher than yours."

"My odds of not being beaten to death are significantly higher than yours. You can't go."

"If you go, I'm going."

"You're such an asshole."

He rolled onto his side so that he faced me, bracing himself on his forearm. "I could say the same thing. What are you thinking, Hadley? What are you planning to do that you don't want me to know about?"

Could he see the pulse at the base of my throat pounding beneath my skin? "Nothing. I'm not stupid."

"I know you're not. Sometimes I think you're too smart for your own good. Your intelligence isn't the problem. Your impulsiveness is. Your anger is."

I snorted. "Don't you lecture me on anger. I was there when you went after Drew. I know what you would've done to him if those guys hadn't pulled you off. And I know what those guys would've done to you if there hadn't been an audience." I remembered how bruised and bloody he'd been, and how much worse Drew had looked. Most people went through life not knowing whether or not they could kill somebody, but Gabriel knew.

"You're not going without me."

"Fine. I won't go."

"Good."

We stared at each other, his eyes hidden behind sunglasses. I was lying, and he probably knew it, but I was still going to try to sell it. If he was stupid enough to show up knowing what would happen to him, then let him. Him getting beaten up was more of a given than me being attacked.

We sat there in silence. Usually, we spent the time talking. Mostly we talked about Magda, but sometimes we talked about other things. This was the first time that neither of us had anything to say.

A little while later Gabriel rolled to his feet. "I have to go to work." He brushed grass off his jeans and picked up his backpack.

I stood as well. "Gabe..."

He looked at me. "Yeah?"

"I...I don't like feeling like you're mad at me."

His shoulders slumped. He dropped the backpack on the grass again and stepped across his sister's grave to stand directly in front of me. I wasn't prepared for him to wrap his arms around me and pull me close. He smelled like sunshine and fabric softener with a touch of sandalwood. I wound my arms around his waist, pressing my hands against his back. Holding him was like holding strength. I could feel it seeping through my clothes, slipping beneath my skin and into my bones. The sadness and helplessness that usually threatened to overwhelm me disappeared. I couldn't even find any anger in my heart.

He rested his cheek against my head. "Please stay away from those guys. I can't lose you too."

Tears burned my eyes, but I blinked them away. I wasn't going to cry on him again, and I wasn't going to let him see how much his words affected me. I couldn't let him see my feelings for him, because I was his little sister's best friend and I knew the love he felt for me was only friendship. I didn't want to lose him. He wasn't just all I had left of Magda. He was all I had left period.

* * *

Like most of the wealthier families in our town, the Bentleys lived on Smith Street. It might have a common name, but Smith Street was one of the oldest streets in town. You could tell how old the houses were by how they were built. The newer houses were large and sprawling, usually white or bluish gray. The older houses—the ones that had been there for a century or more—were red brick or gray stone. The Bentleys lived in a house that was brick that had been stuccoed over.

Zoe and I arrived there around ten o'clock Saturday night. I didn't live on Smith Street, or anywhere near it. My family lived in one of the newer suburbs of town. My mother was an accountant and my father was an engineer. We weren't poor, but we weren't the Bentleys. Mags and I were top of our class in our old school, and we were able to get scholarships. Our parents somehow managed to scrape together the rest of the money for tuition. Magda's grades had slipped after the rape— to the point where the school was going to kick her out. Her suicide saved them the trouble, the unfeeling bastards.

"Are you ready to do this?" Zoe asked. "I mean, it's gotta be painful."

I wanted to say that sometimes pain was better than feeling nothing, but that was really so melodramatic. I shrugged. "It's okay." I didn't know what I hoped to accomplish by going to that damn party. Maybe it was penance for letting Magda down. Maybe I wanted to show that I wasn't afraid. Maybe I thought I could possibly stop another girl from being raped. Maybe I just didn't want to sit home alone.

We walked up the flagstone path. Zoe had driven and promised me she wasn't going to drink. It was a relief to know that

I probably wouldn't have to worry about her. Unfortunately, I still had to worry about pretty much every other girl there.

It was a warm night, and I was wearing cropped jeans and a blouse. I didn't wear dresses or skirts anymore.

We rang the doorbell. We could hear the music inside the house. It was loud, but not so loud that the neighbors would call the police. Not that it would matter if they did. The Bentleys, the Weeks, the Henrys and the Carsons were important families, which apparently entitled them to behave in ways that would get the rest of us in trouble. They were exempt from any kind of responsibility, and that extended to their sons.

The door opened. Standing in the open frame in jeans and a T-shirt that probably cost more than my entire outfit was Jason. A year ago I would've described him as cute. I might've even wanted him to pay attention to me. Now his face had as much appeal as a bowl of maggots. If he ever touched me, I would probably take a cheese grater to the spot just to get rid of the taint.

He smiled when he saw us, though it faltered a little when he looked at me. "Hey," he said, standing back so we could step inside. "Glad you could make it."

I followed Zoe inside. She smiled and thanked him for inviting us. I couldn't do anything more than nod.

"Do you want a soda or anything?" he asked, leading us deeper into the house. The floor looked like marble, and the staircase was wide enough to drive a car up.

"Sure," Zoe said.

"Do you have anything in cans?" I asked. There was no way I was going to let him bring me a glass.

He shot me a glance as though he could read my mind. "Sure. Come into the kitchen."

The kitchen was just as perfect as the rest of the house. There wasn't even a crumb on the stove. A stack of pizza boxes sat on the counter, and I could smell the cheesy, toma-toey goodness.

I wasn't going to eat anything, either.

Jason opened the wide, stainless-steel fridge. "Help yourself."

Zoe took a can of Sprite. I reached in and grabbed a can of diet Dr Pepper. "Thanks."

He closed the fridge door. The action made him step closer toward me. Instinctively I lurched backward, banging my hip against the counter in my effort to avoid contact.

Jason frowned. "I didn't mean to scare you."

I forced myself to meet his gaze. "You didn't." Scare me? No. Repulse me? Yes.

He looked as though he wanted to say something else, but then a small group of people burst into the kitchen. They were all in our class, though one of the girls was a junior.

"Hey, Jay, where's the beer?" one of the guys asked.

Jason went to get it for them, and I took that as my oppor-tunity to escape. Zoe and I followed the music and conversa-tion downstairs into a large finished basement that had the biggest television I've ever seen and a pool table. Patio doors opened up to the backyard, where there was a pool and hot tub. There were kids in each.

Zoe turned to me. "This house is fricking amazing."

"Yeah," I agreed through clenched teeth. The house was gorgeous.

"Hey, there's Anna and Caitlin. Want to go say hi?"

"Yeah." I meant it. I was happy to see the two of them, and not just because there was safety in numbers.

The two girls looked just as happy to see us, and they immediately started talking about how they'd been practicing what they learned in class.

"I think my mother thought we were killing each other," Anna joked. "We almost busted the lamp in my room."

I laughed. I was glad they came. Having them there eased my anxiety. That anxiety came back, however, about an hour later when I saw Drew Carson hovering around the girl I'd recognized as a junior earlier, who was now so drunk she could barely stand up.

A hot prickly sensation ran up the back of my neck, followed by a shiver of ice down my spine. For months I'd thought about what I would do in that very situation. I'd imagined myself walking up to him and beating him stupid. I imagined myself being the girl's savior. Once, I even imagined myself going full-on Kill Bill on them. Never had I imagined myself just standing there, frozen to the spot and shaking with anger. How could I just stand there and not do anything?

I couldn't. With my can of soda in hand—because I was not about to set it down—I started walking toward them. Zoe, Caitlin and Anna were right behind me. Zoe said my name, but it sounded like she was talking to me from the far end of a tunnel.

What was I going to do? Smash my soda can into his face? Kick him? At that moment he hadn't done anything wrong. Of course that was the moment I remembered Gabriel telling me I couldn't fight all four of them.

Suddenly, my path was interrupted by Jason. I hadn't even

seen him approach. One second I had my sights set directly on Drew, and the next Jason was there, blocking me.

"You okay, Angie?" I heard him ask the girl.

"She's had too much to drink," Drew said with a smirk. "She just needs to lie down for a bit. She can use your room can't she, Jay?"

I froze. This cannot be happening. Drew could not be planning to rape this poor drunk girl. Even though I knew him to be the worst kind of monster, I couldn't believe how easily it seemed to come to him.

"Actually," Jason said, glancing at me. "I think Angie needs to go home. I'm going to put her in a cab." He took the girl by the arm and pulled her away from Drew, who had a stupefied look on his face.

The girls and I exchanged glances as Jason steered Angie past us. He had his cell phone to his ear. I heard him ask for a cab.

Drew had been cock-blocked by one of his best friends. His face twisted into a combination of anger, petulance and disappointment. It made me smile.

I followed Jay and Angie, needing to make sure he actually did send her home and didn't take her upstairs instead.

I stood at the opposite end of the hall, near the stairs, and watched. Jason held the girl up, and when the cab arrived, he took her outside and put her in it. I moved closer to the open door so I could watch him pay the cabbie and close the car door.

He spotted me before I could duck away, so I stayed where I was rather than run, as I wanted. I watched him step inside the house, closing the door behind him.

He looked at me. "Did you follow me to make sure I sent her home?"

"Yes." I had no trouble meeting his gaze.

His fists clenched at his sides. "I. Am. Not. A. Monster."

I tilted my head as I looked at him. "Are you trying to convince me of that?" I asked. "Or yourself?" And then I turned on my heel and went back to my new friends. Just because he'd sent one girl home didn't mean he and his friends didn't have another victim picked out.

And it didn't change what he'd done to Magda.

CHAPTER 6

Jason began drinking shortly after our little chat. Every time I saw him he had a drink in his hand. As the evening went on, he became more drunk and obnoxious. More like Drew and his other buddies. The four of them were laughing and being loud, and despite that, girls still flocked around them. It disgusted me.

"What's up with him?" Anna asked.

"Me," I said. "I watched him put a girl in a cab earlier because I wanted to make sure he actually sent her home. He saw me. He knew why I was watching."

The three girls stared at me. I thought maybe they thought I was crazy or paranoid. Zoe spoke first. "You followed him alone?"

I nodded. "To the door, yeah."

Her face flushed, and I didn't think it was because she was too warm. "Are you mental? So all that stuff about traveling in groups doesn't apply to you? Are you, like, Wonder Woman or something? What if he had grabbed you?"

I frowned at her. "I would've punched him in the throat."

She shook her head. "You should've taken one of us with you."

"I didn't think of it, okay? I'm not used... It's been a little while since anyone has cared what I do."

The three of them exchanged glances. I shifted uncomfortably, not sure if they pitied me or thought I was lying.

"Don't do it again, okay?" Zoe gave me a beseeching look. "If you don't want to take one of us with you, at least let us know where you're going so we can find you if you don't come back right away."

I nodded. "Okay. We'll make a deal right now that whenever we're together we'll stay together." But really, how often would we be together? It wasn't like we were best friends. No one could replace Mags.

The girls smiled, and the heaviness inside me lightened a little. I wasn't sure how to feel. Responsibility to another person was something I hadn't had for months. And wasn't Magda going off on her own one of the things that upset me so much? If she had told me where she was going, maybe I would've been able to help her. Instead I'd gone looking for her too late and found her in a bedroom, passed out with her panties wrapped around one ankle and condom wrappers on the floor.

I didn't want anyone to ever find me that way.

I stuck close to my new friends after that. We all stuck together, moving as a group. I met a few more people who I didn't really know that well and talked to some that I did. It felt weird, being social. Zoe told every girl we talked to about the self-defense course. A few of them seemed interested, though a couple wrinkled their noses at the idea of violence. I didn't bother trying to convince them that the class was about protecting yourself rather than hurting someone. They obviously didn't think anything bad would ever happen to them. I wasn't going to be the one to tell them they were wrong.

Shortly before midnight I realized two things: one—Gabriel had obviously come to his senses and decided not to crash the party, and two—Jason had gone missing.

I glanced around the room, mentally counting female heads to see if anyone was absent. It was impossible to tell as the party took up most of the house.

Where was he? At least Drew and Adam were still visible. That didn't mean that Jason and Brody weren't raping a girl somewhere while they waited for their buddies to show up.

It made me anxious. I turned to Anna, who stood next to me, and yelled above the music, "I'm going to the bathroom."

She nodded, then leaned closer to me. "There's one upstairs. Use that. Someone puked in the one on this floor. If you're not back in ten minutes, we'll come looking for you."

I smiled. It didn't matter that I could probably take out one or two guys on my own. The three of them had decided that they were my protectors and that the four of us would protect each other. It was as comforting as it was annoying. I didn't need to be fussed over. I didn't want to be a girl who needed protection. I wanted to be the girl who kicked ass.

I took my soda with me out of paranoia. I moved through the crowd, which had gotten bigger in the last hour and made my way out to the foyer. As I climbed the stairs to the second floor, I couldn't help but feel even more out of place. How did people get this wealthy? It was ridiculous.

My heart thumped against my ribs as I climbed. The house wasn't evil, and it couldn't hurt me, but every step I took away from the heart of the party, the more anxious I became. Would anyone hear me scream up here?

Every door on that floor was shut, except for one. I walked down the corridor toward it, my gaze traveling over paintings and framed photographs that hung on the walls. Some of the paintings looked old, and they had little gold tags at the bottom of their frames that had their names engraved on them. Every one of them I looked at was a Bentley.

I reached the partially open door and pushed it open. As soon as I looked inside, I knew it wasn't the bathroom. It was a bedroom. The bedside lamp was on, and I could clearly see posters on the walls and a guitar in the corner.

I could also see Jason passed out on the bed.

There's a moment—and I believe everyone's had it—when you have to make a decision whether to act or retreat. I could back out of the room and continue my search for the restroom, or I could close the door behind me and take advantage of the fact that Jason was unconscious.

I knew that most people, decent people, would leave. A good person didn't take advantage of someone who was too drunk to fight back. But Jason had already proved that he wasn't a decent person. He and his friends had purposely drugged Magda so they could assault her.

I wasn't a decent person.

I closed the door and locked it. I had no idea what I was going to do, or how I planned to do it. What if he woke up? Cautiously, I moved toward him. He was on his back, limbs splayed. I reached out with my left hand, keeping my right free in case I needed to hit him, and poked him hard in the leg. He didn't even make a sound.

His cell phone was on the bed by his hand. I picked it up and pressed the button to wake it up. It didn't ask for a password, but for a fingerprint. I knew Jason was left-handed from being in class with him, so I took his hand and turned it so that I could press his index finger to the right spot on the phone. Just like that, the phone was unlocked.

I scrolled through his pictures—there were a lot of photos of girls. One of them made my heart thump hard against my ribs and then fall still. *Magda.* It was a portrait of her, taken at school. I don't think she knew he'd taken it, because she didn't look self-conscious. The sight of her, smiling and happy, hurt to the point of physical pain. He'd taken that smile from her, just as he'd taken this photograph without her consent, and he'd been allowed to get away with both.

I stared at him through a veil of scorching tears. There had to be something I could do to make him pay, even just a little bit.

I couldn't rape him. Even if it were possible, I wouldn't. That kind of violation would make me as bad as him, and it would make him a victim. I didn't want anyone to feel sorry for him. I wanted them to mock him and say the kinds of things to him that people had said to Magda after photos and video of her attack had gotten around. I wanted people to see him for what he was.

In my purse I had one of Magda's lipsticks. Her skin was darker than mine, and she'd been able to wear some rich berry colors I envied. The one in my bag was a deep raspberry. I took it out and removed the cap.

I hovered over Jason for a moment, considering my next action. Chickening out wasn't an option. I turned the lipstick and bent down. In block letters I wrote RAPIST on his forehead. I put the lipstick back in my bag and took out my phone. I removed the case first, because I didn't want it to be identifiable. I brought up a Facebook photo of Magda and put my phone in Jason's limp fingers. Then I picked up his phone and switched it to camera mode. I took a photo of him lying there, with his title on his forehead, and Magda's photo right there, so everyone would know exactly who he had hurt. Then I uploaded the photo I'd taken to Jason's social media with the hashtags #rapist #NoJusticeForMagda #GotAwayWithIt and #CarterHigh.

I wiped his phone down before putting it on the bed beside him, then I took back my own and went to the door. I peeked into the hall to make sure no one was there before stepping outside.

Another door down the hall was open, and the light on inside allowed me to see that it was the bathroom. I slipped in and did my business. My legs trembled as I washed my hands. I wasn't sure what I'd just done, or what the consequences would be, but there was no taking it back now.

I dried my hands and opened the door. "Shit!" I cried when I saw someone standing there. I pulled back my fist, but a familiar voice said my name before I lashed out. It was Zoe. Behind her were Anna and Caitlin. They were wide-eyed as they stared at me.

"Have I been gone ten minutes?" I asked, embarrassed to be so on edge.

Anna blushed. "No, but I got worried."

I smiled. "There was someone in here when I came up. I had to wait. Thank you for worrying."

"It wasn't all about you," Zoe remarked with a grin. "I have to pee too."

While we waited outside for her to finish, Caitlin fished her phone out of her purse. I watched as she tapped the screen with her finger, my pulse beating wildly.

"Oh my God!"

Anna whirled toward her. "What?" Caitlin showed her the screen, and her jaw dropped. "Holy shit!"

If I didn't ask it would be weird, and I was already pushing it by having been upstairs when the picture was taken. "What is it?"

Anna couldn't seem to decide if she wanted to laugh or cheer as Caitlin showed me the photo. It was the one I'd taken just minutes before.

I didn't have to fake the laughter that poured out of me. The adrenaline of what I'd done hit hard, making me light-headed and giddy. "Was that taken tonight?" I asked.

Caitlin shrugged. "How should I know? I guess so."

Anna's gaze was bright as it met mine. "Who cares? It's fabulous. Now everyone will know what he did." It was exactly what I wanted to hear. "Whoever took it even left Magda's picture beside him."

On the other side of the door Zoe shouted, "What are you laughing at?" Then the toilet flushed, and we heard running water at the sink. A few seconds later the door opened. Zoe was still drying her hands.

"Check your phone," Caitlin said.

Anna was looking at her own. "I got it too."

Zoe's reaction was the best. Her eyes and mouth opened wide, and then she started to cackle—like a witch who had just performed the perfect spell. "Oh, this is *awesome*." She began tapping at the screen. "Not only am I loving this, but I'm going to *share* it."

We went back downstairs to join the party. When we got there, I couldn't believe the number of people who were looking at their phones, exchanging startled glances, or acting like it was awesome. A few were pissed, but who cared about the douche bags? I'd known the photo would get noticed, it just hadn't occurred to me how quickly.

I found myself looking for Drew, Brody and Adam. The three of them were together in the kitchen, staring at their phones with expressions that were somewhat amused, but mostly pissed. Drew seemed especially angry. I braced myself, waiting for one of them to look at me and point his finger. Surely, they had to know it had been *me*.

"What the fuck?" Drew demanded. His jaw was tight, his eyes narrow. "Who the fuck did this?"

Not one of them looked at me—at least not for any length of time. They looked around the room at the laughing crowd, glaring at everyone who met their collective gaze. I realized then that they were looking for a guy. It didn't occur to them that a girl might do something like this. Did they not think we had the balls to pull such a prank? Did they think a guy would just randomly have lipstick in his pocket? I didn't care which it was, because I'd gotten away with it.

That was the moment I realized what I had to do—for Magda and for myself. I had to get revenge. On all of them.

One down.

Three to go.

Last Year

"Do you have a costume yet?" Magda asked. We were in her kitchen making pizza while Gabe and one of his friends sat at the dining-room table discussing some project for their senior history class. I had a perfect view of his profile from where I stood. God, he was pretty.

"A costume for what?" I asked, slapping pepperoni slices on top of the sauce.

"Drew Carson's Halloween party. He invited us, remember?"

Ugh. She didn't *really* want to go to that, did she? One look at her face and I could tell she did. And she wanted me to go with her. I hated going to rich-kid parties—they always made me feel like trash. My family wasn't poor, but we didn't have a lot of disposable income.

I opened my mouth to tell her I wasn't going—not for her, not for anyone. And then she said, "Gabe said he'd drop us off. He might even stay for a bit."

"Fine," I said. "But only because you and your brother will be the only people there worth hanging out with."

"I'm going as Cleopatra," she announced. "I hope Drew notices me."

Her little smile was so cute I couldn't bring myself to warn her off Drew again. She wouldn't listen anyway. She was going to get her heart broken when Drew hooked up with someone not so obviously virginal as she was.

"He'd be blind not to," I said instead, dumping a handful of grated cheese on the pizza. When she turned that grin on me, I smiled back. "Of course he'll notice you."

I had no idea how much I'd regret saying that.

* * *

I woke up Sunday morning feeling better than I had in months. Even though I knew what I'd done to Jason was wrong, I couldn't deny the happiness it gave me. Maybe happiness was the wrong word. I felt like I had accomplished something, or taken a step to fix a problem.

And was it really wrong to label someone a criminal when you knew they'd done the crime?

Regardless, I felt good. I got up, showered and went downstairs for breakfast. My mother smiled when I kissed her cheek. I hadn't realized how much I'd changed until I saw the surprise on her face. When you're drowning in grief it's hard to see all the people who are trying to save you. And she had her own problems with my father. I thought she was weak to stay with him, but I also understood that this house would be a lot harder to run without his income.

After breakfast, I rode my bike to the cemetery. It was a beautiful sunny day, and I wanted to talk to Magda, but not about how angry or sad I was, or even how much I missed her. I wanted to talk to her about what I had done. When I got there, church had just let out. Magda's mother, Gabriel and his little sister Teresa walked the gravel path from the church into the cemetery. My heart stuttered at the sight of them. For a moment I contemplated running away, so Mrs. Torres's sadness couldn't diminish my sense of accomplishment. I didn't run. In the end, my love for these people won.

Mrs. Torres was an older version of Magda, only a little shorter. She was in her forties, and very pretty. Her husband had walked out on them a few years ago, and the last I'd heard was living in Miami with a twenty-three-year-old. He had nothing to do with the kids, and they had nothing to do with him. Magda had acted like he didn't even exist. I remembered him, but I couldn't remember if I ever even liked him. I certainly didn't like him after he abandoned his family. It made the reality of my own family situation even more bitter. What the fuck was wrong with men? Weren't there *any* good ones in the world? So far, Gabe seemed to be the only one.

Magda's mother smiled when she saw me, even though she had tears in her eyes. She cried a lot. In a way I envied that she was able to get her grief out in a way that didn't require punching someone in the face. She held out her arms, and I stepped into her hug as she told me how good it was to see me.

"It's been too long," she said. "You must come for dinner some night. How does tomorrow sound?"

"I'll check with Mom, but it should be okay."

Mrs. Torres released me. "Come after school. We'll visit. You can help me cook like Magda used to."

My throat was tight as I swallowed. "Okay. I'll check with Mom and call you later." Then I was distracted by Teresa, who also wanted a hug. She was thirteen, and losing her big sister had been very hard on her. Gabriel had told me she was afraid of boys. I didn't know how to help with that, because I had to be honest—I was afraid of them too.

I hung back when Mrs. Torres and Teresa went to the grave. Their grief was a private thing. And I was still clinging to that fading sense of accomplishment I'd woken up with.

Gabriel stayed with me. I should've known it wasn't because he enjoyed my company so much.

"A friend of mine forwarded me an interesting Instagram post this morning," he said, looking down at me.

My heart gave a hard thump. I raised my gaze to his. "The picture of Jason Bentley?" If I told him I had no idea what he was talking about, he'd know for sure I'd been behind it. "Yeah, I saw that too." It wasn't a lie. Zoe had forwarded the photo to me last night.

"Whoever did that to him must've really had it in for him."

I didn't even blink. "I really didn't think about it. But it's the wallpaper on my phone now."

He smiled—just a small tilt of his lips. "Mine too."

I grinned. "I wonder if he'll show his face at school tomorrow."

"He will. They'll make it some kind of smear campaign. It'll take more than this to hurt those four for long."

There went my sense of accomplishment.

"Though this will sting. Whoever did it took a photo from Magda's Facebook page. Makes me think they did this in retaliation for her more than to out Bentley as a rapist."

"Does it matter? I'm not losing any sleep over it." In fact, I'd slept better last night than I had in months.

"No. It doesn't matter at all. Were you there?"

"Yeah. I went with friends."

He looked surprised. I guess he would be. For most of my life Magda had been my only friend. Not that I hadn't hung out with other people, but she'd always been with me.

"Girls from my self-defense class," I told him. I don't know why I felt like he needed to know that detail. "I like them."

Sometimes he smiled at me like he thought I was amusing when I wasn't trying to be. Like we had a private joke, only I didn't know the punch line. "People usually do like their friends."

"Not always. I know girls who seem to hate their best friends."

"Yeah, well, you guys have that whole frenemy thing."

"I've never had one." Now, *that* was a tiny little lie. After Magda died, I hated her for weeks. I was so mad that she'd let them destroy her. I had wanted her to keep fighting. I had wanted her to get past it, which was a laugh because now *I* couldn't even get past it, so how had I expected her to do it? Sometimes I still hated her for leaving me. I wasn't going to tell her brother that.

Gabriel looked away. He was watching his mother and sister. "Be careful, Hadley. I know you think you're smart and strong. You *are* smart and strong, but please don't be reckless. Don't go looking for trouble because you want to avenge Magda."

I stared at him, not quite sure of what he meant. Did he suspect that I was behind that photo of Jason, or was I just that transparent? "You're not going to lose me," I promised. My cheeks burned. I meant his whole family, of course, but mostly him.

He turned to me with a smile, but there was sadness in his eyes, as though he didn't believe me. "Good." Then he held out his hand. "Let's go say hi to Magda."

My fingers trembled a little as I placed my hand in his. His grip was warm and strong, and in that moment I felt like everything was going to be okay.

Even though I knew I was wrong.

CHAPTER 7

Jason wasn't at school on Monday.

I wasn't really surprised by his absence. Most gossip said it was because his family was meeting with the police and investigators and lawyers to find out who'd taken and uploaded the photo. That made me a little nervous, I admit, but there was no way they could pin it on me. Was there? I'd been careful.

Fuck it. I didn't regret doing it, so if I got arrested for it, fine. At least then I'd get a chance to tell them what they'd done to Magda. It didn't matter that Drew had been the one to put something in her drink and lure her away from the party. All four of them had taken turns with her—and took photos. There was a video too.

How could people have forgotten that? How could they feel sorry for Jason, or angry on his behalf? Were they so desensitized to rape that they just shrugged it off? The people who sided with Jason were the same ones who called Madga a slut. How could they believe a girl who had been a virgin would want her first time to be with four guys and recorded? God, it made me so mad I could kill someone.

Both Brody and Drew were in my history class. I sat as far away from them as I could, but the room wasn't that big, and I could hear Drew's obnoxious voice all the way on the other side.

"They don't know who they're messing with," he stated with so much ego I almost gagged. "Whoever did it used his phone to upload it. My father's a lawyer. I told him to have it dusted for prints."

Panic seized me, but only for a second. I'd wiped down Jason's phone and the doorknob. Regardless, there'd probably been close to a hundred kids in the house that night. Good luck trying to figure out who had done it when all of us had left fingerprints all over the place.

"He says he felt violated." Brody snickered. "I told him that's what happens when you're a pussy."

"Nice," I said before I could stop myself.

The two of them looked at me. The rows of seats between us had started to fill up, but we made eye contact.

Drew sneered at me. He was one of those guys who thought he was better than everyone else. Entitled. "No one was talking to you."

I smiled. I don't know how I managed it, but it felt good to smirk at him. "If he talks like that about Jason, don't you wonder what he says about you when you're not around?"

Drew shot a sharp glance at Brody, who looked slightly panicked. "I don't say anything about you. Honest."

I snorted. "Yeah, but you kind of have to say that, don't you?

I mean, no one's going to admit to their face that they talk about the person behind their back."

"Shut up," Brody told me.

It was at that moment that Mr. Stiles, our teacher, walked into the room. He turned on Brody. "Mr. Henry, that's quite enough. If you would like to remain in this class, you will apologize to Miss White, or you will leave."

Oh, that didn't feel good at *all*. I had to bite the inside of my cheek to keep from grinning as Brody glared at me. "Sorry," he said sullenly. It was obvious he didn't mean it, but I didn't care. He still had to say it.

At lunch I met up with Zoe, Anna and Caitlin. Caitlin turned to me as soon as I sat. "What happened between you and Brody today? Rebecca Thomas said you totally told him off in history class."

"*What?*" Zoe and Anna chorused.

You just had to love high school gossip. "I didn't tell him off. I just called attention to the fact that he's a complete prick."

Anna shook her head. "That's an insult to pricks everywhere."

We laughed.

"No, seriously," Zoe said. "What happened? Give us details so we can set people straight if they start talking smack."

I sighed and told them what'd really happened.

"Wow." Zoe shook her head. "You really know how to talk to people."

I shrugged. "They raped my best friend. You think I should be nice?"

Her face went completely white, then red. "Oh my God.

Hadley, I'm so sorry. I didn't think. I was just trying to make a joke. I'm such a bitch."

"No. I'm the bitch. I didn't need to put it that way, and I should've known you were only teasing. I'm sorry." She looked at me uncertainly. I didn't like myself much at that moment. "Seriously. We're good. I know you didn't mean to upset me, and I apologize for upsetting you."

"I didn't. I really didn't."

"It's okay." I put my hand on her arm. "Really."

Thankfully, Anna changed the topic. If she hadn't, I think Zoe and I might have kept on going for the rest of lunch. "So, any ideas as to who took the picture? It certainly wasn't Jason."

"Somebody with balls," Zoe commented. "Especially to do it in his own house."

"Ovaries," I corrected. "Somebody with ovaries did it."

Her eyes twinkled as she looked at me. "You're right. It was a girl."

"I want to be her best friend," Anna commented. "Seriously."

"Don't look," Caitlin whispered close to my ear. "But Brody's giving you the stink eye."

Of course I looked. She kicked me under the table. I didn't even wince. Brody was watching me with a hateful expression, and he didn't seem to care that I noticed.

I did the only thing I could under the circumstances; I stuck my tongue out. It was stupid and childish, but it felt completely right. Did he think he could scare me? What could he possibly do to me? He and his friends could rape me and try to destroy my reputation, but I'd recover. They'd already taken my best friend; there wasn't much else they could do.

My friends burst into loud laughter that carried throughout

the cafeteria and made heads turn toward us. I laughed too, and went back to my lunch. Anticipation twitched through my veins.

One down.

I wanted to make Brody number two.

Gabriel wasn't home when I arrived at his house Monday afternoon. Teresa was, though, and she was very happy to see me. She practically flew at me when I came into the house, and wrapped her arms around my waist. She was getting so tall, so grown-up. I worried for her.

Then, I noticed the earrings she was wearing. They were little pink plastic lips. I recognize them because I had made them for Magda as a gift for her fourteenth birthday.

Teresa must've noticed the look on my face, and where I was looking, because her hands immediately went to her ears. "Mom said I could wear them."

Mrs. Torres looked up from something she was stirring on the stove. She gave me that sad smile. "I hope you don't mind, Hadley. Magda had many nice things, and Teresa feels closer to her when she wears them."

"I don't mind at all," I said. And it was true. The earrings had only caught me off guard. It was nice to know somebody would wear them since Magda no longer could.

"Come with me," the older woman said, setting her spoon in a holder on the stove.

I had a sense of where we were going, and I wasn't wrong. She led me into Magda's bedroom, which looked as it had the day before she took those pills. I'd only been in it once since then, and that was to help her mother pick out a dress to bury her daughter in. My skin tingled uncomfortably. I didn't like being in this room. It felt so empty.

Mrs. Torres opened the jewelry box on the dresser, and the closet doors. "I have taken all the things I want to keep of hers. Gabriel and Teresa have taken what they want as well. Eventually, I will give the rest away to family, or donate it to charity. Magda would like that, I think. But before I do, I would like you to take anything you want, so that you will always have something of hers."

I was dangerously close to tears. I looked around at the white and lavender room. Magda and I had painted it a few years ago. I'd slept over many nights in this room. It was as familiar to me as my own. Part of me wanted to scream at her for giving Magda's things away, while another part of me wanted to take it all home.

Mrs. Torres seemed to understand what I was feeling. She patted me on the shoulder. "I'll leave you alone to go through things. Teresa, go do your homework, baby."

Her daughter didn't argue, and neither did I. I stood there in the middle of the room, staring at the open closet. I probably looked brain-dead, but in reality my mind raced with too many things to even sort out. I tried to push the noise aside and stepped up to the closet. My hands shook as I reached inside and started going through the clothing there, hanger by hanger.

I took a couple of tops and sweaters, then a pair of shoes and a pair of boots. Our shoe size was one of the things we had in common. I didn't touch her jeans because none would fit, but I did find a cute miniskirt. I put these things on the bed before turning my attention to the jewelry box. Magda had liked jewelry more than me, and had a lot of earrings. I took a few pairs of those as well, and a ring that had a big flower on it.

Her makeup bag was on the dresser. Her favorite lip gloss was on top. I took it. Then I wrapped the makeup and jewelry in the clothing and carried the bundle out to the kitchen. Mrs. Torres looked pleased that I had found things, and gave me a paper bag in which to put it all. I set it by my shoes so I wouldn't forget it. It was like my own personal little treasure.

"Can I help you make dinner?" I asked. She had mentioned us doing that like she and I and Mags used to.

"Of course," she said with a smile. "You can chop the onion for me. You are always so good at that."

I smiled. "That's because none of you can do it without crying."

Helping her cook was something Magda and I often did. I envied their mother-daughter relationship. It wasn't that I didn't love my own mother, or that we weren't close. But Mrs. Torres seemed to understand Magda—and Teresa—in a way my mother didn't understand me. There were times I thought Mom had forgotten what it was like to be a teenager. Mrs. Torres remembered. She tried to pay attention to modern music, current events, even TV shows. I knew that she took an interest in everything Teresa did, but never seemed to do it in an overbearing way.

We cooked, and we made dessert for later. We talked—sometimes about Magda—and sometimes not.

"Hadley," she said, turning toward me. "I would like to ask you something, and I would like it if we could keep it just between the two of us."

"Okay," I said. I was a little worried where this might be going.

"I am worried about my boy."

"Gabriel?" As though she had another son. "Why?" Gabriel was smart, got good grades, worked part-time, was nice and absolutely gorgeous. What could she possibly be worried about?

"Since Magda…left us, Gabriel has become more and more withdrawn. He seems so angry. I'm worried what he might do if he can't let go of that anger."

"I'm not sure I'm a good one to talk to," I replied honestly. "I'm angry too."

"We're all angry. You should be angry when someone you love is taken from you too soon, but there is also sadness that comes with grieving. I see it in you, and Teresa. I see it when I look in the mirror. I do not see it in Gabriel. He has not grieved for his sister. He won't allow himself to do it."

I thought of all the times Gabriel had hugged me when I cried over Magda. All the times he had been there for me. I'd thought I'd also been there for him, but maybe I hadn't been. I couldn't remember ever seeing him cry for his sister. I don't remember having seen him cry at all. I thought he had because of the anguish I'd seen on his face, but had his eyes ever been actually wet?

"Do you want me to talk to him?" I asked.

"Would you?" She looked so relieved. "I don't know if he'll open up to you, either, but if he decides he wants to talk, I think you are the only one he will talk to."

I wasn't sure I wanted that responsibility. Wasn't sure I was strong enough for it. I was so overwhelmed by my own grief, my own anger, and I didn't think I had room to shoulder anybody else's. But this was Gabe, and I had to be there for him if I could.

"Okay. I'll talk to him."

"Thank you. You're such a good girl."

I wanted to correct her on that, but I couldn't. Let her think it. If I'd been so good, I would have watched over Magda better that night instead of being pissy. I would have been more understanding, and then she wouldn't have killed herself after her best friend had been such a thoughtless bitch.

Everyone said it wasn't my fault that Magda killed herself. It was because of the rape, because of the bullying. But I knew, in my heart, that the way I'd spoken to her that day had been the last straw.

She had said it all in the note she left. "Tell Hadley I'm sorry she got pulled into all of this." Pulled in, like I hadn't had a choice. I hadn't made Magda feel like I wanted to stand beside her, and in the end, Mags had felt completely alone.

I had to live with that.

Gabriel arrived home shortly after five, as dinner neared completion. I followed him into his room, closing the door behind us. He looked startled when he turned around and found himself alone with me.

His dark eyes narrowed. "Mom sent you in here, didn't she?"

I didn't bother to lie. "She's worried about you. She thinks you're so full of anger you can't properly grieve for Magda."

"That's because I can't just hand over everything to Jesus, and expect it to be okay." He looked disgusted. "She thinks if she prays enough we'll all find peace. She thinks my sister's in heaven hanging out with God and the Apostles, a couple of saints too, probably. She thinks that's wonderful. I would rather have my sister here than imagine her with a halo and wings."

"Believing that makes it easier for her. She needs to believe that there's a heaven, and that Magda's in it. It doesn't matter what you think of that. You need to find a way to stop being so angry at your mother, at Magda."

He laughed, but it was a harsh sound. "Really? That's rich coming from a girl who has to beat people up several times a week to even feel remotely normal. I don't think you're the best person to lecture me on anger and letting go of it."

I shrugged. "You're right. I'm not. But I'm trying, and I think it might finally be working."

"Well, good for you. How nice that you're just able to forget what those bastards did to her and let them get away with it."

"I haven't forgotten *anything*." I jabbed him in the chest with my finger. It probably hurt me more than him. "I have to see those assholes five days a week. I have to sit in the same room with them. I have to listen to them talk and laugh. I have to watch them *live*, while knowing Magda is gone. So, don't you get snotty with me, Gabriel Torres. The other day they were all in a car together, and for a moment I was terrified they were going to grab me and do to me what they did to Magda. That's not something you have to think about."

His face hardened. The muscle in his jaw stood out beneath his cheek. "If one of them so much as touches you," he growled, "I'll kill him."

He trembled with anger. I didn't know what to do about that, and I was too astounded by his confession to do anything more than stare at him. He lifted his hand and touched my hair, rubbing the strands between his fingers. My breath caught in my throat. This was not like our hugs, or even when we sometimes held each other's hands.

Gabriel took a step toward me. We were already close, and he made us even closer, so that we were no more than a fist apart.

"Promise me you'll be careful," he beseeched, his dark eyes full of emotion. "I don't know what I'd do without you."

I swallowed. My mouth and throat were dry, and my heart was beating so hard I thought I'd wake up with bruises tomorrow morning. "You're not going to lose me. Not ever." My voice was strained, strangled by the tightness in my throat.

He let go of my hair and slid his hand around the back of my neck. His palm was warm against my skin. Our gazes locked as I tilted my chin up. I knew what he was going to do, and I wasn't going to stop him. I would never stop him, no matter how far it went.

Gabriel lowered his head. My eyes began to close as my lips opened. I could barely breathe. I wanted him to kiss me. I wanted to kiss him back. I could feel his breath—it smelled of peppermint. My hands clutched the front of his T-shirt. I felt like I was on fire, and he was rain.

Just as his lips were about to touch mine there was a knock n his door. We froze, breathing each other's air.

"Gabe? Hadley?" It was Teresa. "Dinner's ready."

"We'll be right there," Gabriel replied.

I let go of his shirt and tried to step backward, but he still had his hand around my neck and he held me fast.

"You need to know," he murmured, "that if she hadn't knocked I would've kissed you. And the next time I get the chance, I'm going to. Are you okay with that?"

Wasn't it obvious? God, he was so incredible. "Yes," I rasped.

He let me go then, stepping back so that I could leave the room before him. He didn't say anything. He didn't have to. We both knew what was going to happen the next time we were alone.

And I was so okay with it.

CHAPTER 8

I didn't see Gabriel again for the rest of the week. Part of me was disappointed, but there was another part that was glad to avoid him. It was the part that felt guilty for feeling anything other than anger when my best friend was dead. Rationally, I knew Magda wouldn't want me to be like this, and that she would laugh about me having a crush on Gabriel. She would want me to be happy. It was me who didn't want to feel it.

I knew if I was going to continue down this road, getting whatever revenge or payback I could for her, I was going to have to find a way to conceal my identity. I was just lucky that Jason hadn't woken up and seen me. I couldn't count on Adam, Brody or Drew being drunk, or even stoned, when I went after them.

So Thursday night before defense class—it would be my third martial arts class that week—I was sitting in my closet digging through a box of winter gear. I had to dig to the bottom to find what I was looking for, but I did find it. I pulled it out of the box and held it in both hands, smiling at the sight of it.

It was a pink ski mask that Magda had bought me last Christmas when we'd decided we were going to take up skiing. We never did ski, and I'd never worn the mask. It seemed right to me that I would wear it in her honor when I confronted her rapists.

Maybe the mask was too flashy, but I'd seen a stack of them at Target, and at a kiosk in the mall. I wouldn't be the only woman in town to own one, and since I'd never worn it before, there was little chance of anyone figuring out it was me beneath it.

I closed the box and shoved it back in my closet. Then I hid the ski mask in my underwear drawer. When I went downstairs, my father was in the living room. He'd arrived home earlier that day from a trip. He was gone more than he was at home, and I didn't mind it.

"Where are you going?" he asked with a frown.

"Self-defense class," I replied. "At the dojo."

"That's your fourth class this week. You're not going. Upstairs and your homework instead."

I stared at him. "It's my third." And how the hell did he know about it anyway? "My homework is done, and I have to go because I help teach the class."

He looked like he didn't believe me. Maybe if I gave him a roundhouse kick to the head he wouldn't be so dubious. "They can do without you for one night. You've been out too much."

Before I could stop myself I asked, "How would you know how often I've been out? You're never here. I'll be back by ten." I turned to walk away.

"You're not going."

I sighed and faced him once more. His cheeks were flushed

with anger. I don't know why he'd decided to make this some kind of power struggle between us, but he had.

"Look, Dad, this class is important. If you don't want me to go, you can call Detective Diane Davies and explain to her that you don't think training girls to protect themselves from muggers or rapists is important. Otherwise, I'm going. You lost any right to order me around when you chose your job over my sixteenth birthday."

All that redness in his face drained away, replaced by the stark pallor of guilt. Did he honestly believe his absence had gone unnoticed?

"Anything else?" I asked. "I don't want to be late, but if you need some father-daughter bonding, we can totally do that."

He stared at me like he didn't recognize me. I could tell him it was mutual, but I was going to be late. So, I said nothing. I left him sitting there, grabbed the keys off the hook by the door, went outside, got in the car and drove to class. I got there with five minutes to spare and the urge to hit something hard gnawing at my insides.

There were four new girls there when I walked in. Anna, Zoe and Caitlin were already there, and they introduced me to the newbies. One was Zoe's cousin Julie, who went to a different school. She'd brought her friend Kelsey with her. The other two girls—Megan and Holly—had seen a flyer for the class at Starbucks. It was nice to have new faces. Nice to know that there were girls out there who wanted to know how to protect themselves.

Detective Davies smiled when she saw me. "I wasn't sure you were going to make it," she commented.

"Wouldn't miss it." I put my bag to the side near the wall

and did a few stretches before the class started. As she had last week, Detective Davies talked a bit before getting started with the physical instruction.

"Statistics tell us that approximately one in five women are raped in this country every year. Personally, I think that's a low number. I believe in reality it's closer to three out of five women who experience some sort of sexual assault in their lifetime. Men are sexually assaulted, as well. Statistics say one in seventy-one. This is probably a low number as well, as men are even less likely to report an assault than women.

"Almost every one of these victims reports a feeling of isolation. They believe they are going through this alone even though there are far too many people out there who know exactly how they feel. My goal in this class is to help keep you from being one of those people. But I'm not just here to teach you how to fight, or defend yourself. I want this class—you girls—to be a place where you can feel safe and express yourself freely. I want you all to be there for each other. This class is not just about protecting yourselves, but protecting other women and girls who may not be able to protect themselves."

I watched her as she paced a bit in front of us. She made eye contact with all of us, but I felt as though she were talking directly to me, as though she knew what I had done, knew what I wanted to do and was giving me *permission*. Rationally, I knew that she wasn't singling me out, and that as a cop she would not condone any of us taking the law into her own hands. That wasn't going to stop me, however.

Maybe it made me a terrible person, but I didn't regret what I'd done to Jason. It wasn't as though I stripped him and posted naked photos. It wasn't like I made it look like he used a stuffed

sheep as a sex toy. He and his friends had done far more damage to who knows how many people. All I'd done was remind
them that there were consequences for their actions. And I
was going to keep reminding them until I thought they'd had
enough. Posting that photo of Jason had alleviated some of
the guilt I carried. I might not have saved Magda, but I could
show those assholes that they couldn't get away with what
they'd done.

I felt powerful, but more than that, I was hopeful. For the
first time since Magda's death, I was starting to feel like my
own life might be worth living. That I might have a purpose,
and only some of that hopefulness came from almost kissing
Gabe. Yes, I might get into trouble if I was caught. I was aware
that what I was doing, and planned to do, might backfire on
me, but I was willing to risk that and face my own consequences if necessary.

"Tonight," Detective Davies said, "we're going to go through
some techniques for fending off an attacker. You know how
girls are always said to fight dirty?"

We all looked at each other and nodded.

"Well, I don't think that's a bad thing. When there's a very
good chance that your attacker is stronger than you—and let's
face it, there are very few of us who are as strong as a guy our
own age or size—you have to do whatever necessary to escape
harm. You do that by pulling hair, jabbing eyes, kicking balls."
A nervous collection of laughter rose up from the girls.

Detective Davies smiled. "If any of you are ever faced with
physical danger—I hope to God you're not—I want you to
be able to put as much hurt into your attacker as possible, as

quickly as possible, so that you can get away. In short, ladies, I'm going to teach you to fight like a girl."

We cheered, grinning like idiots. What this woman offered us was an escape from fear. Before Magda's attack, I'd never really given much thought to sexual assault. I think a lot of us lived in a little bubble where we assumed it would never happen to us. And sometimes I think women, particularly girls my age, don't always know when they're being assaulted, because assault doesn't necessarily mean rape.

But even though I had never worried about being raped myself, I have always been aware of the fear. Girls and women are told not to walk alone after dark. We're told to travel in groups. Don't go to a public bathroom alone. Don't drink too much. Don't smile too much. Don't wear a dress that's too short. Don't wear pants that are too tight. If you do, you're asking for it.

I've never had to ask what *it* is. We all know, and we know from a time when we're very young. We're told that if we are attacked we probably did something to invite it. But I have never heard of a boy being told that he shouldn't inspire the fear, that he shouldn't behave in a way that causes fear or pain.

"I've never heard anyone at any time say to a guy 'don't rape anybody,'" I said out loud. The girls nodded. "But almost every girl I know has been told by friends, family or the media, 'don't get raped.' How did the responsibility fall on us, when we're not the ones doing the harm? If somebody gets robbed, they're not put in jail for it." To my surprise this was met with more cheers and applause.

"That's right!" one of the new girls cried. "I'm so sick of it."

I looked up at Detective Davies. She was smiling at me in

a way that was almost maternal. Like she was proud. I smiled back. "Can I help you demonstrate, Detective?"

"Yes, please, Hadley." She rolled her shoulders and stretched her neck from side to side. "Since you're all of the same age group, I'll play the part of the attacker. Now, if I come at you like this, what do you do?"

She came at me fast, grabbing me around the neck in a chokehold that bent my spine backward. For a second I panicked as I gasped for breath. Then I tried to picture it in my head. I couldn't reach back and hit her in the body, but her head was close to mine.

"I can scratch your arm," I said.

"Good. What else?"

"I might be able to smash your face with my head if I can loosen your grip a bit. I can reach back and pull your hair. And I can stick my thumbs in your eyes." I demonstrated all three of these as effectively as I could without being able to see what I was doing. Several of the girls groaned when I went for the detective's eyes.

Detective Davies released me and turned to the class. "All these things are effective. Now, Hadley, put your arm around my neck and I'll show you some other things."

By the time she was done with me, I'd been elbowed in the gut, had my eyes gouged, my nose gouged, my toes broken, my knee dislocated and had been kicked in my hypothetical balls. And the girls were all laughing.

"Do not stop at that first attack," the older woman instructed. "Once you get an opening, you exploit it until you've rendered your attacker incapacitated. I don't care if it's gross— and you won't, either—go for the eyes and go for the nose.

When his eyes are watering, you kick them in the junk. You do whatever you need to do to get free. You scratch, you pull hair. If you have to, bite, but that's a last resource. Step on toes, kick knees, kick him in the stomach. Hit them with your purse. Hell, hit him with your shoe. Put him down, get out of there and call 911. Now, let's partner up and practice."

The girls jumped to their feet and quickly found partners. The odd number left me partnered with Detective Davies again. We practiced a few of the things that I hadn't thought to do when she was my attacker.

"Were you at Jason Bentley's party?" she asked me.

I nodded, taking the hand she offered to help me to my feet after she knocked me on my butt. "Yeah. I saw the picture that got uploaded."

Her face was serious, her eyes seeming to look right through me. "Do you know who took it?"

"No." The lie rolled easily off my tongue. "I'm glad they did it, though."

She smiled the tiniest bit. "I bet. Any idea where he got that photo of Magda? It looked like she posed for it."

My spine stiffened. "If you think he took it, you're wrong. It was her brother Gabe. She never would have smiled like that for Jason."

"Was Gabriel at the party?"

Shit. Did she suspect Gabe? "No. He knew it wouldn't be a good idea."

The detective nodded. "No, I suppose it wouldn't be. If you hear anything, will you let me know? Even if it seems like nothing?"

I considered my answer for a moment. "Detective, you seem

really awesome, but if you think I'd turn in the one person who seems to care about what happened to Magda, you're mental. Even if I knew who it was, I wouldn't say a word."

"You probably shouldn't tell me that," she reminded dryly.

I shrugged. "I try to be honest."

"Let's just forget I asked."

I shrugged agan. "Fine by me." Then she had me come around the class with her and see how the other girls were doing.

If I decided to get a little revenge on Brody, I was going to have to be very careful to make sure suspicion didn't fall on Gabriel. I would never forgive myself if he got blamed for my actions. And I wanted Brody—and his buddies—to know that the person coming after them wasn't a guy, but a girl.

A girl in a pink ski mask who was going to make sure they paid for what they'd done to Magda Torres.

CHAPTER 9

That Friday was when I officially became a stalker. I had a couple of classes with Brody, and I eavesdropped on his conversations. It turned out that he and Drew, and Adam and Jason, liked to go out drinking on Friday nights. They went to a small bar a couple of towns over that was popular with college students. Apparently they had some pretty good fake IDs to back them up.

Obviously, even if I could get into a bar, I wasn't going to go to one where my best friend's rapists liked to hang out. I didn't have a fake ID, and to be honest, getting drunk held no appeal to me. I was terrified of it, of the control I would lose. It was too easy to be a victim when you were drunk, and I wasn't going to be a victim.

I told my mother I was going out with Zoe, Anna and Caitlin. The three of them had invited me to go out with them. They were just going to hang out at a coffee shop or something. I told them I'd meet up with them later if I could.

At 11:45 that night, I was sitting in my mom's car one

parking lot over from the bar. I'd chosen that lot because it didn't have any cameras. However, it had a very good view of the bar's entrance.

I had a moment, while peeing behind a Dumpster, when I wondered, *What the hell am I doing?* I was intentionally lying in wait for someone. What was I going to do? Brody was going to come out of that bar with his buddies. I couldn't take on all four of them. I could only hope that he left last, or that he wouldn't notice if I followed him home. That wasn't really an option. It was always a bad idea to fight someone on their own turf.

That aside, I didn't know what I was going to do to him once I had him. Beating him up would feel awesome, but would it avenge Magda, would it change him in any way? Would he regret what he'd done? Would he pay?

I'd heard that Jason was embarrassed about the photo, and that he'd become a little withdrawn this past week. The fact that someone had sneaked into his room and done that to him without him knowing freaked him out. Good. Maybe he'd think about how Magda had felt. I liked knowing he felt vulnerable.

Now, to repeat the process with his friends.

It was just a couple of minutes before midnight when I saw the four of them come out of the bar. Brody barely made it to the bottom of the steps before he doubled over and puked in a bush. I could hear the others laughing from where I sat with my window down.

Jason was the only one to approach Brody in what looked like a helpful way—like he was going to try to help him walk. Brody waved him off. Jason rejoined the other two, and they

staggered toward a little red car I recognized as Drew's. They
were all drunk.

Now what the hell did I do? I couldn't just let them drive
off, could I? What if they hurt someone? I drew a deep breath.
Getting mad because stupid drunks were going to interfere
with my plans for revenge was a little mental. There was a
line—a moral line—I couldn't cross. Maybe it was cliché, but
even though I wanted them to pay, I wasn't willing to allow
myself to become like them.

I could have sexually humiliated Jason the week before.
He'd been passed out. I could've stuck something in his butt.
I could've left him naked. There was part of me that very
much wanted to assault him, to make him feel like Magda
had when she saw the photos they posted of her. But when
given the opportunity, I simply couldn't do it. It wasn't in me
to violate someone, and I hadn't yet decided if that was a trait
I was glad to have. Regardless, I wasn't like them, and I could
live with that.

Drew backed his car out of the parking spot. With the lights
on, I could read the license plate. It was easy to memorize.
Who could forget RCH BOY?

I waited until they pulled out of the lot before I dialed 911.
I needed them to not be near the bar when the cops pulled
them over. I could've left it at that. Getting Drew arrested for
drunk driving certainly qualified as revenge. But regardless of
my moral line, I needed to be a little more upclose. I needed
to look them in the eye if I could.

At this point, Brody was trying to walk to his own car. I
jogged through the parking lot as he braced himself on the
trunk and puked again. Before I reached him, I pulled on

the ski mask Magda had given me. I couldn't get caught before I took care of Adam and Drew. I was being as smart as someone without a criminal background could be. At least, I thought I was.

The bar parking lot was paved, so he didn't hear me approach. He didn't look up until my shadow fell across him, his eyes unfocused, a string of vomit hanging from his lip. He was known as one of the hottest guys in school, but he just looked pathetic and gross to me.

"Who the fuck are you?" he demanded, pushing himself upright.

I didn't say anything. I just stood there and looked at him. I was wearing head-to-toe black—nothing easily identifiable, except for the mask. There was no way he could recognize me, especially if I kept my mouth shut.

"You trying to scare me or something?" he demanded, weaving on his feet.

I didn't speak.

"You took that shot of Jay, didn't you?" Brody asked, bringing my attention back to him.

He lunged at me, and to my shame, caught me off guard. His fist slammed into my jaw. It would've hurt more had he been sober. As it was, his aim was a little off, and he almost fell down when he swung. He might have gotten the first hit, but as pain exploded in my jaw, rage unfurled in my stomach. My teeth had cut the inside of my cheek, and I tasted blood. I didn't think; I just struck.

One of my favorite places to hit an attacker is the throat. I'd never actually done it to someone who was actually attacking me, so when I did it to Brody, I took a moment to watch what it did to him. He clutched at his throat, wheezing for breath.

I realized something else for the first time at that moment; adrenaline could counteract booze, because when he came at me next time, he was a lot more steady. I deflected the punch and hit him again—this time in the sternum. Then I punched him in the gut. He doubled over, puking again. I didn't hesitate, I swung around with a roundhouse kick that put him down.

I'd knocked him out. I'd never knocked anyone out before. My hands shook as I hooked him under the arms and dragged him to his car. He was heavy, but I had so much adrenaline racing through my veins that I think I could've picked up a truck; I felt that powerful.

His keys were in his pocket, so I unlocked the doors and then heaved him into the backseat. I had to go around to the other side to pull him all the way in. Once I had him there I moved as quickly as my shaking limbs would allow.

It was a warm night, so he was wearing a button-down shirt and jeans. My fingers fumbled with the buttons of his shirt, but I finally got it undone and pulled it off. Then, I took off his shoes and sock, leaving him in his jeans. I took his clothes and his keys and threw them in the Dumpster behind the bar before returning to the car.

Magda's lipstick was in my pocket. My body heat had softened it, made it smooth and creamy. I smeared the color across Brody's lips before turning his body into my personal message board. He didn't have any chest hair, so it was easy to write on his skin. In big block letters I wrote RAPIST over and over again, until he was covered in pink. I put my phone—showing the photo of Magda from her Facebook page—beside him. Then I took a picture—with his phone, of course. He had an Instagram account as well, linked to his FB and Twitter, so it was easy for me to upload. God, I loved technology and guys who were dumb enough not to lock their phone.

I posted the photo with the hashtags #prettyinpink #rapist #cats #onfleek #hot…and anything else I could think of to get it as many views as possible. I also mailed a copy to everyone in his contact list. Then I wiped down the phone and tossed it on the seat beside him.

That done, I made sure the car doors were locked when I shut them—tugging my sleeve over my hand so I didn't leave prints. No matter what kind of monster he was, I wasn't going to leave him as an easy target for another.

I took the lipstick with me. I was probably going to need a new tube. Then I jogged back to my car, pulled off the mask, got in and drove away. I didn't feel like going home. I was too jacked-up for that. So I texted Zoe to see what they were up to. It was just after midnight, but most of us had late curfews on the weekend. She called a few minutes later. I pressed the button on the dash screen to take her call through speaker.

"Hey, Zoe. Are you still out?" I could hear noise in the background.

"Yeah. We're at that artsy coffee shop that's open until two. You want to join? It's open mic."

I couldn't tell if that was supposed to be an enticement for me to come or warning to stay away. It didn't matter. "You mean the Bare Bean? I'll meet you in a few minutes."

"Yay!"

I laughed and hung up. My hands weren't shaking quite so much now. I pulled into the coffee shop parking lot ten minutes later and went inside. My three new friends had a table not far from the stage area. I got a vanilla-cinnamon latte and walked over to join them. Then I saw Gabe.

He was sitting at a full table toward the back. I recognized two of the guys with him as friends he'd had since high school. The others I didn't know, especially the girls.

It shouldn't have bothered me, but the girls were pretty. They were college girls, which shouldn't have made a difference, but it did. Maybe they were only a couple years older than me, but they were still older. Why would Gabe want to be with a stupid high school kid who was a reminder of his dead sister, when he could be with someone his own age who didn't have that kind of sadness clinging to her?

I wasn't going to talk to him. I wasn't going to let on I'd seen him. But first, I had to stop staring at him. Because if he turned around he'd probably see everything I felt for him plainly written on my face.

"Hadley!" Anna cried. "You made it!"

I hoped she didn't see me wince. The three of them didn't know Gabe, and they certainly didn't know that I had a thing for him. So Anna couldn't have known that he was the last person I wanted to notice me. But it wasn't like my name was a common one, and of course he looked up. He looked right at me.

I expected him to nod at me, maybe wave. I didn't expect him to stand up in the middle of a conversation. And I didn't expect him to make a beeline for me with a look on his face that scared me a little.

"Hi," I said uncertainly. He made scowling sexy. Sounds stupid, but it was true.

"Who hit you?"

Before I could lie and say I didn't know what he was talking about, I gave myself away. My fingers instantly went to the spot where Brody's fist had connected. It was a little tender, and I still had a bit of that blood taste in my mouth, but I hadn't even looked at it in the car mirror. How bad was it?

"Sparring partner," I lied. Gabriel used to take martial arts, as well. I couldn't tell him it had happened at Thursday night's class, because he knew a fresh hit when he saw one. "Forgot to pull her punch."

He stared at me, his almost-black eyes impossible to read. I couldn't tell if he believed me or not. Sometimes I thought he could just look right into my soul and know what was truth and what wasn't. That terrified me, because what if he knew how I felt about him? Knowing I liked him was one thing, but I was afraid my feelings went deeper than that.

"Next time use a different partner," he suggested. "I don't like the idea of someone actually hitting you."

My heart fluttered in my chest. Maybe he meant it in a brotherly way, but it didn't *feel* brotherly. It felt...warm. Tingly.

"Sometimes you get hit. You know that," I reminded him. "It's no big deal. I'll be fine."

He touched my cheek. His fingers were warm and gentle. I had to fight to keep my eyes open, and not lean into him.

"I don't like seeing you hurt," he said softly. "If I had my way, no one would ever hurt you. Be careful, Had, please. For me."

He killed me. I couldn't speak. Couldn't think. All I could do was nod.

He gave me a little smile. "I'll see you later."

Gabriel walked away, leaving me standing there probably

looking stupid. I mentally shook my head and continued to the table where my friends sat. All three of them were staring at me.

"*Who* was *that?*" Caitlin demanded, her eyes huge. "He's gorgeous."

I glanced at him, sitting with his friends once more. He smiled at something one of the girls said, then laughed when she said something else. My chest ached. He'd told me the next time we were together he'd kiss me—and he hadn't.

"He's a friend," I told them. "He's just a friend."

CHAPTER 10

Zoe had asked me to go to the mall with her on Saturday, to help her pick out some new clothes. I hesitated to say yes. I hadn't gone to the mall with anyone since Magda was alive. Going with someone else felt wrong. Like I was betraying my best friend, even though she wasn't there, and probably wouldn't care if she was. Mags had tried to push me away many times after her rape, and I thought I'd keep her if I just refused to give up. But I abandoned her anyway, without ever taking a step. And now, I was the one left alone.

So, I could stay home and alternate between punishing myself and feeling pissed, or I could go out. Oddly enough, the second choice won out. I actually wanted to leave the house and spend time with another person who wasn't Gabe.

My mother, happy that I had actually made a friend, gave me some money so I could shop too. Zoe picked me up at noon. We went to Starbucks first to caffeinate before hitting the mall. I'd covered up the bruise on my face with some makeup, and it wasn't all that noticeable. Thank God for drunks with bad aim.

"Did you hear about Brody?" she asked when we were sitting at a table drinking our lattes.

"I saw the photo. I might print it and get it framed."

"Oh yeah, what she did is awesome."

My heart skipped a beat and then began pounding out a hard new rhythm against my ribs. "She?"

Zoe's eyes widened. "You haven't seen the video?" She pulled her phone out of her purse and began swiping and tapping the screen. "You've got to see this." She handed it to me.

On the screen—smudged with fingerprints—played a somewhat grainy video taken at night using only ambient light. It wasn't very good quality, but you could see Drew's car drive away, and me approaching Brody in all my grainy, ski-masked glory.

Oh, *shit*. Stunned, I watched Brody hit me and my responding kick. Someone had filmed it, I hadn't even noticed them. What if I hadn't been wearing the mask?

The person filming the video didn't come any closer until after I made my escape. They didn't follow me. Instead, they went to Brody and tried to open the car door but couldn't. I was glad I'd locked it. I could hear them laughing as they filmed him through the window.

"Rapist." It was a male voice. "Dude, I would not want to be you." And then the video stopped.

I glanced at the bottom of the screen. The video already had fifteen thousand hits. I felt sick...

"Isn't that amazing?" Zoe asked. "Did you see how she kicked him? I want to be able to do that."

I almost offered to teach her, but then remembered it wasn't in my best interest to admit that I could do that kind of stuff. "Yeah, me too." I stared at my latte, my mouth very dry. "How did you find the video?"

"Oh, Anna sent it to me. Her mother saw it on Channel 7's website."

I was definitely going to puke. I took a sip of my drink instead. Probably not a bright idea; coffee was horrible when it came back up. "Why would Channel 7 care about some hazing?"

"Hazing?" She looked at me like I was a little slow. "Hadley, Brody's father is a corporate lawyer. This is a big deal around town. Why aren't you more excited? Somebody is targeting the guys who hurt Magda. I would've thought you'd be into all of this."

I wanted to confess to her right then and there, tell her my little secret. I didn't. I couldn't. It wasn't just about protecting myself, it was about protecting her. If she knew what I'd done, she'd get in trouble if she didn't tell.

Part of me wondered why she didn't ask me about it. If this situation was reversed, I'd wonder if Zoe had decided to avenge her best friend. Surely it was only a matter of time before the police showed up on my doorstep.

I needed to cover my ass.

"I'm not sure how I feel about it," I told her. "None of this is going to bring Magda back, is it?" The words felt heavy on my tongue, the reality of them settling hard on my shoulders. What was I doing? "Outing" Jason and Brody made me feel better at the time, and I did feel like I was getting a little bit of payback for Magda. That I was providing consequences for what those assholes had done. But in reality, it was too little, too late, and I might end up in a lot of trouble if I got caught.

The craziest part was that I knew I *wasn't* going to stop. As frightened as I was of getting caught, I was still going to go through with it, even though it wouldn't bring back my friend. I still had to get Adam and Drew. I couldn't get caught before that.

Zoe looked at me sympathetically. "No, it won't. I'm sorry. I…I didn't mean…"

"I know what you meant." I said it with a bit of a smile so she wouldn't think I was upset with her. "And yeah, it does feel good to know that someone is at least trying to make them pay."

"Do you think Detective Davies would teach us how to do that kick?"

I laughed. "Maybe." Hopefully she wouldn't ask me to demonstrate it.

"I just think it's cool that it's a girl. Or a woman, whatever. I'd be so afraid to do what she's doing. What if Jason had woken up? What if Brody hadn't been drunk? They could've hurt her."

I tilted my head. "I don't know. She looks like she can take care of herself."

My new friend took a drink from the tall paper cup in front of her. "She's smart to wear a mask. I wonder if we know her?" Her eyes got wide again.

I almost choked on a mouthful of latte. What would I say if I really had no idea who was behind that pink mask? "It's not that big a town. We could know her, I guess. I wonder if she goes to the dojo? She's obviously got martial arts training."

"Maybe it's Detective Davies."

I laughed. "I doubt that."

"Why? She's about the right height and build, and it has to piss her off that she arrested those guys and then they got off because Brody's dad got them a shark of a lawyer."

"Don't remind me. That asshole tore my, Gabriel's and Magda's reputations apart." He'd made Gabe sound like an overly protective brother, prejudiced against a boy Magda liked. He'd made me out to be jealous, and just drunk enough that I didn't know what I saw. And Magda…he'd made her sound like a sad little girl trying to get a boy's attention and then crying wolf when it didn't work out the way she wanted. The charges were thrown out because of him. For a moment, I entertained adding him to my list, but even I wasn't that reckless.

How could he sleep after saying those things about her?

"You must miss her."

I nodded, my throat suddenly tight. "I do." I hoped she'd take a hint and not say anything else about it.

"So," she began with a sly smile, leaning over the table on her forearms. "Who was that hottie you talked to last night?"

My cheeks warmed. I hoped I wasn't blushing too hard. "That was Gabriel. He's Magda's brother. I've known him since I was five."

Zoe grinned. "Yeah? How long have you been in love with him?"

My jaw dropped. How had she figured that out? "I'm not."

She laughed at me. "You tell yourself that, but I know you're lying. I could tell from the way you looked at him that you were more than just friends."

"We are just friends." I wanted to believe there was more between us, but I was his little sister's best friend, and he hung out with beautiful girls his own age. Why would he want me? Forget that he'd flirted with me. Maybe he thought I was cute. Maybe he wanted me, but that didn't mean he had feelings for me. As awesome as he was, he was still just a guy.

The smile drained from Zoe's face as she stared at me. "Wait, you don't think he likes you?"

"Not in the way you mean, no."

She shook her head. "You may be smart when it comes to books, but you're incredibly dense when it comes to guys."

"I know. Otherwise, I wouldn't have let Magda go off with Drew."

"That's not on you. And it's not on her, either. You know who's to blame for what happened to her. Don't use guilt to deflect the subject. If you can't tell that that guy likes you, then you're just plain clueless."

I shrugged. "I guess I am."

She rolled her eyes at me but didn't push the topic.

A few minutes later we took what was left of our coffees and went to the mall. Zoe had her mother's credit card and proceeded to do some damage with it. I picked up a couple of black shirts, some extra leggings and a pair of jeans from the sale racks.

Every store we went to Zoe had to try on a ton of stuff. She made me come into the dressing room with her, so I could give my opinion on every outfit. She took selfies of herself in front of the mirror wearing different combinations and posted them to her social media sites.

"Why do you do that when you don't even buy half the clothes?" I asked her.

She smiled. "Sometimes a girl just needs to be told by people she hardly knows that she looks fabulous."

I couldn't argue with that logic.

It was almost 6:00 p.m. by the time she dropped me off. I took my bags up to my room and was hanging stuff in my closet when someone knocked on my bedroom door.

"Come in," I said, assuming it was Mom.

The door opened and then closed again. I stepped out of the closet when the silence dragged on. It wasn't Mom. It was Gabriel. He did not look happy.

"What are you doing here?" I asked. I was suddenly very aware of what a mess my room was, and also of the fact that he was the only boy to ever step foot in it.

He walked toward me in a way that reminded me of a cat stalking a bird. I wanted to back away, but that little part of me that refused to be intimidated wouldn't take a step.

"Was it you?" he asked, his voice very, very low.

"Me, what?" I wasn't that stupid. I knew exactly what he was asking. He'd seen the video.

Apparently, he knew I wasn't that stupid, either. "You know what I'm talking about. Did you go after Brody Henry last night?"

I looked him right in the eye. "No." Lying to him felt so *wrong*.

He came closer. "Really? Because the girl in that video looked a lot like you."

This time I did step backward, but not because he scared me. "The girl in that video was dressed in black and wearing a mask. She could be anybody."

He tilted his head, dark hair falling over his shoulder. "Anybody with a pink ski mask, a wicked roundhouse and legs I'd know anywhere? You were dressed in black last night, and you've got a bruise right where she got hit."

I shrugged. "Coincidence."

Gabriel moved fast, closing the distance between us. I stepped back, but there was nowhere to go. I was pinned between him and the wall—his forearm braced above my head, his other hand between my waist and arm. There was barely enough room to breathe between us. I could feel how warm he was through my clothes. His entire body was taut, like a snake about to strike.

"I don't think it's a coincidence that you have a bruise, and a pink ski mask, and that the guys being targeted are the same bastards that hurt my sister."

I tried to meet his gaze, but I could only hold it for a second. His eyes were black, glittering like stones. "I don't care what it is, and neither should you. Just be happy someone's finally doing something about it."

His chest touched mine. "I would be happy if I wasn't terrified someone was going to hurt you."

"No one's going to hurt me." I lifted my chin, and this time I had no trouble making eye contact. "I can take care of myself."

His eyes seemed fathomless as they stared down at me. "I know you can. You could take any of those guys. But what if they attack you together? You can't take all four of them."

His words brought back memories—terrible ones—of listening to Magda tell me every detail of what she could remember them doing to her. They'd drugged her, so she didn't remember much. I was glad she didn't remember the whole thing, because what she did remember was sickening. Gabe and I had held each other's hands while we listened to her story.

"Don't worry about me," I told him. "I'll be okay." Even if the four of them did the same thing to me, I would be okay. I wouldn't let them get away with it. If the law let them off, I wouldn't kill myself.

I'd get my own justice.

The hand he braced between my waist and arm moved to my hip. My heart jumped. He lowered his head so that it touched mine. "I'd kill anyone who hurt you."

My mouth was dry, and my heart was pounding. His hand on my hip burned through my clothes. He smelled like cinnamon, and being this close to him made me a little dizzy. It made me brave.

I looked up at him. "The only person who has the power to hurt me is you," I whispered. And then, before I could think, or before I could stop myself, I came up on my toes and kissed him.

He tasted like cinnamon too—and sugar.

Gabe froze, and for a second—a terrifying second—I thought he was going to push me away. But then he pushed his body against mine, pressing me between him and the wall. He kissed me hard. I opened my mouth at the touch of his tongue, my heart pounding so hard I was sure he could feel it.

I couldn't think. My head swam. Every inch of me tingled with electricity. He felt so good against me that I wanted to push him onto my bed and rip off his clothes. I didn't even care if we made it to the bed. I'd made out with other guys, but not like this. No one had ever made me feel like this.

Suddenly, I was lifted off the floor as Gabe swept me up into his arms like something out of a movie. He carried me to the bed and set me on it. I reached for him, pulling him down on top of me, wrapping him up in my arms and legs. I was overwhelmed by a feeling of intense urgency that pushed all common sense, all thought of anything but him from my mind.

We found a rhythm, every inch of us pressed together from lip to hip. My heart felt like it might burst straight out of my chest as I clung to him. Every second made that feeling of urgent desperation stronger. And stronger.

And stronger.

Oh. My. God.

Gabriel went still. He lifted himself up on his hands, breaking the kiss. I shivered as the parts of me that had been pressed against him cooled.

His hair hung around his face, and from my perspective his eyes were completely black, bright and intense. He was as breathless as I was.

"Tell me it was you," he said, voice hoarse and low.

I stared at him. Really? How could he ask me that now?

"No." I couldn't tell him the truth. He'd try to stop me, or worse he'd want to help. I couldn't put him in danger. I would never forgive myself if something happened to him.

I saw the disappointment in his eyes. He knew I was lying. He knew everything. When he pulled back, I let him go. I sat up as he stood. He walked to the door, then stopped and looked at me over his shoulder.

"I'm your friend, Had. I want to be more than just a friend. I think you want that too, but it's not going to happen if you can't trust me. Lie to yourself if you have to, but don't lie to me." He walked out, the door clicking shut behind him.

I sat there on the bed, trembling inside. I couldn't even begin to understand how I felt. There was only one thing I knew for sure—I had just hurt the one person who mattered most to me.

And I didn't know if he would ever forgive me for it.

CHAPTER 11

They had a brief story about me on the news Monday night. I wouldn't have seen it if my mother hadn't been watching.

"Police report that there have been attacks on two local teenage boys. The boys were marked and photos of them uploaded to their own social media accounts. While police cannot give the names of the victims, sources say the boys are connected, and that both were involved in the investigation of an alleged sexual assault earlier this year."

"Alleged?" I echoed. "They did it."

My mother gave me a pained look. "You don't know that, Hadley."

I was still wounded from Gabe walking out on me yesterday, so my temper jacked up surprisingly fast. I pulled out my phone, accessed the gallery and showed her the photo I tried to never look at, but kept as a reminder of what they'd done. It was a photo of Magda and the bastards who raped her. Jason was the one running the camera while Adam had my friend draped over the footboard of the bed. He was behind her.

Drew was in front of her, his fists in her hair. Both of them were violating her while Brody waited his turn, making lewd faces at the camera.

"Does that look consensual to you?" I demanded, shoving my phone in Mom's face.

She winced and turned her head. "That's terrible."

"You're right it is," I ground out.

"She shouldn't have gone off with them. That poor girl."

I remembered the look on Magda's face when I told her she'd made a stupid mistake going off with Drew. It shamed me.

"They shouldn't have raped her," I corrected. "It wasn't her fault. It was theirs."

She gave me a pitying look. I'd never wanted to punch my mother in the face until that very moment. "Every girl knows the risk. Magda must have known what they wanted from her. Look how short her skirt was. If she went with him, of course he'd think she wanted sex."

"So what if she did?" I challenged. "It doesn't mean she wanted to have sex with all of them, Mom, Jesus."

Her lips thinned. "There are consequences, Hadley. There are always consequences for everything we do. I'm not saying that Magda deserved what happened, but some of the responsibility of it falls on her shoulders."

I stared at her. Was she really that stupid? My God, she was only in her thirties. She had to have more sense than that. I used to think her being so young—eighteen when she had me—meant she was more progressive in her thinking, but it only seemed to make her more messed up.

Eighteen. Who the hell wanted to have a baby at eighteen? She told me once she hadn't known Dad for long when they

got married. She made it sound romantic. Now, I did some math. She had to have been already pregnant with me when she got married. I thought it had happened on their honeymoon.

"Was I a consequence?" I asked her with a sneer. "A 're-sponsibility' you and Dad had to own?"

Mom flushed. "We met at a party. I'd had too much to drink. I flirted with him. We ended up in his car. When I told him I was pregnant, he asked me to marry him. He could have abandoned me. Most boys wouldn't have stepped up like that."

That wasn't the whole truth, I could tell. "My God. I'm here because you got drunk and the guy who took advantage of you couldn't be bothered to use a condom. That's just *awesome*." No wonder he was always gone. We were the family he got stuck with.

"I do not regret having you," she insisted, looking me dead in the eye. "You may not have been planned, but *you* were not a mistake, and you never will be."

"You say that to me now, but every time you say Magda should have known better, what you're telling me is that I was a mistake, Mom. A big one. I'm going out." She didn't try to stop me.

I went to Starbucks. On my way there, I studied almost every woman I saw. How many of them had been told whatever happened to her was her fault, or she'd been asking for it? Had the woman walking toward me been assaulted at a bar? Maybe the next one had been harassed at her work. Or another might have been told she could pay a debt with sex. How many women did I see every day who had been assaulted

in some way—used as objects—and been made to feel like somehow they were to blame for it?

I hadn't been. Not yet. What a sad realization. Sadder was knowing that it would probably happen to me more than once before my life was over. Someone would at least try to violate me just for the sheer fact that I had a vagina instead of a dick.

Had Gabe used sex to punish me the day before? If he'd been the girl and me the guy, people would say he teased me. Left me with blue balls. If I'd gone after him—the real, female me—and made him have sex with me, would anyone think that was wrong? Most guys would make it a joke. Because the only thing better than forcing a girl to have sex with you, was one coming after you on her own.

Either way, we girls were going to get hurt and the guys were going to slut us up. No way around it. We wanted it as much as they did—wasn't that the defense they used?

The thing was, some of us did want it. We just wanted to be in charge of who we did it with and when.

By the time I got a latte and sat down, I was vibrating with anger. I needed to take it down a notch, or I was going to lose it.

"You look like you want to kill someone."

I looked up, even though I didn't have to. I'd know his voice anywhere. Gabe. My jaw was tight as I stared at him. "You volunteering?"

His left eyebrow rose. "Actually, I wanted to apologize. Can I sit with you?"

I shrugged. "Do what you have to do." My heart was pounding, but I couldn't tell it if was because I was happy to see him or because he'd pissed me off.

He sat across from me. His foot brushed mine beneath the table. I tried to force my jaw to relax. He looked perfectly calm. "Look, I'm sorry for yesterday. I shouldn't have come over. I shouldn't have let things go as far as they did, and I shouldn't have left like that."

"You're probably the first guy to ever turn down sex, but then how else were you going to punish me for not doing what you wanted?"

Gabriel's jaw dropped. "Is that what you think I did? Punish you? Manipulate you? Jesus, Hadley, I *like* you. I wasn't trying to hurt you, I was trying to protect myself. Would you have sex with me if you thought I was keeping things from you?"

Yes. God, what did that say about me? "That would depend on whether or not it was any of my business."

"You getting revenge on my sister's attackers *is* my business."

"Would you tell me if it was you going after them?"

"No, but that's not the same thing."

"It's exactly the same thing."

"They can't rape me."

"You're not naive enough to believe that." I kept my voice low. "Rape isn't about sexual preference."

"Fine. I think I could protect myself better than you can."

"That's probably true. You're bigger, and stronger, and you have a couple of years of training on me. You'd also be tried as an adult. I don't think you'd be safe in prison, Gabe. You're too pretty."

He placed his forearms on the table and leaned forward. "You know everything you say tells me it was you in that video."

"What if it is?" I challenged. "What are you going to do? Stop me?"

"Yes."

I smiled. "I don't need protection."

"No. You need to give your head a shake and stop taking risks."

"Not going to happen. You're right—it was me in that video." I watched the surprise play over his face. He hadn't expected me to admit it. "I took the picture of Jason too. Now what? Are you going to stake out my house? Follow me everywhere I go? You have college and a job, and I'm not about to give you my schedule."

He stared at me. "I don't know if I want to shake you or kiss you."

I smiled, and leaned over the table so that our faces were only a few inches apart. "Try either and I'll put you on your ass."

His lips curved. "You liked it yesterday."

"Yesterday I thought you meant it."

Gabe's smile vanished. "I did. I just don't get involved with girls who lie to my face."

"Sure you do. You guys don't care what we say. You'd like it better if we didn't speak at all."

He pulled back like I'd slapped him. "You think I'm like them?"

I shrugged, leaning back in my chair. "Aren't you? You barged into my room and tried to intimidate me. You're trying to make me behave like you think I should, and telling me that I should behave differently because I'm a girl. You're not treating me like someone you like and respect, Gabe. You're acting like you want to control me."

His eyes hardened; they were like black stones boring right into me, so sharp they had to leave a mark. "You know me better than that." He pushed back his chair and stood up. "You know what? Do whatever you want. Get yourself hurt or worse."

"Whatever happens I asked for it, huh?"

"Fuck you, Hadley." He turned on his heel and walked away. I watched his back with a hollow feeling in my chest. Whatever.

I didn't need him anyway.

Last Year

I couldn't believe Magda had bailed on me. She left me standing there alone at the party like an idiot while she went off with Drew. Gabe hadn't stuck around for long—he'd probably met some girl who was far more sophisticated than his little sister's best friend—and I was totally on my own. God, I just stood there, looking like an idiot.

Until Michel showed up. He was cute and French, and I was full of spite. I'd show Magda. She was off making out with Drew? Well, I'd make out with Michel.

We did more than make out. *Much* more. Afterward, I felt… weird. Disappointed. It certainly wasn't what they talked about in books, but I had the oddest feeling that it was supposed to be *more* than what I'd just experienced. Michel didn't seem to know what to do afterward, either. He asked if I wanted him to drive me home, but I couldn't leave without Magda.

When I returned to the party, I saw Drew with his buddies,

but I didn't see Magda. I asked around, but half of the people there didn't know who she was. Finally, I went up to Drew.

"Where's Magda?" I yelled over the music.

"Who?" he asked, laughing.

"Cleopatra!"

He and his friends laughed some more. One of them—Jason Bentley—looked uncomfortable. He smiled, but didn't look at me.

"She's sleeping it off," Drew shouted in my ear. "She had a busy night."

They laughed again. A shiver of unease ran down my spine. I hurried away from them, and their mocking laughter. I looked in every room downstairs and then moved upstairs. I walked in on a couple making out in the bathroom—it was Michel and another girl. I shook my head at him. "You really get around, don't you?"

Before he could answer, I closed the door. It wasn't like my feelings were hurt by his apparent attempt to set the world record for hookups in one night—I hardly knew the guy. He'd just been a way for me to lose my virginity and get back at Magda for abandoning me, which seemed stupid to me when I thought about it.

I opened a bedroom door and walked in. It smelled like booze and barf inside. I almost backed out, until I saw the girl on the bed. She was passed out, and her dress was up around her waist, the top pulled down so one breast was bare. Her panties were wrapped around one ankle.

Oh, God.

"Magda?" My voice was little more than a whisper. My hands shook as I closed the door behind me and walked toward the bed. The lamps were bright, and as I drew closer, I saw a smudge of what looked like blood on her thigh—more on the white of her dress. Condom wrappers littered the bed and floor—there had to be at least six of them, and they were all empty.

What had they done to her? I was cold with shock and anger. This couldn't be real. But it was real. They'd raped her—Drew Carson and his three friends—maybe even more.

The bastards.

"Magda?" I gave her a shake. She turned her head, and that was when I noticed the vomit on the side of her face. She'd thrown up on the bed and then had been allowed to lie in it. She had circular bruises on her breast and on her thighs.

Bite marks.

"Oh my God." I had to get her out of there. Had to get her to the hospital. I did the only thing I could think of—I called Gabe. Then, I cleaned her face and fixed her clothes. I had her somewhat awake by the time her brother arrived. I also had her downstairs and at the back door.

I caught a couple of guys looking at us. They looked down at a cell phone, then back to Magda and laughed.

"What?" I demanded, glaring at them.

One of them—he was dressed like a zombie—held up his phone. I couldn't see it that well, but it wasn't hard to tell that it was a video of someone having sex with a girl dressed like…Cleopatra.

"Your friend's a star," he said with a laugh.

I would have punched him in the face if I hadn't been the only thing holding Magda upright.

My cheeks burned. I looked around. Was everyone looking

at us? At their phones? Girls laughed and made rude comments. A few looked at Magda with sympathy, but no one came forward to help me get her outside.

No one tried to help her at all. Just me, and I was too late.

When I arrived at the dojo Thursday night, there were even more girls than there had been the week before. There were thirteen of us now. Detective Davies looked as surprised and pleased as I felt.

"Isn't this amazing?" she asked.

I nodded. "It's awesome. Do you think I could have a couple minutes to talk during class? I have an idea I want to share."

She looked intrigued. "Sure."

I wanted to ask her what she knew about the video of me, but was too afraid. If she thought it was me she'd question me, wouldn't she? She'd at least look at me differently. Right?

Maybe she was really good at hiding it and was waiting for me to slip up. I was just glad the bruise on my face had faded so she couldn't ask me about it.

I recognized the new girls from school. When Detective Davies asked them what made them join the class, they said they'd seen the video of "that girl who knocked out Brody Henry." They wanted to be able to fight back too. Or just fight. I found it hard to look at some of their faces, because it was obvious some of them had been hurt in the past, or were afraid of being hurt in the future.

Detective Davies gave them a tight smile. "Just to be clear, this class is not to teach you to beat up boys. I know some of you think that girl's a hero—but what she's doing is wrong."

"Why?" Zoe challenged. "She's letting them know they can't get away with rape."

"That's not her job," the cop responded.

"No, it's yours," Zoe shot back, looking her in the eye.

"Yes, it is. Sometimes my hands get tied. You think I don't hate letting rapists walk free? But people can't take the law into their own hands. Someone's going to get hurt."

"Yeah," said another girl. "Rapists."

"I heard the girl in the photos killed herself after those guys got away with raping her. Is that true?"

"It is," I said before I could stop myself. Everyone—including Detective Davies—looked at me. "She was my best friend. But this class isn't about her. It's about making sure what happened to her doesn't happen to any of you."

"Wouldn't the best way to do that be to teach guys not to rape?"

"Yeah," I said. "Good luck with that."

Detective Davies stepped up. "While I could waste my breath defending myself, I won't. The law decided there wasn't enough evidence to charge Magda Torres's alleged attackers with rape. Do I agree with that? It doesn't matter. I have to uphold the law. It's my job, and sometimes I don't like it. That's why it's important to me to teach classes like this one, so let's get started, okay?"

Then she recapped some of the things she'd taught in the previous classes, then began on a new lesson. I paid attention to only half of what she said. Thankfully, I was already familiar with the physical aspect of the class. I couldn't stop thinking about the look on Gabe's face when I accused him of trying to manipulate me. He'd been so hurt and angry. I'd been the one who started it—I'd kissed him first. He could have just as easily accused me of trying to use sex to stop him from asking questions. And then when he did ask, I lied. Right to his face, looking him in the eye.

I'd been so angry and upset over the conversation with my mother that I'd been a complete and total bitch to him when he tried to apologize for something that wasn't entirely his fault. I had to fix that. He didn't deserve to be treated like shit.

"Hadley, you had something you wanted to share?"

Detective Davies's voice snapped me out of my thoughts. "Uh, yeah." I stood up and went to the front of the room where she stood. "Hi. I'm Hadley White. So, you know my friend Magda killed herself after being raped at a party. No offense, Detective Davies, but there was nothing alleged about it. I know what happened to her, because I was the one who found her when they were done with her. I was also the one who found her when she overdosed."

There was a murmur of sympathy. I blinked back tears. "As girls we're taught that we're in competition with each other. You know it's true—we compete for grades, for guys, for the best hair… I think it's time we stopped being against each other, and be there *for* each other." I had their attention now.

"I want to start something called The Girlfriend Watch. We can look out for each other at parties. Make sure we all get home safe, that kind of thing. Even if I'm not at a party, if Zoe calls me because she's had too much to drink and some guy is pestering her, I can go get her. And if something horrible does happen, we can take care of each other and make sure one of us doesn't get painted with the slut brush." Someone actually laughed.

I held up the clipboard I'd grabbed from José's office. "If you're interested, write down your name and cell number. I'll send each one of you a contact list. Share it with your girlfriends and add them to it, as well. The more of us looking out for each other, the better."

I turned to Detective Davies. "Can we add you to the contact list, Detective?"

"In this room I'm just Diane," she answered. "And yes. Each and every one of you can call me if you're in trouble. I will answer, and I will come for you. Thank you, Hadley, for coming up with such a wonderful idea. Once you've written down your information, grab a partner for sparring. That is, if Hadley's finished?"

I nodded. "I am. Thanks."

My name and info was already on the list, so I just stood back as the girls added themselves one by one before partnering off. I went to my bag and took out my phone. I selected Gabe's number and wrote, Want to apologize. I was an ass. Can we meet? I hit Send before I could change my mind.

I was just putting my phone away when the notification that I had a text popped up. It was from him. Come over when you're done. My heart somersaulted. He was probably still mad, and that was okay. At least he wasn't so mad he didn't want to see me. I'd take that as a win.

When class was done, Zoe suggested coffee, but I bailed so I could go see Gabe. It wasn't a long walk to his house, so I slung my bag over my shoulder and set off.

I was walking past a small bar that had been around since the fifties when I heard a girl's voice. "No!"

I stopped, jerking my head in the direction of the cry. Quietly, I crept toward the dark alley between the bar and another building. In the murky light, I could see a guy pinning a girl against the side of the building. He had her arms behind her back and was kissing her neck as she cried.

I don't know why I was shocked. Given the last few months, I would probably be more shocked if he *wasn't* trying to force himself on her. There were good guys in the world—I knew that, but why did so many have to be complete and utter pricks?

The ski mask was in my bag. I pulled it out of the side pocket where I kept it and pulled it over my head, stuffing my hair inside so no one could see what color it was.

I slipped into the alley, keeping to the shadows. The girl's crying was louder now, her struggles more frantic.

"C'mon, baby," the guy urged. "You know you want it as bad as I do."

"Hey, asshole," I said, my voice low.

He stopped, lifted his head and turned around. He was medium height and build, with a face that might have been nice to look at if it wasn't for the fact that it belonged to a jerk. "You're that freak from the news."

The girl sagged against the wall, digging in her purse, probably for a phone. I turned my attention to her attacker. "And hey, you're that asshole who doesn't understand the word 'no.'"

He snorted. "What are you going to do about it?"

"This." I kicked him in the balls. "And this." I kneed him in the face when he doubled over.

"What the hell's going on?" A new voice—male—shouted.

There was a flash of light that made stars dance before my eyes. I tried blinking them away, but suddenly I was grabbed and slammed into the side of the building with the force of being hit by a small truck.

"Little bitch," the new guy growled. "Let's see how you like it." The stars cleared just in time for me to dodge a punch. He hit the wall instead. I heard his knuckles crunch just before he screamed.

The guy I'd kicked had gotten up. He grabbed me as I tried to run by. He punched me in the stomach, knocking the breath out of me. It hurt. It *really* hurt, but I'd been punched before. I came up with a punch to his throat, turned on my heel and started running for the street. The girl was gone, and I wasn't stupid enough to test my luck against two full-grown men. Besides, there were probably more of them.

I was tackled to the ground, putting up my arms just in time to keep my face from grinding into the pavement as all the breath exploded from my lungs. My attacker seized my shoulder and rolled me over. This time, I didn't manage to avoid the punch. I could only turn my head and take it on the cheekbone rather than the nose. Still, it hurt like hell.

He called me names—ones I would never repeat, they were so awful. It was meant to degrade me, but every ugly thing that came out of his mouth just made my anger stronger. He had one knee on the ground beside me, his foot on the other side. He probably felt secure like that, but it gave me plenty of room to move. I tightened my core, pulling my legs up fast. I rolled up onto my shoulders, bringing my feet up. I kicked him in the back of the head, and when he listed to the side with a grunt, I used my feet to send him sprawling.

I jumped to my feet, every inch of me screaming in agony.

First I'd taken a beating in class, and now this. I had to have a death wish.

His buddy was on his feet, and he came after me when he saw his friend groaning on the ground. I ran. I ran as fast as I could. He chased me. And then I heard the other join in.

Being chased down the street while wearing a bright pink ski mask was not how I would normally choose to spend a Thursday night. Or any night. I understood why Gabe had been worried now. There was no way I could take both of those men, and it pissed me off.

Okay, and it terrified me too. What were they going to do to me? Beat me? Rape me? Take away this power I'd just found?

My lungs burned as I ran. My ribs hurt. My face hurt. The only thing that didn't hurt was my left foot. I ran as fast as I could. It wasn't going to be fast enough. They were gaining on me.

Headlights blinded me as they went past. Great. Someone had seen me. Then the screech of brakes and the car backed up. The passenger door opened. "Get in!"

It was Gabe. Oh, thank God or whoever watched over angry and reckless teenage girls. I dived into the car and slammed the door. We peeled away from the curb as the first guy ran up. I'd escaped, but just barely.

I fastened my seat belt, gasping for breath, every inch of me sore and on fire. The sides of my hands were raw where they'd scraped pavement.

Gabe glanced at me. I still had the mask on.

He smirked. "So, Hadley, I don't suppose that was you in the video with Brody, huh?"

He couldn't be too mad if he was making jokes. I started

laughing. God, it hurt. I pulled off the mask, my hair falling over my face like a tangle of blond spiderwebs. "No," I said, flashing him a grin. "It wasn't me at all."

CHAPTER 12

We went back to Gabe's house. Teresa was in bed, and his mother was reading. I said hi to her before continuing up to Gabe's room. I'd spent so much of my life in that house, she didn't even think twice about me being there late on a school night.

His room was at the end of the hall. I hadn't been in it very often since I was a kid. Once Gabe realized Magda and I were snooping around in there—we were eight—he started locking the door. The walls of his room were white, but almost every inch of them was covered in drawings, magazine clippings, music art and movie posters. There was a to-scale illustration of the interior of the human body that was both gross and intriguing. I studied it while he retrieved the first-aid kit from the bathroom.

"Push up your sleeves," he commanded. I did.

He used a warm, wet facecloth to clean my hands and wrists, then he patted them dry and applied antibiotic cream before wrapping them in some gauze.

"You don't have to wrap them," I said.

He shot me a look that told me I shouldn't argue. "Leave these on overnight. You can take them off before school so people don't ask what happened. You'll have to think of something else for your cheek."

Right. That jerk had hit me on the same side Brody had. I was going to have another bruise. "I can blame it on self-defense class."

"Yeah, I guess telling people you were trying to take on two men in a fight would be stupid."

Our gazes locked. "I saved a girl from probably being raped," I informed him. "There was nothing stupid about it at the time."

"You're very brave." He put the cap back on the cream. "You're also an idiot."

"Would you say that to a guy?" I asked, scowling.

He hesitated. "Probably not."

I rolled my eyes. I hurt all over, and I just wanted to go to bed. "At least you're honest. I don't need or want a lecture, Gabe. I know what I'm doing."

"Do you?"

"No, I just enjoy getting beaten up. Look, do we have to do this again? I don't want to fight with you. I don't like it."

"Neither do I." He put the gauze back in the kit and closed it. "What do you want to do with me?" His voice was low and a little raspy.

My stomach fluttered as my cheeks warmed. "I liked what we did in my room," I whispered.

Gabriel smiled—a slow curving of his lips that made my insides turn to goo. "So did I."

He kissed me. His lips were soft and warm. I slid my hands over his shoulders, wrapping my arms around his neck as his closed around my waist. He felt so good. Maybe it was stupid, but my life had become dark since Magda died. No, that was a lie. My life started getting dark when Magda was raped, and it had kept getting darker until I couldn't see. Gabriel was like a light in that darkness—a flickering flame that drew me in with promises of lighting my way and seeing me through the black.

His mouth lifted from mine. I opened my eyes to find him looking down at me. "What?" I asked.

"I want you," he said, his low voice sending a shiver down my spine. "So bad."

I wanted him too. A little part of me was afraid, but mostly I just wanted to push him onto his bed and do whatever came to mind. "Do you have condoms?" I asked.

He went still. "God, Hadley. Don't ask me that."

"Why not?"

"Because it's too fast, too soon. Isn't it?"

"No."

Gabe's forehead lowered to mine. "You kill me," he said. "I'm trying to go slow and do the right thing."

Suddenly, my eyes filled with hot tears. They burned as they spilled down my cheeks. Gabriel lifted his head and looked down at me in horror as I frantically swiped at my face with my hands.

"What?" he demanded. "What is it? Did I do something wrong?"

I shook my head. I was such an idiot. "No."

"Then why are you crying?"

"Because you're a good guy." I sniffed and wiped at my

cheeks. I could only imagine how stupid I sounded. I hope he found bawling, beaten idiots sexy, because that's all he was getting.

His arms went around me again, pulling me against his chest. "There are a few of us out there," he murmured. "Not all of us are assholes."

I wanted to believe him. He couldn't be the only one, could he? I didn't want to think so, but at that moment, I couldn't think of any other guy I knew who was half as decent. Even my father was a prick. I cried harder.

Gabe held me tight, his cheek resting on the top of my head. "It's okay," he murmured.

But it wasn't, and we both knew it. It wasn't going to be okay at all.

I woke up a little earlier than usual Friday morning so I could do the homework I didn't get to the night before. I sat at the kitchen table bent over my notebook while my mother made breakfast. She had the small TV on the counter set to a local channel as she worked.

"Another attack by a mysterious female in a pink ski mask," said the woman on the screen. I lifted my head, heart rate accelerating. On the TV, the pretty, blonde morning-show host looked vaguely amused. "Last night a local man was attacked outside a local nightclub by a woman in pink. The man had allegedly made unwanted advances toward a female patron of the establishment, which led to him being viciously beaten. We were sent the following footage by the woman who claims to have been attacked, but wishes to remain anonymous."

I stared at the screen as they switched to the cell phone video.

It wasn't very good—it was dark and she'd been drinking—but there was a very clear image of me kicking her attacker in the balls. I had to admit, I looked pretty badass. Luckily for me she hadn't stuck around to see me almost get my bad ass handed to me—or worse.

The screen went back to the anchorwoman's face. "Police are asking townspeople to report the vigilante if they see her. Detective Diane Davies responded to questions about the woman in pink earlier this morning."

Detective Davies's face came up on screen. A reporter had obviously caught up with her on her way into the police station. They were standing on the steps of the building. The detective had a large paper coffee cup in her hand.

"This person may seem like a hero," she said into the microphone held in front of her face. "But taking the law into your own hands is never a good idea. Not only is she risking her own safety, but the safety of others. Combating violence with more violence doesn't change anything."

It was as though giant fingers reached into my chest and pinched something—hard. Her words cut me deep. Was she right? Was I simply making things worse? I couldn't believe it. The law had failed Magda. I wouldn't. I'd already made sure the world saw Jason and Brody for what they were, which was more than the cops had managed.

The image on screen changed to two girls on the local college campus. "What do you think of this pink-masked vigilante?" a female voice asked them.

One with pretty auburn hair replied, "I think she's awesome. I wish she'd shown up at some of the parties I've been to."

The second girl was a bit more serious. "Somebody has to

do something. The cops aren't. I know of at least two girls who were raped last year, and another one who was slut-shamed so badly she dropped out. If school administrators won't protect us, and the police can't protect us, then it's up to us to protect ourselves." She looked directly into the camera. "If you're watching this, Pink Vigilante, I say thank you."

Pride rose inside me. Last night with Gabriel I'd had a moment of weakness, wondering if I was doing the right thing. Now I knew for certain that I was.

The blonde anchorwoman was back on screen. "So, there you go. Local police urging people to report the vigilante if they see her, and young women wanting to thank her."

The camera panned back to reveal her cohost, a man in his forties, whose teeth were unnaturally big and white. "Thank you, Anna Beth. I don't blame the fellow for not wanting to appear on TV. I'd be embarrassed to be beaten up by a girl, as well." He chuckled. I wanted to kick him in those horse teeth.

Anna Beth shot him a sideways glance. "Well, Charles, keep your hands to yourself and you won't have to worry about it." She said it with a smile, but there was a little bite in her tone. Her companion looked surprised.

Mom set a plate of toast and eggs in front of me. "That wasn't very professional of her to say that to him."

"He's a jerk. Detective Davies could totally kick his ass. He wouldn't be joking about being beaten up by a girl then."

My mother made a face. "I don't like it when you talk about beating people up."

I wasn't going to apologize, and she didn't stick around to hear it. She went back to the counter and poured herself a cup of coffee. I'd already had two.

I ate my breakfast as I finished my homework and then packed my books up for school. When I arrived, Zoe, Caitlin, Anna and some of the other girls from class were outside. Zoe was wearing an off-white moto jacket with a big pink V drawn in marker just above her left boob.

"What's that for?" I asked, raising a brow. "You haven't started some kind of virgin initiative, have you?"

The girls laughed. "No," Zoe replied. "It's for the Pink Vigilante. What do you think?"

Honestly? I fucking *loved* it. I didn't tell her that. Instead, I shrugged. "I think people—mostly guys—are going to look at it and ask you about your vag."

She grinned. "I hope they do. Then I can try out some of the things we've learned in class on them." The girls laughed again. I frowned. Some guy making a stupid remark was hardly a reason to punch him in the throat. And did Zoe really think that after just a handful of classes she was ready to take on a guy?

"Hey," Caitlin said. "Draw a V on me." She turned her back as Zoe dug a pink Sharpie out of her bag, presenting her right shoulder. Some of the other girls exclaimed that they wanted one too.

I forced a smile. I wasn't sure what was going on, and it made me feel weird—like my balance was off. Surreal. When Zoe asked me if I wanted her to draw a V on me as well, I shook my head. The bell rang so we all filed inside.

"Hey," Zoe said, falling into step beside me. "Are you okay?"
I nodded. "Just tired."

A sly smile widened her lips. "That's right. You went to see your guy last night. Did he keep you up late?"

Heat rushed to my cheeks. "A little." Of course, I wasn't

going to tell her about the kissing and the crying and the more kissing. Or the fact that Gabriel wanted to take things slow. That was private.

But Zoe didn't push, and she didn't ask any more questions. I was starting to really like her. I wasn't sure how I felt about that. Nobody could ever replace Magda. She'd been my best friend forever, and she always would be, but Zoe made me feel like being social again. She made me feel like maybe the rest of my life wasn't going to be so damn lonely.

On our way to homeroom we walked by Drew, Adam, Brody and Jason. They stood against the wall with their little cluster of sycophants. The group seemed smaller than it had at the beginning of the year. Brody and Jason didn't look as cocky as they used to.

"What's the V for?" Drew asked, leering at Zoe's chest. "Virgin?" His remark was so close to what I had said just a little while ago that I felt sick.

"No." Zoe smiled at him before turning her amusement on Brody and Jason. "You guys know what it means, don't you?"

Jason flushed and looked away. Brody glared at her. "Fuck off, bitch."

All eyes were on Zoe. People actually stopped in the hallway and watched what was going on. My friend laughed. "Poor Brody. How long were you in that car before somebody found you? Did you have to bathe in makeup remover to get all the lipstick off, Revlon?"

A few of the people watching laughed. Brody took a step away from the wall toward Zoe, his fists clenched at his sides.

I took a step forward, about to put myself between the two of them and maybe kick him in the head again. But Zoe closed the distance between them, so that they were almost nose to nose.

"Go for it," she taunted, flashing him a mocking smile. "I'm sure everyone here would love to see you get your ass handed to you by another girl, you pathetic sack of shit."

Brody's face flushed dark. He didn't hit her, but he grabbed her by the throat, shoving her across the hall into a row of lockers that rattled with the impact. I dropped my books and lunged for him, but stopped when he suddenly released her. I glanced down and almost laughed.

Zoe had grabbed him between the legs and given his balls a little twist. Okay, so maybe she was ready to take on a guy.

"Touch me again," she warned, "and I'll take these off." She gave him a push and moved away from the lockers. I picked up my books as some of the people around us laughed and cheered. It wasn't all supportive. I heard at least two guys and one girl called Zoe a bitch, and two other people urged Brody to hit her. I grabbed her arm and pulled her through the crowd. I didn't stop or let go until we reached homeroom.

Just before we went inside, I turned on her. "What the fuck was that about?" I demanded. "He could've hurt you."

She looked surprised. "I had him. You saw that."

"You had him by the balls, yeah. And he had two fists free that he could've used on you. You humiliated him in front of his friends. The whole school will know about this in less than an hour. He's going to want revenge. What the hell were you thinking?" God, I sounded like Gabriel. I was suddenly very aware of what it was like to be worried for someone I cared about.

Zoe frowned at me. "I can take care of myself."

"You've had three self-defense classes. If he hurts you…"
I ran my hand through my hair. "I don't even want to think
about it. You know what he did to Magda. And she hadn't
done *anything* to him. He just thought raping her would be
fun." I shook my head.

Zoe's eyes were wide as she stared at me. "I'm sorry. I just…
I just wanted to stand up to them, because of what they did
to her. What they did to you."

I blinked. "What they did to me?" I frowned. "They didn't
touch me."

Her expression was sympathetic, pitying almost. "Oh, Hadley. They didn't have to." Then she walked into the classroom,
leaving me alone with her words echoing in my head.

CHAPTER 13

The next week passed by uneventfully. Gabriel had to work on the weekend, so I didn't see him at all, not even when I went to Magda's grave. It was raining, so I didn't stay as long as I normally did, but that was okay. I didn't need to be at her grave to feel like she was with me.

Zoe and I went to a movie on Saturday, and then I spent the rest of the weekend studying for a test on Monday.

That week, nominations for Homecoming King and Queen strutted around the school like getting a cheap crown and their photo taken might actually impact their lives. I didn't really know the three girls up for queen, and Jason and Adam were two of the three guys in the running for king. One of them was going to win, and it was probably going to be Adam. Jason had gotten quiet since I made him infamous. I actually felt a twinge of conscience because of it—but just a small one. He deserved to be outed. He deserved the way people looked at him now—as though he wasn't to be trusted. They looked at

Brody the same way, and soon they'd see Adam and Drew as they really were too.

I went to the dojo almost every night and pounded on a Wavemaster until my shins were purple and my fists ached. That's what I was doing on Thursday when the self-defense class came in.

"Wow," Zoe said. "You're good."

I shrugged, sweat dripping down my back. "I've been doing it for a while."

"Have you ever beat up a guy?" another girl asked.

I didn't hesitate before answering because Detective Davies was watching. "Only in competition or class."

The girl looked disappointed. Part of me wanted to blurt out that I was the goddamn Vigilante and that what they'd seen was only a taste of what I could do, but getting arrested wasn't part of my plan. Detective Davies was already looking at me like she suspected something. She cornered me after class.

"Hadley, do you know anything about this vigilante?" she asked when we were alone. She was direct and to the point, I'd give her that.

"Should I?" I countered. "I know she's getting justice for Magda."

"She's going to get in a lot of trouble, is what she's going to get," the older woman countered.

I stared at her. "So? Maybe she thinks it's worth it."

Her expression softened. "Those boys aren't worth an eighth of the trouble she's going to get into if she's caught."

"*If* she's caught." I looked her right in the eye, daring her to accuse me, or something.

Detective Davies hesitated. "Do you think Magda would want this violence being done in her name?"

"Magda's dead," I shot back. "Because four guys raped her and got away with it. What she wanted hasn't mattered at all, so why start now?"

She looked like I'd just sucker punched her. "If it's you, please stop. I can't protect you."

"It's not me, and I don't expect you to. I know you tried to help Magda, but the only people the cops have protected are the guys who raped my friend. Even if you could protect me, I wouldn't want it. I gotta go."

I left her standing there and walked away, terrified she'd arrest me before I made it to the door. She didn't. I was almost disappointed.

Friday night was the Homecoming dance. I wasn't going to go, but Zoe, Caitlin and Anna gave me a hard time over it. I texted Gabe and asked if he wanted to come with me. He answered a few minutes later.

Who are you and what have you done with Hadley?

Funny, I typed.

Sure. Pick you up at eight. And that was it, I had a date. I bought tickets during lunch. I couldn't help but wonder what Magda would say about her brother taking me to a dance. She probably would have laughed. I liked to think that wherever she was, she was at least smiling.

Gabe did pick me up at eight. He was wearing a white shirt and black pants. His hair hung in effortless waves that I envied. I wore a vintage black minidress that had belonged to my grandmother in the sixties. It was cute, and I dressed it up with some sparkly jewelry and heels.

Gabe smiled at me. "You look amazing."

I think I blushed. "Thanks."

He opened the car door for me and I climbed inside. When he got in, he didn't immediately start the engine. Instead, he leaned across the console and kissed me, bringing every nerve in my body screaming to attention.

"I've had to wait too long to do that," he said.

"You could always do it again," I suggested. "To make up for lost time."

He smiled and kissed me again.

We arrived at the school at twenty past eight. The dance had already started, though the "court" wouldn't be announced until nine. School dances didn't run very late, and usually there was a party planned for afterward. Jason Bentley's father had rented a place for that night. He was that certain his son was going to be king. Actually, he'd probably guaranteed his son would be king by offering us a place to party. Gabe and I hadn't talked about whether or not we were going to go.

The gym was decorated in the school colors, with streamers and balloons and other tacky favors. Really, it looked like something better suited to an eighties movie, but no one but me seemed to care, so I kept my mouth shut. We found Zoe and the others a few minutes after walking in. Music blared so loud I could feel the bass throbbing through the floor, and beams of light cut through the relative darkness.

"It's like a bad rave," Gabe shouted.

I laughed.

Zoe's date turned out to be a guy who had gone to school with Gabe. His name was Alex, and he was tall, blond and cute. Caitlin was there with Rick, a guy from our grade, and Anna was on her own. I didn't even know if there was a guy—or girl—she liked at our school. I didn't know much about her at all. I was too caught up in my own crap.

Drew, Adam, Brody and Jason were across the gym from us, thank God. Gabe spotted them almost immediately. I think he'd made a point of seeking them out.

I intertwined my fingers with his. He squeezed my hand. I had a pretty good idea of how he felt looking at them. The two of us could probably take the four of them, but we were no match for their friends, as well.

"Do you want to go?" I asked, raising my voice just enough to be heard over the music as I leaned close to him.

He shook his head and turned to look at me. "No. We came here to have fun. Mags would want us to do that."

I smiled. He was right. Before the rape, Magda had been fun and full of joy. I've never met anyone who thought life was as fabulous as she had. Everything had been an adventure. Things that I was afraid to do were nothing more than a chance to try something new to her. She had made me more brave than I ever thought I could be. I went on my first roller coaster with her. Did my first zip line with her. I'd even contemplated going on that thing at the amusement park that threw you into the air like a slingshot, but had been saved by the fact that it cost twenty bucks.

Magda made me want to be brave, and now I was running around like Batman, beating up sexual predators. What would she think of that? Was Detective Davies right that Magda wouldn't want me to do it? Or would she back me up and tell me what a good thing I was doing?

Or would she ask me why me and my fists of fury hadn't been there when she needed them?

We danced. Mostly it was just the girls, but the guys joined occasionally. When the time to announce the king and queen arrived, and the stage lights came on, I felt good. Happy, even.

The principal stood in front of a microphone, smiling condescendingly at the crowd. The vice principal stood just behind her with crowns and banners in hand. "It's time to announce this year's Royal Court. Our first runner-up and prince is…" She glanced down at the page in her hand. "Adam Weeks!"

Cheers and applause echoed through the gym. Gabe and I stayed silent.

As Adam climbed the stairs to the stage, smiling that stupid smug smile of his, the principal went on, "This year's Homecoming King is Jason Bentley!"

More applause. More cheers. Jason look surprised as he climbed the steps and received his crown from the vice principal. I didn't blame him—I hadn't thought he'd win after what I'd done to him. Didn't it mean anything? Didn't anyone care?

My happiness took a nosedive.

"And now for the ladies. This year's princess is Ashley Swanson!"

I didn't know Ashley well, but she seemed nice enough. Her family was rich, so she had perfect teeth and perfect hair. Her dress was probably designer, as well as her shoes. A year ago, I would've been so jealous of her. I would've wanted to be her. Now, I could only stand there and feel sorry for her because

Adam was looking at her like it was his birthday and she was his present.

"And now for our queen." The principal smiled. "This year's Homecoming Queen is…Magda Torres?"

I felt like someone yanked the floor out from underneath me. I think I might've even stumbled. Gabriel's hand tightened around mine. Confused laughter and bewildered voices rose up around us. I felt a hand on my arm. It was Zoe.

"Oh my God," she said. "Hadley, Gabriel, are…are you guys okay?"

I couldn't answer her. I couldn't even open my mouth let alone find my voice. On the stage the principal scowled. "What is this?"

My gaze fell on Jason first. His face was red, and Adam was laughing at him. Then, I turned my attention to Drew and Brody. Brody looked confused, but Drew grinned like he'd done something to be proud of, and he looked right at Gabe while he did it. I knew then that he was responsible for this. That this was his idea of a joke.

"She can't be the queen," he shouted at the principal. "She's dead!"

Dark red crept up the principal's neck and cheeks. She looked like she was about to explode. "I don't know who's responsible for this," she said into the microphone, "but when I find out, you can expect disciplinary action."

I watched as Drew shook his head and laughed. He wasn't worried. His father was a powerful man. If he could make rape charges go away, he could keep his kid in school.

"As of this moment, Homecoming is canceled." Groans and

shouts from the crowd didn't faze the principal. "There is no Royal Court, and the dance is now over. Go home."

For a moment I thought there was going to be a riot, but then the lights came on and everyone looked around at each other, blinking and confused.

Zoe stood in front of me, a worried look on her face. "Are you okay?" she asked again.

"I...I don't know," I answered honestly. My brain had been shut off. I felt cold and empty. Shock, that's what it was.

That's when I noticed that Gabriel no longer had hold of my hand. In fact he wasn't beside me, either. Shock immediately gave way to panic. I whipped my head around. I didn't have to look for him—I knew where he had gone. He was too far away for me to stop.

Drew and Jason were arguing. Drew had his back to the rest of the gym, but I could see him shove his finger into Jason's chest. Jason looked pissed. Gabe came up behind Drew and tapped him on the shoulder. When Drew turned around, Gabe punched him in the face. He fell to the floor, his head bouncing off the polished wood. Adam made a move toward Gabe, but apparently changed his mind. No one else did anything. Not even the principal. They let Gabe turn around and walk away. Then Adam dropped to his knees beside Drew.

"Call you later," I said to Zoe before going after Gabe. Instead of coming back to me, he'd walked out. I knew he needed time to cool down, but I wasn't leaving him alone in case some friend—or six—of Drew's decided they wanted a little payback after all.

I found him outside, around the back of the school where he and his friends had hung out when he was a senior. He was sitting on the grass, his back against the building as he rubbed his hand.

I didn't speak. I just sat beside him and took his right hand in my left, gently rubbing my thumb over his knuckles.

What Drew Carson had done was beyond cruel. How could anyone be so mean? He hadn't done it to get at Gabe, because there was no way he could've known Gabe was going to be there, and he had to have put this in motion days ago.

No, Drew had done this because he thought it would be funny. He wanted to make a joke at Jason, who was supposed to be his friend. He wanted to make fun of Magda—because he hadn't hurt her enough, apparently. He was a fucking psycho.

I leaned into Gabe's shoulder. A few seconds later I felt his head rest on mine. I lifted his hand and kissed the back of it. "He's going to pay for this," I whispered. "I promise you, I'm going to make him sorry."

I expected Drew's father to send the cops after Gabe, but he didn't—or at least he hadn't done it by the time Monday rolled around.

Martin Carson had done a fabulous job of keeping his son's name out of the press—and of protecting the other boys, as well. It had been Madga's name dragged through the mud. She'd been the one called a slut and a whore. Once, the mother of a classmate walked right up to her and told her she ought to be ashamed of herself. The only thing that had stopped me from breaking the woman's nose had been Magda. She didn't want trouble.

Drew's cruel prank at the dance only made me want vengeance even more. What I honestly wanted was to beat him to death with a brick, starting at his feet so I could drag it out. Magda wouldn't approve, but she wasn't there. If she was alive, I wouldn't feel this way. Would I?

How had he managed to pull it off? People had to have helped him. The thought of someone on the voting committee actually helping him make a joke of Magda made my gut churn, sour and hot. You don't realize how mean humans could be until that meanness was directed at someone you loved.

A few months ago, I did a Google search for Magda. A lot of photos of her came up, including that awful one I had on my phone. There were articles about her suicide and "alleged" assault, and screenshots of some of the horrible things people had said about her. There was nothing about her rapists. Nothing.

I couldn't let Drew get away with this latest douche-baggery. If what I'd done to Jason and Brody hadn't been enough of a message, I would have to strike a little closer to home.

Monday morning, I printed several copies of one of the most common photos of Magda—it was her school photo from last year. I wrote *Remember her?* across the bottom of one in black marker and folded the paper into a small square. On my way to first class, I stuck it between the door and edge of Drew's locker. I had to pass his locker six times that day, and every time, I left a new photo. The last one, I actually managed to leave taped to his locker door. The hall was so crowded, I managed to leave it without anyone seeing. The other ones I'd left were gone. I wished I could have seen his face when he found them.

Tuesday morning when I got to school, Zoe was there waiting for me. She had a funny look on her face.

"What is it?" I asked.

"Go home sick," she suggested, her tone pleading.

I frowned. Instead of taking her advice, I walked into the school. She followed me. Caitlin and Anna converged on us in the hall, but by then, I'd already seen some of what Zoe hadn't wanted me to see.

Black-and-white photos of Magda papered the walls and lockers for as far as I could see—one or two here, a couple there. Most of them were the same one I'd left for Drew, and on every one of them was a word written in red. Words like *Slut*, *Whore*, *Dead* and *Sloppy*. That last word really pissed me off. It was what someone had said in a comment when photos of the rape went viral. They'd said, "That thing's just sloppy. Time to hose the whore down."

On several of the photos, someone had drawn a crown. Homecoming Queen.

I was so cold inside, my legs trembled and my fingers felt numb. I'd done this. I poked Drew and he retaliated. I'd made a stupid mistake.

No. I didn't do this. Drew had done this. He was an entitled asshole who thought he could do whatever he wanted, because he'd always gotten away with it. I couldn't let him get away with this. I was the only person who could make him pay. I *had* to make him pay.

"I'm so sorry," Zoe said. I could hear tears in her voice. "We took some of them down, but…there's a lot."

"They're all over the place," Caitlyn added. Anna smacked her arm with the back of her hand.

I walked over to the nearest wall and started taking the photos down. A few seconds later, my friends started on the lockers and sections of wall farther down the hall. I was aware of people walking by—commenting on the display. I didn't hear what they said. I didn't care.

"Look," Zoe said a few minutes later.

I turned my head. Along the entire length of the hall were other girls—even one or two guys—ripping the photos from the wall and lockers. We stayed even after the bell for home-room rang, though a few ran off to class. We moved together like a train, dipping into bathrooms and alcoves to remove what had been left there. Both the first and second floor hall-ways had been "decorated" and we climbed the stairs to fin-ish the job.

I was working on removing a huge collage in the main hall upstairs when the principal found me. I didn't look at her. I didn't care what she said to me or what she did. I wasn't going to class until I'd taken every last one of those fucking photos down.

To my surprise, she started helping me. I did pause then, and turned my head toward her. She met my gaze and nod-ded. I wasn't sure exactly what that meant, but I didn't ask.

Later, when I'd finally made it to class, the teacher was inter-rupted by an announcement over the PA. It was the principal.

"Your attention, please. Given recent events, anyone caught vandalizing school property, or defacing school property in any way, will be immediately suspended."

A few people groaned. A couple laughed. The principal continued. "Let me be perfectly clear. Not only will you be suspended, but the infraction will be added to your permanent record, and if the offense includes defamation of a student or school employee's character, you will be brought before the disciplinary review board. Thank you."

I supposed it was good that she'd made that announcement, but why hadn't she made it when Magda was being harassed? Where was she when my friend really needed her? She'd been hiding, just like everyone else, and this was too little too late as far as I was concerned. And now it meant I'd have to be a bit more careful in my own campaign against Drew, Adam, Brody and Jason.

That night, on my way home from aikido, I spotted Adam's car at Starbucks. I parked a couple blocks away and ran back, mask in hand. The coffee shop was in a shopping complex, so it was fairly well lit, but there were plenty of shrubs around, as the town wanted to make what was effectively an upper-crust strip mall seem inviting and pretty. I crouched behind one of these shrubs and pulled on my mask. I didn't know if there were security cameras or not, but it was probably a safe bet. I crept through the bushes and in between cars, using them and the shadows for cover. Finally, I found myself between Adam's car and another. I took my keys from my pocket and went to work on the passenger side, starting near the rear tire. I gouged hard and deep, making the letters as big as I could, all the while, keeping my ears attentive to the sound of someone approaching.

I finished and crept back the way I'd come. I wondered when Adam would notice.

He hadn't noticed by the next morning. I had a little laugh over it when I saw his car in the school lot. Several people were gathered around it—a couple taking photos. It was probably all over Instagram and Snapchat by now. I got the pleasure of seeing Adam discover it for himself a few moments later.

I had to admit, I dug my phone out and took a photo for my own enjoyment. My smile grew when I looked at it: His face was red, twisted in anger as he stared at his car, and the word RAPIST carved into it, and signed with a big V. I could hear him swearing—promising that someone was "going to pay for this"—as I walked away.

It was the happiest I'd been in months.

CHAPTER 14

Thursday afternoon there was an assembly. The teachers didn't seemed surprised by the announcement that we were to go to the auditorium, but the students were.

I heard Zoe call my name when I entered the auditorium. I found her sitting with Anna and Caitlin about six rows back from the stage. They had saved me a seat.

"What's going on?" I asked as I sat down. "You know why we're here?"

They all shook their heads. "No clue," Caitlin said.

We sat there, looking around as the auditorium filled up around us.

Anna, who sat between Zoe and Caitlin, chuckled. I followed her gaze and saw Drew, Adam and Brody sitting down. "I heard Adam's car needs to be repainted. He's been coming to school with Drew."

"Do you think it was *her* who keyed it?" Caitlin asked.

"It had to have been," Zoe said. She looked at me. "What do you think, Hadley?"

Did she suspect me? I wasn't going to admit to anything—not there. Not anywhere. If she didn't know for sure, she couldn't tell. And she wouldn't have to lie.

So I shrugged. "Probably. She's been stirring up a lot of shit."

Anna glanced around at the students filling the room. "She could be here right now." There was an element of wonder to her voice that surprised me. I wasn't a hero. In fact, it was really hard for me not to humiliate them as thoroughly as they had my friend. I wanted to debase and hurt them. I wanted to ruin them, and completely lose myself in it.

Maybe I wanted to ruin myself too. Punish myself.

The others looked around as well, and I made myself take a look. I had to keep reminding myself that I needed to act as though I didn't know who the vigilante was, either.

Once everyone was in the auditorium, teachers closed the doors and stood sentry beside them. A few moments later the principal walked across the stage to the microphone in the center. She was dressed in a black suit, and she wasn't smiling. "Thank you all for coming." Chatter in the room died down, but only because we were all so curious. "I called this assembly because I feel there needs to be a discussion of recent events. Over the next month, we're going to have periodic assemblies during which we will hear from different people on the topic of bullying, stalking, violence and sexual assault."

Some idiot in the back of the room actually cried, "Woot!"

The principal arched an eyebrow. "Today we have our first guest who will be talking to you about sexual assault and how to prevent it."

"Close your legs!" another voice shouted. Laughter followed this. I looked over my shoulder at the same time as everyone else. A few rows back, a junior I didn't know sat surrounded by laughing friends. What a dick.

"Mr. Matthews," the principal said, "would you please escort that young man to my office and have him wait there until I can return?"

Suddenly the kid's expression went from smug to scared. I smiled. Served him right. I hope she reamed him a new one. A smattering of applause broke out when Mr. Matthews—one of the younger and more buff teachers at school—took the kid by the arm and practically dragged him down the steps to an exit. I clapped too.

"If there's anyone else who would like to display their ignorance by making a sorry excuse for a joke, please do so now, or save us all from having to hear it, and leave." The principal's voice boomed through the microphone. "A teacher will escort you to my office where you can wait your turn to have a little chat."

The room went silent. She waited a beat, sweeping that unflinching gaze over all of us. That was power. That was strength. I wanted to be her. She dared anyone to make a noise, and no one—not even Drew—called her bluff.

"Our speaker today has more than fifteen years of experience in law enforcement. She has worked with victims of sexual assault and has advocated for programs to help survivors. Currently she's teaching a self-defense course that is free to anyone who would like to join. She will provide you with information at the end of the discussion. Please welcome Detective Diane Davies."

Most of the applause was polite, but you could tell who was in the class, because they cheered and whistled. Even though my heart was pounding in anticipation of what the detective might say, I had to give a little shout-out too.

When Detective Davies walked out onto the stage, my jaw dropped. She was wearing a black skirt that ended just above her knee, black pumps and a white shirt that fit her more closely than the T-shirts she wore in class. A couple of guys whistled.

Diane's brows rose as she stepped up to the microphone. "Thank you, Principal Tate, and thank you to whoever just whistled for helping me jump right into the topic of sexual harassment and assault, which I like to define as uninvited sexual attention and behavior." She went on to give stats that made the room fall dead silent.

"Principal Tate told you I teach a self-defense course. I started it so that I could teach girls to better protect themselves from sexual assault, but that's not what I'm here to discuss. Today I want to talk to you about preventing sexual assault. Do you know the best way to prevent a rape from happening? And no, it's not keeping your legs closed."

Silence. We all stared at her as her gaze wandered over the crowd.

"The best way to prevent sexual assault or rape is to not assault or rape anyone."

I swear to God every female in the place went nuts at that moment. The shouts and applause were deafening. There were guys shouting and clapping too, but it was mostly just the girls. I'd never felt so much a part of something huge as I did in that moment.

Detective Davies held up her hand and we quieted. "That remark wasn't just for the guys in the room, though most sexual assaults are committed by men against women. Men also assault other men, though it's a smaller percentage, and there are women who have assaulted men, and other women. I'm not here to make this a female versus male debate, or accuse all men of being potential rapists. I'm here to tell you what behavior is not okay, what you can do to prevent sexual assault, and how to report one should you witness it."

She was awesome. If I liked Detective Davies before this, I freaking loved her at that moment. She talked to us, not like victims and violators, but as people who should be looking out for one another. Who should respect one another.

"Someone who has been raped has been through a traumatic event. I've known women who have PTSD from their attack, who take years to recover, whose lives have been ruined. Do you want to be the person responsible for that? You aren't stupid—you know what no means. And if someone is too drunk to say no, or passed out, that is automatically a no. If you are found guilty of rape, you will go to prison, where *you* might very well become a victim of sexual assault yourself.

"By the same token, I want you to imagine the worst thing that has ever happened to you. Now, imagine that everyone in this room knows about it, but instead of giving you sympathy and support, they're laughing at you, and leaving messages on your social media that what happened was all your fault—that you deserved it. Can you imagine telling someone it's their fault their mother died of cancer? That they're to blame for a traffic accident simply because they were sitting in a car? No, you probably can't.

"As a society, we tend to blame the victim of a sexual assault. We say they asked for it because they wore something revealing, or because they'd been drinking. If I took my side-arm and shot one of you right now, would it be the victim's fault for being in the same room as a person with a gun? No, that's just foolish. You blame the person with the gun."

"What if the person asks you to shoot them?" Oh, God. It was Drew. I'd know his douche-bag voice anywhere.

Detective Davies looked right at him. I knew that because I saw her jaw tighten when she made eye contact. "I've had people try to use me as a way to commit suicide, and I've never once pulled the trigger. If someone asks to have sex with you, that's an invitation. They still have the right to change their mind. Without consent, it's rape, Mr. Carson."

I could have marched right up onto that stage, grabbed her by the hair and kissed her right on the mouth. Oh, that amazing woman, to stand there alone, under the bright stage lights, and call him out. She was my hero.

"Are you an expert in sex, Officer?" Drew asked.

There was a small burst of nervous laughter from the crowd.

"Detective," she corrected. "Rape has little to nothing to do with sex, but I am an expert, unfortunately, when it comes to victims. I've never raped anyone, though, so I'm not an expert in that. How about you?"

Silence. I resisted the urge to look over my shoulder at Drew and his friends. Instead, my gaze settled on Jason Bentley, who was sitting in the row across the aisle from mine. He stared at Detective Davies, his face pale. Since the Homecoming dance I hadn't seen him with Drew much at all. He'd become quiet and withdraw. Maybe, he was developing a conscience.

But that didn't mean I had any sympathy where he was

concerned. He'd helped drive Magda to suicide, and for that I hoped he suffered for the rest of his life.

As for Drew, I wished I had my phone out so I could take a picture of his red, angry face. I couldn't help but look at him. He still wore that smirk of his, but he looked pissed off.

Detective Davies was talking again, having shut Drew up. She talked a little more about how guys should behave—how anyone should behave—and then gave advice on how to protect yourself. She ended with information about the self-defense class and various hot-line numbers.

And then, she said, "One last thing. You've all heard of the person the media calls the Pink Vigilante. We know she is definitely responsible for attacks on a few guys, and maybe responsible for a few more incidents. A lot of people agree with her actions—" hoots and whistles cut her off "—but some of what she's done is against the law. No one, no matter how noble the motive, is above the law. If you see this individual, call the police."

My heart skipped a beat, even though I heard a lot of people say they had no intention of turning me in. I knew then that I couldn't trust Detective Davies, no matter how much I liked her. She was a cop, and she didn't understand.

At the end of the assembly, we all stood up to go to our scheduled final class of the day.

I had just stepped out into the aisle when I heard someone say my name. It was Detective Davies. Stomach fluttering, I approached her.

"I'll just keep you a moment," she said. "I wanted to ask if you could come early tonight. I think we might have a large influx of new girls, and I want to coordinate lessons with you."

The fact that she treated me like a partner in the class was awesome. It was also confusing. "Sure," I said with a shrug. "It's your class."

"Our class. I couldn't do it without you. That's what makes this next bit difficult."

Shit. Here it came. I stared at her.

"I'm sure you've noticed that so far the vigilante has targeted three boys who allegedly assaulted Magda Torres."

"There's nothing *alleged* about it," I informed her.

She nodded. "I know. I still have to say it, just like I have to ask you if you can account for your whereabouts the nights of the incidents."

Fuck. "Yeah, I can."

Her shoulders relaxed a little. "That's good—just in case someone questions you. You'll want to be able to give them details."

Wait…was she telling me to make sure I had my story straight? I blinked. "Okay."

"Good." She smiled. "See you tonight, then."

"Yeah, sure. See ya." I turned and walked away. I would make sure I covered my ass as much as possible in case the police did want to question me. But more important, it was time for the Vigilante to pick a few new "targets" so Magda's rape wasn't so obviously the motive behind her—my—actions.

It shouldn't be hard—a lot of people had posted about their own experiences on the video the girl had uploaded of me fighting the guy outside the club. Some had even given names. If that didn't work, I could always see if Gabe would take me to a college party. It was sad, but I was pretty much guaranteed to find a rapist-in-training at a kegger.

Good thing I had class tonight. The Vigilante needed to get to work.

CHAPTER 15

Detective Davies had been right. Our little self-defense class increased in numbers again that night after she spoke to the school assembly. She had me bring the new girls up to speed as the more experienced girls practiced the newer moves.

My plans to extract further justice for Magda were being thwarted. Drew, Adam, Brody and Jason rarely spent time apart, and since the keying incident, they'd been hyper vigilant. Vigilant against the Vigilante. Oh, the irony. But that was okay. I was patient. And the longer I waited, the less Detective Davies looked at me like a suspect and more like someone she trusted.

That night after class I went looking for trouble. And I went out looking every night after that too. Sometimes I found it, sometimes I didn't, and sometimes it found me. Very little of it was actually reported. The incidents where the girls were sober and coherent, those were the ones that got mentioned on the news, but the ones where the guys were the only witness? Not so much.

Turns out that guys aren't so eager to report being beaten up by a girl, especially when they were trying to hurt another girl. Not all the girls reported on me, either. I didn't know if it was because they were trying to protect me, or because they were ashamed. I didn't ask, because to be honest, I really didn't want to know.

Mostly, I spent a lot of time putting up posters and signs that I'd been careful not to make on my own computer. I bought colored paper at Staples and made the signs at the local internet café.

The paper was pink and the posters said things like: RAPE IS NOT A SPORT and WHAT PART OF 'NO' DON'T YOU UNDERSTAND? My favorite said V IS FOR: Vigilance, Vengeance, Vehemence, Venerate, Veracious, Veritable, Verge and VIGILANTE. Of course, there was always some douche bag who hand-wrote *vagina* on them. It never failed.

I made stickers too. Most of them just had a big pink V on them. I put them on the wall inside the stalls of every girl's bathroom at school. I was careful not to put them anywhere else in case I got caught because of the principal's vandalism rules. But outside school, I put them everywhere—the library, the local fast-food restaurants, the tiny movie theater, gas stations, the coffee shops, town bulletin boards, the park…everywhere I could. And then I started noticing them on binders and textbooks, messenger bags and backpacks. People were making their own.

Adam Weeks made a T-shirt that said "V is for violate, bitch." Principal Tate stopped him in the hall and told him to go home and change. Over the next few days a dozen girls came to school wearing shirts they decorated themselves. One had *vigilante* written in script in pink bubble paint. Another was glittery. Some just had a big pink V on the front or back. Zoe showed up at the next self-defense class with enough shirts for every girl there to have one. It was just a plain white tee, but the front said—in pink, of course—I Am Vigilant.

When Zoe gave one of them to Detective Davies, I held my breath. I expected her to refuse or to say that we shouldn't wear them. I didn't expect her to put it on over her sports bra. And when we were all sitting together as class began, I didn't expect her to ask what she did.

"How many of you have received unwanted sexual attention?"

We all looked at each other. Some of us raised our hands, others looked at the floor. And a few girls who were either very lucky, or liars, shook their heads.

Detective Davies nodded. "Quite a few of you, then. Most of you know that I spoke out against the woman the press have called the Pink Vigilante. That is such a stupid name. What does pink have to do with it? Because her mask is pink? It's like they're trying to make her sound cute. If it was a guy would they call him the Blue Vigilante? No, they'd just call him Vigilante, or fucking Batman. I'm sorry, I shouldn't have swore."

"No," I said. "You're right. Not about the swearing, but about it being different if it was a guy."

"More guys should step up," Zoe joined in. "I hate thinking some guy is cute and wanting to get to know him, but at the same time being afraid that he might hurt me."

"The assholes make it hard for the decent guys." That came from Anna.

"Are there any decent guys?" asked Sarah James, one of the newer girls.

"Hadley's got one," Zoe replied with a smile.

I felt them all look at me, and heat rushed up my neck to my cheeks. "Yeah," I said softly. "There are decent guys."

"Hadley's right." Detective Davies smiled at me. "There are a lot of good men out there. I married one. I work with several. There are also some bad ones, like the guys the vigilante has targeted. I don't agree with her methods, but I love the fact that she's empowering you girls, that she's uniting you, because you're all stronger together than you are apart. And mostly, it gives me great satisfaction in seeing these men be held accountable for their actions.

"I couldn't put the guys who raped Magda Torres in jail." She looked right at me when she spoke. "That eats at me every day. I will say this only in this place, our little sanctuary where we can be completely honest with each other and everything said stays within these walls, there is a part of me—a large part— that wants to thank the Vigilante for doing what I couldn't."

I stared at her. My mouth might've even been hanging open. I wanted to hug her. At that moment I wanted to tell them all that I was the Vigilante. I wanted to confess so bad, but I didn't. I just sat there, silent, because for all I knew it could also be a trap.

Detective Davies wasn't done. "I was raped when I was seventeen. I went to a beach party, had too much to drink and ended up on my back in a tent with a guy from the chess club on top of me. I didn't say no, but I hadn't said yes, either."

Now we were all staring at her—in stunned silence.

"When I told a girlfriend that I hadn't wanted to have sex

with him, she went and told him that. His response? 'The bitch wanted it as much as I did.' Not all rapists are jocks or rough guys. My attacker was the school valedictorian that year. I ran into him at the reunion a few years ago. He didn't recognize me at first, and when he did, he gave me this little smirk like we shared a secret. I'll never forget the look on his face when I told him I was a cop, and that if he kept smiling at me like that I was going to find a reason to shoot him."

We all cheered. She smiled. "I don't condone violence. What I do believe in is giving you the power not only to defend yourself, but to stand up for yourself. I know it's difficult to come forward and admit what someone did to you. I regret every day not reporting my rapist, or going to the hospital and having a rape kit done. I had been drinking, and I thought it was my fault. It wasn't my fault, and it's not your fault. And if your rapist attacks someone else, that's not your fault, either. He is the one who is to blame, not you. Never you."

I'm not sure who went next, but one by one, those who wanted to share their stories started talking. When it came around to me, I was sure what I was going to say, but then I opened my mouth. "My best friend was raped by four guys I have to see almost every day. She killed herself. I blame myself because I wasn't there to help her. I was off with a guy, not being raped."

They all looked at me in sympathy. Some of these girls had shared terrible stories about what had happened to them, and yet they felt sorry for me? I couldn't deal. I thought about what Zoe had said to me—that Drew and his friends hadn't needed to physically rape me—they'd already done it emotionally. They took away something inside me that I would never get back.

Detective Davies smiled as she looked at all of us. "When I look at you, I don't see victims. I see survivors. Now, on your feet. We're going to do some punching and kicking."

We all jumped up. I don't think there was even one of us who didn't feel like throwing as many punches and kicks as we could. I just had to picture Drew's smirking face in front of me and I gave it all I had.

After class I headed toward the local college where Gabriel was studying. He'd texted me earlier, asking if I wanted to meet up around 10:00. I said yes. Like I'd ever say no. I hadn't seen him much lately, as he was working on some project for one of his classes. We were going to meet at a pizza place just off campus in about half an hour.

The college had turned a bunch of old Victorian houses into student living space a few years ago. I was walking past a row of these when I heard what sounded like a whimper followed by male laughter. It was a sound that was both frightening and infuriating. My hand closed around the mask in my bag as I slowly moved toward the sounds.

Was it too much to ask that the one night I wasn't looking for trouble, I didn't find any?

Lights were on in two houses that had a narrow alley between them. It was dark in that alley, but there was enough light from the windows that I could see four guys together in a circle. As my eyes adjusted to the dim light, I could see that they were clustered around a girl, and that there was actually a fifth guy on the ground with her. He had his hands under her skirt trying to remove her underwear. His friends cheered him on as she cried. I could tell she was drunk. She was also terrified.

There was no way I could take on five guys in a fight, but I wasn't about to walk away, and I wasn't about to let them hurt her. I had my bag behind some bushes and pulled my ski mask over my head, tucking my ponytail inside. I had two sets of brass knuckles that I had borrowed from the dojo—we sometimes used them when we staged fight scenarios. I put them on, simultaneously psyching myself up while part of me wondered if I was completely insane.

I crept back to the strip of darkness between the houses and drew a deep breath. "Hey!" I yelled as loud as I could.

The circle jerked back, revealing more of the guy and girl on the ground. He had her underwear around her knees and was ripping them off as she kicked at him.

One of the guys turned toward me. "It's that pink-masked bitch from the news. You picked the wrong party to crash, baby."

"Really?" I asked. "Because it seems like you guys were about to start without me." Something about putting on the mask made me ballsy. When I wore it, I felt like I was actually the badass people thought I was.

The guy came at me. He made it easy for me. I punched him hard in the nose, then slammed an uppercut into his jaw. His nose crunched under the brass knuckles, spurting blood down the front of his shirt. He fell to his knees with a cry of pain. I whipped my leg out and snapped him with a controlled kick that sent him sprawling and knocked him out.

When his friends saw what I'd done, two of them decided to come at me, followed by a third. The guy on the ground was still trying to get between the crying girls legs. I sent up a little prayer to the universe that I could get through these three guys before he managed to rape her. I seriously wanted to beat him bloody.

If they didn't beat and rape me first.

The trio rushed me, driving me out of the alley. *Fuck.* In the open they would be able to surround me. I punched one, kicked at another, but the third got behind me and grabbed my arms. I threw my head back, hoping to connect with his nose, but he moved and I ended up connecting with what felt like his cheekbone instead. He grunted but didn't let go of me. He pulled my arms behind me, locking them so I couldn't pull free. I kicked at his shins and struggled against his hold, but then one of his buddies punched me in the stomach, knocking the wind out of me. I bent double, gasping for breath. I could feel the guy behind me grinding himself against my ass.

"We're going to have fun with you," he said to me, laughing. "We'll see how much of a hero you are when a video of me fucking you like a dog goes viral."

I probably should've been more scared than I was, but what actually went through my head was sadness that so many guys thought this way. Where did it come from? How could I have thought that I could ever fight it? It was like a disease. A worldwide epidemic of men and boys who thought that violating a woman was not only their right, but a pleasure.

Another punch knocked that thought right out of my head as a hard fist connected with my jaw. Stars exploded before my eyes as pain blasted through my skull. He hadn't broken my jaw—at least not yet. When he came at me again I was ready, and I caught him with a kick to the gut that knocked him backward into his buddy. That made them both mad, and I desperately tried to think of some way to save myself as I watched the two of them prepare to come at me together.

I braced myself for their attack, running possible defenses in my head. I didn't have much going for me, but maybe I could get angled around so that I could slam the guy behind me into the side of the building. I drew a deep breath as the first one lunged...

Then I heard it. At first it was faint over the muffled cries of the girl in the alley, but it was a shout—more than one. My opponents paused, turning their heads in the direction the sound had come from. Under the streetlights, I saw three girls running toward us. It was Zoe, Anna and Caitlin. I didn't know whether to scream at them to run or to burst out laughing in joy at the sight of them.

"Let her go!" Zoe's eyes blazed. She looked fierce with her frown and clenched fists. Anna and Caitlin flanked her—they looked like a badass girl gang.

"Fuck off," the guy behind me growled. "Or you'll be next."

Zoe actually laughed. I think I loved her a little bit at that moment. "I don't think so, asshole."

I watched in amazement as these girls who I'd begun to think of as true friends went Kill Bill on the two guys who had been about to come at me. They were brutal and beautiful. What they lacked in proficiency they made up for in ferocity.

The arms that held mine slackened. I could feel my captor's indecision. Did he hold on to me, or did he help his friends?

I made the decision for him.

I pulled my arms free and pivoted around to punch him hard in the mouth. I was still wearing the brass knuckles, and I felt teeth shatter as they connected. I didn't take time to enjoy it. I punched him again in the nose before kicking him hard between the legs. When he doubled over, I brought my knee up, smashing it into his face. He fell to the ground and didn't get up.

While my girls took care of his friends, I headed into that dark crevice between the houses. I heard a front door open, voices raised. I ignored it. On the ground, the girl lay unconscious, her legs splayed as her attacker unbuttoned his fly. Rage rushed up from somewhere deep inside me. I wanted to kill him. It was only the knowledge that Magda would be so disappointed in me that kept me from bouncing his head against the concrete foundation of one of the houses.

That didn't stop me from kicking him, though. Not in the head, but in the ribs. I think I felt a couple of them snap beneath my boot. He screamed and fell onto one of the girl's legs. I kicked him again, this time in the ass. Then I kicked him in the kidneys, and the ass again, and the thigh. I even kicked him in the foot. I kicked him everywhere I could that I knew would hurt but not knock him out, and not cause serious injury.

The sound of sirens made me stop.

"Hey!" came Zoe's voice from behind me. "Someone called the cops. You've got to get out of here."

I whirled around. She had blood in the corner of her mouth, but other than that she looked gorgeous. There was real concern on her face, and in that moment I knew that she knew it was me beneath the mask.

I ran out of the alley. "Stay with her, please." I looked Zoe in the eye as I spoke. "Make sure she tells the cops what happened. You tell them what happened. Don't lie for me."

"You're not the boss of me." She said it with a smile. "I'll take care of it. Now will you just get the hell out of here?"

The sirens were getting louder. I grabbed my bag from where I'd stashed it and ran. A crowd gathered outside both houses. Someone shouted as I ran by, and someone else made a grab for me, but I escaped.

"Let her go!" Caitlin shouted. "She didn't do anything wrong!"

I ran across the street, bolting for the darkness behind the library. Only when I was sure I was hidden from any cameras or windows did I pull off the mask and stuff it in my bag. My fingers shook as I pulled the elastic from my ponytail and combed my hair into less of a mess. I pulled a mirror from my bag and squinted at myself in the darkness. I didn't look too bad except for the blood on my lips. My teeth had cut the inside of my mouth when that asshole punched me. Other than that, I was okay.

I didn't take the time to think about the fact that being punched wasn't a big deal to me anymore. Instead, I took a couple of deep breaths, put on some lip gloss and walked off in the direction of the pizza place, leaving the sirens and flashing lights behind me.

CHAPTER 16

Earlier This Year

"Let's go to a movie," I suggested.

Magda stared straight ahead, her greasy hair falling over her forehead. How long had it been since she'd showered? I could smell the BO from where I sat. "I don't feel like it."

"You can't just stay in bed," I told her. She was still in her pajamas—something that had become all too common since the charges against Drew Carson and his friends had been dropped. Basically, everyone in town believed Magda had willingly had sex with all of them, even though they'd found GHB—the "date rape drug"—in her system.

The lesson here was that rich boys could get away with rape and poor girls deserved it.

"I don't feel like it, Hadley. You go."

"I don't want to go alone. I want you to come with me."

"Leave me alone!" she snapped.

I stared at her. She'd never yelled at me. Never. It hurt—

and it pissed me off. She'd turned her back on me lately, and I didn't know what to do. "Fine. Stay here and rot," I retorted. I jumped off the bed and stormed out of the room.

Gabe found me in the kitchen. "What's up? She still in bed?"

I nodded, not trusting my voice as tears burned the back of my eyes. It was five o'clock in the afternoon on a Saturday. Normally we'd be out doing something, or making pizza for that night and picking out movies to watch. Who was I trying to kid? We hadn't done much of anything since That Night.

He gave me a hug. "I'm worried about her too," he said. "Hey, I was going to make a pizza and watch a movie tonight. Why don't you stay? Maybe she'll come around."

I nodded, brushing away a tear. I wasn't going to feel sorry for myself around him, or anyone in the family. His mother had taken his little sister Teresa to his grandparents' house for the weekend, just to get her away from the gossip. The entire Torres family was suffering thanks to Drew Carson and his friends.

A little while later, while I was opening a can of pizza sauce, I heard Gabe on the phone. "Sorry, Jenn, but I can't take you to Todd's party tonight... No, it's my sister... Well, yeah, she *is* more important to me than you are... She did *not* ask for it... Forget it, we're done."

When he came into the kitchen, he looked angry enough to punch someone. "You okay?" I asked.

Gabe shook his head. "Not really, no."

I set the open can of sauce on the counter. "We'll be not okay together then."

He smiled at me and stole another little piece of my heart. The pizza had just come out of the oven when Magda walked into the kitchen. She'd showered and was wearing leggings and a sweater. Her wet hair was up in a clip. She looked more like her old self. "Is that pizza?" she asked.

Gabe and I exchanged a glance. "Yeah," I said, keeping my tone casual. "Want some?" She'd lost so much weight since the rape she was practically skeletal.

She nodded. "Yeah. I'm hungry. I'm sorry for being cranky with the two of you."

"It's okay," Gabe said, giving her a smile. "I'll get some soda."

The three of us sat in the living room, eating pizza and watching a movie. I tried not to notice that Magda barely ate, and that she laughed way too hard at the funny bits. She was faking being okay for me and her brother, and I wasn't going to take that away from her. I hoped that maybe she was getting better.

I was wrong.

I hadn't told Gabe what happened on campus when I saw him Thursday night, so I wasn't surprised to get a text from him Friday morning that said Come over tonight. We need to talk.

He could be as angry as he wanted. It wasn't going to stop me. And it wasn't going to make me let him be my partner, or whatever. It was bad enough that Zoe was now involved. Since the cops didn't come to arrest me, I can only assume she hadn't given me up. I hoped she wasn't in too much trouble.

She was waiting for me by my locker when I got to school Friday morning. She had a bruise high up on her cheekbone that was even angrier looking than the one on my jaw. Her eye was even a little swollen. She smiled when she saw me.

"Did you see us on the news?" she asked.

"No, but I heard my mother talking to a friend about it this morning. She doesn't know what the world is coming to." I said this with a wry smile. I loved my mom, but she was completely out of touch. Maybe being married to my father had broken her.

"Detective Davies showed up. She said she was proud of us. And then she asked us if we knew who the Vigilante was."

"What did you tell her?" The pulse of my throat pounded hard.

"First of all, we hadn't said anything about the Vigilante being there. The guy who tried to grab her told the cops that she ran. He also told them that I said for him to let her go."

"Fuck," I muttered. "How much trouble are you in?"

She shook her head. "None. I told Detective Davies that I thought the guy was going to hurt the girl in the mask, and that was why I told him to let her go. I also told her that we didn't know who she was. She didn't push."

Detective Davies had to suspect me now, especially with Zoe, Anna and Caitlin being involved. Didn't she?

Zoe continued. "A couple of the male cops gave us a hard time for 'putting ourselves in danger.' Davies told them to back off. She said if it weren't for the three of us—and the Vigilante—those guys would've raped that girl."

I put the things I didn't need for my first class in my locker and slung my bag over my shoulder as I closed the door. A couple of girls squeezed by us to get into their own lockers. Zoe and I stepped out into the corridor and started walking toward class. "Did they say on the news if the girl is okay?" I asked.

"She was on the news."

I looked at her in surprise. "Seriously?"

"Yeah. She said she planned to press charges. Apparently the guys slipped something in her drink at a party. She also publicly thanked the Vigilante—and the three of us—for saving her from becoming a statistic. Apparently the college is going to conduct a review into their security since there was supposed to be a car patrolling that area."

"I'm glad she's okay." Glad was an understatement compared to what I felt at that moment. It didn't make up for me not being there when Magda needed me, but I felt like I had redeemed myself a little bit by saving someone else from going through what she had. "She really thanked the Vigilante?"

She shot me a sly look. "Yeah, she did. I don't mind telling you that I'm convinced pretty much all guys are shit right now."

"I know. I've seen the Not All Men posts online. There are good guys out there, it's just hard to see them when you're just looking for the bad."

"Lucky for you, you have a good one." She glanced at me—I saw her head turn out of the corner of my eye. "You don't have do this alone."

I nodded. "Thanks." That was all I was going to say.

"I heard there's a pit party this weekend. *Everyone's* going."

Anticipation danced to my stomach. "Yeah?" We stopped outside homeroom. By everyone I assumed she meant Adam and Drew and the others. "What time?"

"It starts at nine. We're going if you want to come along."

"I might." She followed me into the classroom. Her desk was the one behind mine. I turned to look at her. "Thanks."

Her eyes brightened, and I knew she understood that I wasn't talking about the invitation. "Anytime."

I turned around. Right then I made up my mind to go to the party, but I wasn't going to let Zoe or anyone else get tangled up in my actions. My need to avenge Magda wasn't taking anybody else down with it. I hoped Zoe would forgive me for cutting her out, but I wouldn't forgive myself if another friend got hurt because I wasn't paying attention.

I had homework to finish before going to Gabe's. I didn't want to do it, but I also didn't want it hanging over my head for the weekend. Also, I was procrastinating. I was anxious about seeing him, but the longer I put it off, the more anxious I became, so finally I grew a pair and decided to go. I got to his house shortly after eight.

He answered the door in a T-shirt and jeans. He didn't look angry, but he didn't smile, either.

The house was quiet when I stepped inside. "Is your mom working?"

"She and Teresa went to my grandparents' for the weekend."

"Oh." So we were totally alone. Whatever he had to say to me, he didn't want anyone else to hear it, or see my reaction. Shit. "Look, I know you probably saw video of what happened last night—" I didn't get a chance to finish, because he took my face in his hands and kissed me. It wasn't a gentle kiss, either, but hard and urgent—the kind of kiss that made my heart pound and my head swim. The kind of kiss that lit my nerves on fire.

I wrapped my arms around his waist, pressing my chest to his. I could feel his muscles beneath his T-shirt, firm and warm beneath my hands.

We were both breathing a little heavy when he pulled back.

"You're reckless and brave, and I want to be angry at you for putting yourself in danger, but I can't be mad when you are so *fucking* incredible." He kissed me again.

It was like someone opened a window inside me and let the sun in. I kissed him like my life depended on it, and when he started moving us toward the living room, I kicked off my shoes without breaking stride.

We ended up on the sofa, facing each other. I was on the outside, but I wasn't worried about falling off. As we kissed, Gabe ran his hand up my leg and over my hip, then up my back. It was like he couldn't believe I was real and needed to make sure I was all there.

He kissed my face and my neck as his hand slid beneath my shirt. I gasped when his fingers brushed my skin. I grabbed at my shirt, pulling it over my head so he could touch more of me. It didn't take long for his shirt, and both our jeans to follow. He held me tight, like he was afraid I might disappear. It wasn't difficult to tell he was as into me as I was into him. I knew where this was going to lead, and it was like someone had dumped a bucket of cold water on me. I couldn't let this happen without being honest with him.

I put my hands against the warm skin of his chest and pushed, breaking our kiss. "I have to tell you something."

His hair was a mess from my hands. His eyes were like melted chocolate—warm, with the promise of something delicious. I don't think I'd ever seen anything more beautiful in all my life than Gabe looking at me like he was at that moment. It made me feel both special and terrible.

"What is it?" he asked, coming up on his elbow.

"I'm not a virgin," I blurted.

He smiled. God, he was hot. "Neither am I."

"No, I need to tell you."

"Hadley, it doesn't matter. I'm not jealous—well, I kind of am, but your past is your past."

"It was Michel le Duc."

"The French exchange kid?"

I nodded.

"Mine was Christi Bennett." He moved to kiss me again, his fingers slipping beneath the waistband of my underwear.

I grabbed his hand. "Don't." For a second—and only one—I was afraid that he wasn't the good guy I thought he was.

Frowning, he removed his hand and leaned back so that we could see each other clearly. "What is it?"

"The night I had sex with Michel was the night of Drew Carson's party. I was outside in Michel's car." I forced myself to meet his gaze, hoping he would fill in the blanks so I didn't have to confess.

Gabriel didn't disappoint me. "You were with him when Magda was attacked." His voice didn't even crack.

I nodded. "I was jealous that she was getting all the attention, so when Michel hit on me, I was stupid and I went outside with him. I didn't even really want to have sex with him. I just figured, why not? Virginity is tedious. He was cute and safe, and once he went back to France I'd never have to see him again."

"Why are you telling me this?"

"Because if I hadn't been a jealous bitch, I wouldn't have gone with him, and I might have been there when Magda needed me." A tear slid down my cheek. "I couldn't let this happen without telling you the truth, not when the first and only time I've ever had sex was such a terrible night."

"Did he hurt you?"

"No." I swiped at my eyes. "He was nice. It just…it wasn't what I hoped. When I went back into the party, I couldn't find Magda. I figured she was having fun. When I found her—" My voice broke and suddenly tears streamed from my eyes. I sobbed so hard, my shoulders shook.

Gabe gathered me against his chest once more. He shushed me as his hands rubbed gentle circles on my back. "It's okay. Hadley, it wasn't your fault."

I hadn't realized how much I'd needed to hear him say that. I'd been carrying that guilt with me for months, convinced that nothing would absolve me of it, and Gabe managed to do it with a hug and a kiss to my forehead.

Eventually, I stopped crying. I had to sit up to grab tissues from the box on the coffee table. My nose was so full of snot it was threatening to drip. Damn, I was sexy.

He sat up as well, and put his arm around me as I dried my face. "You okay?" he asked.

I nodded. "I think so." I turned my face to look at him. "You don't hate me?"

He smiled gently and gave my shoulder a squeeze. "No. I don't think I could ever hate you."

We sat there for a little while—until my nose cleared and my eyes stopped burning. I probably had makeup all over my face. Then Gabe rose to his feet and offered me his hand. I took it and stood up. He led me out of the living room to the stairs. I didn't care that I was in my underwear—so was he. I wasn't self-conscious or embarrassed because I knew he liked my body. More important, he liked *me*.

We climbed the stairs and went to his room. Streetlights shone through the window, casting a golden glow over the room that was almost like candlelight.

He took me into his arms again. "I'm sorry your first time was disappointing. I'd like to fly to France and fuck that guy up."

I smiled. "It wasn't his fault."

"Yeah, it was." He kissed me, and the moment his lips touched mine I felt that explosion of want in my stomach again.

He undid my bra and slipped it off my shoulders. It fell to the floor at my feet. I tried to press myself against him, but he held me back. "I want to see you," he said. He wanted to touch me too, and I let him, because I wanted to feel his hands on my skin.

A few minutes later, our breath mingling, we were in his bed. Gabe rolled onto his back, taking me with him. "We're not going to do anything you don't want," he said.

I think that was the moment I realized I was in love with him, when he left everything in my hands. I smiled. "I know what I want," I said, lowering my head to kiss him as I slid my leg over his.

And this time I wasn't disappointed.

CHAPTER 17

Before I left his place Friday night, Gabe informed me that he was going to be my date for the pit party. I wasn't about to argue. I drove home with a stupid grin on my face. That night with him… Well, I couldn't describe it. And the more I thought about it, the more mixed my emotions became.

What had happened with me and Gabe had been incredible. That wasn't the problem. The problem was that I wanted to share this incredible thing with Magda. Okay, so she might be a little icked out by the fact that it was her brother I'd slept with, but we'd told each other everything. Almost everything.

And then I thought about the fact that Magda's first time hadn't been disappointing like mine, but tragic and violent. Because of Drew Carson and his friends, my best friend would never know what I was feeling at that moment. She would never know what I knew, that sex with the right person could be amazing. Knowing that made me sad, and when I crawled into bed that night—my own bed—I cried for her and all the things she would never experience. I cried for myself too, and all the firsts I would have and never be able to share with her.

The next morning I woke up to a text from Zoe asking how I was getting to the party that night. I texted back and told her I was going with Gabe, to which she replied that I was a "lucky bitch" and asked if he had a friend. I told her I would ask.

I got out of bed, showered, dressed and went downstairs. My mother was baking something when I walked into the kitchen.

"Look who's up before noon," she quipped, looking up from the mixing bowl. She frowned at me. "What happened to your face?"

My face? What the hell was she talking about? Oh, she meant the bruise from the guy at the frat house. How sad was it that I was becoming so used to having bruises that I didn't even remember where they were?

"I had class at the dojo last night. I got hit."

She was still frowning. "It looks awful."

"It looks worse than it feels." I went to the cupboard for a box of cereal.

"I don't like you walking around with bruises on your face."

I got a bowl, as well. "I'll slap some makeup on it later."

"Who's teaching this class? I'd like to have a talk with them about what they're teaching you."

Seriously? "It's Diane Davies. She's a detective, you know, a cop." I watched as her frown turned into a grimace.

"She should know better than to let the boys in her class get so rough with the girls."

Didn't she listen to anything I told her? I went to the fridge for milk. "It's an all-girl class." It didn't matter that a guy had actually given me this bruise. It could have just as easily come from a girl with a good right hook.

"She shouldn't be teaching this stuff anyway. I've seen the news reports about that crazy pink-masked girl. And now I see that three girls got into an altercation at a college party a couple of nights ago."

I took my cereal to the table and sat so I could see her. "So you think girls are to blame for what's been going on in this town?"

Her blue eyes narrowed as she looked at me. I think it was the first time in my life that my mother ever actually *saw* me. "All these stories about groups of girls going around beating guys up. What do you think that's going to solve?"

"First of all, those girls saved another girl from being raped. In fact, the one thing all of these 'stories' you're talking about have in common is the fact that the guys—the ones you seem to think are the victims—have all been sleazebags who had sexually assaulted somebody in the past, or were about to."

She paused then. "Really?"

"Yes, Mom." God, I sounded so patronizing.

"The news made it sound like it was all random." Her gaze narrowed at me. "How do you know so much about it? Hadley, tell me you aren't going around beating up boys."

My heart kicked my ribs. "What if I was?"

Her eyes widened. "I…I don't know."

"Would you be proud of me for standing up for what I believe in? Or would you be mad? Would you call the police and turn me in?"

"I don't want you to get hurt."

"Would you call the police?"

She looked completely thrown off. "No. No, I wouldn't. Are you beating up boys?"

"Yes," I admitted. Shit, it felt good to let it out.

Whatever she was making was forgotten for a moment as she slumped into a chair at the table. "Oh."

"I have to do it, Mom."

"This is about what happened to Magda, isn't it?"

I nodded. I thought she might start crying.

"Your father would blame me for this."

"Dad's a douche bag."

She actually laughed. "I guess since we're confessing, I can tell you I filed for divorce."

That was more surprising than it ought to have been. I guess part of me didn't believe she'd actually break it off with him completely.

"Can you afford a divorce?" I asked.

"Yes. I had a job interview last week, and they called yesterday to offer me the position. You and I are going to be just fine. Better than fine." But as she spoke, a tear trickled down her cheek.

I put my hand over hers. "Are you okay?" I asked. Stupid question. She was shaking.

"I will be." Her fingers tightened around mine. "Sweetie, you have to stop this. Magda wouldn't want you to get hurt— or worse, arrested."

"Magda's dead," I whispered. "It doesn't matter what she wants."

My mother tilted her head as she watched me. "That's what those boys thought."

It was like a sucker punch to the throat. I literally couldn't think—couldn't speak. I pushed my chair back and stood up.

"Hadley!" Mom cried as I walked out of the room. "Hadley, come back! We need to talk about this!"

No, we really didn't. I was done talking. Done listening. Everyone just needed to shut the fuck up and let me do what needed to be done.

The pit was an old quarry on the edge of town that was owned by the DOT. It was where they got the gravel to do road repairs, and where bored high school students had been partying for years.

Gabe and I went together, as he'd promised. There was no way he was letting me go alone knowing Drew, Adam, Brody and Jason were going to be there, especially since he knew the four of them were the only reason I was going.

I didn't really have a plan. My ski mask, which was starting to look a little dirty, was tucked into the waistband of my jeans. It was a cool night, so I had on a jacket that concealed the bulk beneath my shirt. Other than keeping an eye on Drew and his minions, I didn't know what I was going to do. I suppose I'd figure it out if the opportunity arose. It hadn't steered me wrong so far.

What I knew for certain was that I wanted to get Adam before Drew. I was saving Drew for last, though I hadn't realized it until that moment. Drew was the one who had given Magda the spiked drink. He was the one who took her upstairs. And in all of those awful photos, he was the one who had degraded her the most.

So, yeah. He was going to be the grand finale. I wanted him

to know I was coming for him. I wanted him to look over his shoulder and wonder when I would strike.

We got there around nine. It was dark up where we parked, but everyone knew where the road into the pit was. We followed Zoe and her date—a surprise named Paul—and Anna down into the open area where someone had already got the fire burning. There were sticks set aside for hot dogs and marshmallows—sticks that had been there since before I started going to these parties—and magically these food staples always seemed to appear.

People had brought coolers full of beer and soda. I had a bottle of cola, and so did Gabe. Neither one of us were big drinkers—not anymore. Before Magda's attack it was pretty much a guarantee that I was going to get drunk at every party I went to. Nothing like a friend's gang rape to make a girl more cautious. I think Gabe just didn't like to lose control.

As we approached the fire, the scent of another kind of smoke hung heavy in the air. God, pot smelled like skunk. I never got into it, but I knew a lot of girls who did because they liked it better than beer, and they didn't have to pee as much.

Caitlin was already there with her boyfriend, Rick, and they came to meet us as we approached the fire. I was glad that we were going to hang out with them, and Paul. Lately I'd been paying so much attention to guys who were rotten douche bags that spending time with ones who were good was a welcome change. It was nice to know that Gabriel wasn't an anomaly.

Anna had brought stuff to make s'mores, so we gathered close to the fire to indulge in sticky chocolatey goodness. I'd just made my first one when Jenny, a girl from defense class, approached. She said hi to all of us, but her attention was mostly fixed on Anna. And Anna batted her big, anime-like eyes back at her. No one else seemed surprised that Anna was into girls. Had I been that self-absorbed that I didn't even notice the people around me?

Yes, I had been. I purposefully ignored people so I didn't have to know about them, or care. I was stupidly afraid of making a friend and losing them—or worse, doing something stupid and having something horrible happen as a result. It didn't matter how many people told me that Magda didn't kill herself because of what I'd said that day; I still believed she'd be alive if I hadn't said it. Or maybe she would have lived long enough for me to see she needed help.

Someone had brought a sound system, filling the pot-laced air with a throbbing bass beat. I looked around at the others gathered around the fire. There were girls wearing clothes that were completely inappropriate for the setting, and guys being idiots putting each other in headlocks. That was going to escalate to full-blown wrestling as the evening progressed. It wasn't a pit party until somebody went too far and play fighting turned into the real thing. I'd seen guys who were best friends when they walked into a pit party leave bloody and battered and hating each other.

There was a track, or road, around the mountain of gravel in the center of the pit. The other side of this mound was where people went to make out. The scrub on the bank was where you went to pee. What I liked about the place, was that even though you could find a little bit of privacy, sound carried. If a girl started screaming, we were all going to hear it, even over the music, because we tried to keep quiet enough that no one called the cops.

My gaze kept searching the crowd. Beside me, Gabe nudged my arm with his. "They're not here yet," he said.

I turned my head just enough to look up at him and smiled. "That obvious?"

His lips tilted on one side. "Little bit." Then he took my hand in his. His fingers were warm and strong. When I thought about them touching me, my entire body started to tingle.

"Don't look at me like that," he said with a laugh. "I've never been big on sex in cars, but you could change my mind."

I smiled. It sounded like a great idea to me, but I wasn't into voyeurism, so maybe in a more discreet location.

We hung out, singing and laughing, eating way too much sugar and chocolate. Anna and Jenny were really hitting it off. She seemed to be a nice girl. She was in the school band and drama club, and she looked at Anna like she was the most beautiful thing she'd ever seen. That was good enough for me.

Around eleven, Drew and his crew made an appearance. I watched them as they stood around the fire, talking to the mindless few who flocked to them like drones to a queen bee. Someone said something to Brody and then laughed. Brody didn't look impressed, and gave the guy a shove. My ego immediately determined that the guy had said something about the night I'd left Brody covered in lipstick and locked in his car.

They didn't have as many hangers-on as usual. Maybe their popularity was actually waning. Could it be? Detective Davies had dealt a major blow against Drew's social standing when she pretty much called him a rapist in front of the school. She'd done more in those few minutes than I had in the last month with my pink ski mask. I wasn't jealous—I was thankful.

I wanted Drew Carson's fall to be a hard one.

CHAPTER 18

I watched Adam for what felt like hours. In fact, it was just over an hour. Finally, he left the group and walked off into the shadows. I figured he was going to take a leak. I had a small window of opportunity in which to act.

I told my friends I would be right back, and walked away. Gabriel was talking to some friends, so he didn't notice me leave. Once I was sure no one could see me, I got my ski mask and pulled it over my head. I took off my jacket and stashed it behind some shrubs.

It was dark—really dark—so it took me a couple of seconds to find Adam. By the time I came up behind him, he had just zipped up. He must've heard my footsteps, because he looked over his shoulder and said, "Get your own rock, man. Or are you a faggot?"

I didn't say anything. I kicked him in the back, sending him into the mound of rock and gravel he had just pissed on. Then I went at him with a couple of shots to his kidneys and to the back of his head. I lost my footing on the gravel and stumbled. I had to back away to get my balance again.

My stumble gave Adam time to get up. He turned toward me with a glare, one of his hands pressed to the back of his head. "What the fuck?" His gaze narrowed. "It's you. I've been waiting for you, bitch."

My heart gave a little thump in my chest as adrenaline coursed through my veins. This was my favorite part.

I didn't speak. I didn't move. Instead, I waited for him to come at me. Better to use his own energy against him than waste mine by going on the attack. He didn't disappoint me. In fact, he came at me with a roundhouse that I barely managed to duck. Shit. Of course he would be the one who could actually fight. Thank God he was drunk.

I kicked him in the knee. He cried out and stumbled. I didn't think anyone would be able to hear him above the music, but I was on guard all the same. I punched him twice before he managed to punch me in the stomach. I doubled over, gasping for breath. God it hurt."

"Did you think I'd be easy like those other two pussies?" Adam demanded, coming at me—a shadow with clenched fists. If only there were a bit more moonlight. "I'm going to make you wish you'd never been born, bitch."

He swung again, but I dodged. His fist struck me in the shoulder, rather than the chest. Stars exploded behind my eyes as he landed a punch just above my ear. How twisted was it that I was glad that at least that bruise wouldn't show?

I had to end this quickly. People would be wondering where I was. People would be wondering where he was. So, when he came at me again, I used my Krav Maga and aikido training to use his own force against him, and clotheslined him. He fell hard onto his back on the gravel.

I dropped to one knee and punched him in the face, feeling something split beneath my fist. He sat up suddenly, and I felt a burning pain in my ribs.

"How does that feel?" he demanded. The pain intensified, and I cried out. "Yeah, that's right."

I punched him as hard as I could. He fell back, unconscious. Reaching down, I found something sticking out of me. Oh fuck, he'd *stabbed* me.

I was shaking. I didn't know if it was shock or adrenaline. I pulled it out and used the light on my phone to look at it. It wasn't a very long blade, and I didn't think he'd hit anything vital. Still, I was pretty freaked out. I wiped the blade on my sock—I didn't want to leave any evidence behind.

My thumbs shook as I texted Gabe to meet me at the car. Then, when the light from my phone hit Adam's face, I knew what to do. The bastard tried to kill me. I remembered everything he done to Magda in those photos, in the video. I remembered what she told me he had done—what little she could remember. I remembered all the terrible things he'd said to and about her. Leaving him in his underwear, or naked, was too good for him.

I still had the knife. I leaned closer, shining the light on his face. I swallowed, took a deep breath, and then I went to work. I worked fast, ignoring the churning in my stomach every time the blade pierced his flesh. When I was done, I folded the knife and put it in my pocket. And then I grabbed his phone to take a photo, but it was locked. Damn. I wiped it down and tossed it on the ground beside him.

I stood up and started walking. My legs trembled with every step, making me stagger like I was drunk. I got my jacket and put it on so no one would see the blood soaking my side. I stuffed my mask inside to stanch the flow. Was that my blood on my hands, or Adam's?

Vomit rushed up my throat. I'd barely fallen to my knees before it poured out of my mouth, hot and sour. My body twitched as I wretched, adrenaline and shame battling it out. What had I done? Beating Adam was one thing, but I had *cut* him. I didn't have to do that. I could have just made the V out of lipstick like I had with Jason and Brody.

"Oh, God," I whispered, closing my eyes. "Oh, God." I was going to die. I was going to get caught. I was going to jail. Something. There were going to be consequences for this. I couldn't just walk away. Could I?

Jesus Christ, I'd cut Adam's face! I wretched again, tasting acid and chocolate and burnt marshmallow.

Gabe would know what to do. I swiped my sleeve across my wet mouth and staggered to my feet. The blood on my hands was getting sticky, and the spinning in my head was getting worse. The parking lot wasn't far. I had to get there before I passed out. I walked as fast as I could.

Gabe was already there when I made it to the car.

"What the hell happened?" he demanded. "Where were you?"

I lurched toward the car. "I went after Adam."

"Are you crazy? What if someone had seen you?"

I met his gaze as I opened the passenger door. "You can lecture me all you want later. Right now, we need to get back to your place. He stabbed me."

All the color drained from his face. His dark eyes were wide. "Stabbed you? Fuck, Hadley, you need a hospital."

"No! He knows he cut me. If he tells the cops… They're already looking at me." I climbed into the car and shut the door. "Fuck, Gabe. I cut him too."

Gabriel was still swearing as he got in and slammed his own door shut. He started the car and peeled out of the lot.

"Is your mom home yet?" I asked. Now that I was in the car, the feeling like I was going to pass out had waned.

He kept his eyes on the road. His jaw was clenched, and I knew he was so pissed with me. "No."

"Good. Can you stitch me up?"

He swore some more. "You need to be examined to make sure he didn't hit anything vital."

"We can't go to the hospital."

"I know somebody." That was the last thing he said to me until we pulled into the driveway on the edge of town. The house was small and in need of repair. There was a pickup truck parked outside. A dog barked from inside the house.

I got out of the car. Gabe came around and took my arm. "I can walk," I said.

He didn't respond. His fingers gripped me tight enough that I would probably bruise, but I didn't try to pull free, because I needed his help to get up the steps to the front door. It wasn't that I felt weak, it was just that my legs were still shaking that bad.

A dog barked when Gabe rang the bell. A few minutes later the door opened, revealing a young guy in nothing but a pair of track pants. He was ripped. He also had dark circles under his eyes, and a scar on his chest that look like a bullet wound. A gray pit bull sat beside his right foot.

"Gabe," he said. "Little late, isn't it?"

"Sorry, Chris. We need some help. The no hospital, no cops kind."

Chris nodded and stepped aside for us to enter. The dog wagged its tail when Gabe patted it on the head.

I smiled, feeling a little drunk even though I hadn't had anything to drink. "Nice puppy," I said.

Chris glanced from me to Gabe. "She on anything?"

Gabe shook his head. "Nothing. She got stabbed."

"Get into Mom's room. I'll get my stuff."

I stumbled as Gabe half carried, half dragged me through the kitchen into a small hallway, and then into a small bedroom. He turned on the lamp, bathing the room in a dim golden glow. It was definitely a woman's bedroom, and it smelled of dust and perfume. I don't know how I knew, but I knew then that Chris's mom had died, and he hadn't been able to bring himself to pack her things away yet.

"Can you stand?" Gabe asked me.

I nodded. "I think so." I sounded a lot more confident than I felt. When he let go of me, my right knee sagged a bit. But I managed to stay on my feet with the help of the bed's footboard. He came back a few seconds later with a large black garbage bag and a towel.

"You're not gonna let him cut me up and put me in that, are you?" I asked.

He didn't even look at me. He simply laid the plastic bag on the bed and then placed the towel on top. Then, he removed my jacket and shirt and tossed the ski mask on top of them on the floor.

"Lie down," he said, helping me onto the bed.

I did as I was told. "How bad does it look?" I asked.

Gabe's face was still pale, and in the dim light his eyes were as black as ink. "Bad," he whispered.

Oh, shit.

A few moments later the overhead light came on. I winced at the sudden harsh light. Chris nudged Gabe out of the way. In his hands he had a medical kit, but not the kind you kept under your bathroom sink. His looked professional.

"Chris was a medic in the army," Gabe told me.

That was great, but I still felt weird letting him see me in my bra. "Gabe says it looks bad."

Chris shot me a faint smile. "That's because he's a wimp. Let me take a look."

I sucked in a sharp breath when his fingers touched my skin—not just because his hands were cold, but because it hurt. "How big was the knife?" he asked. "Just the blade."

I held up my hand, spreading my thumb and index finger apart until they were the distance of the blade. It had felt bigger when I pulled it out of me.

Chris continued to poke around my side for a bit with his cold hands. "You're lucky. It looks like the blade hit one of your ribs and then deflected upward."

"Meaning?" I asked.

Chris gave me another smile. At that moment, if he told me the sky was pink I'd believe him. He was just one of those people that inspired confidence. "Meaning the wound is long, but not serious. Be glad that the person trying to hurt you didn't know jack shit about how to use a knife. I'm going to clean this up and stitch it. It's going to hurt some, but you're going to be okay."

Tears of relief burned the back of my eyes. "Thank you," I said. "If I ever have any children, I'm naming one of them after you."

He chuckled and glanced over his shoulder at Gabriel. "You sure she's not on anything?"

Gabe shook his head, a reluctant smile curving his lips. I could tell he was just as relieved as I was. "Yeah, she's just special."

I met his gaze. "I'm sorry," I whispered.

He nodded. "Don't do it again."

"I won't," I promised.

"I hope you got the son of a bitch back," Chris commented as he dampened a cloth with that yellowish stuff they put on surgical wounds.

I was still looking at Gabe. "I did."

Chris cleaned my wound. I tensed when I saw the needle in his hand. His smile was kind. "No way around this, sweetheart. It's going to hurt. But I guess the Pink Vigilante is tough enough to not let a few stitches get to her."

My entire body jerked. I stared at him in horror. "What did you just call me?"

"Relax. You're safe here. I'm not going to turn you in. I loved her too, you know. Take a deep breath. Now let it out, slowly."

I watched his face, rather than his hands as I released the air in my lungs. The needle pierced my skin. Oh, shit it hurt.

"You're the guy she used to write to," I wheezed.

He smiled sadly but didn't look up from his work—I could've used the break. "I am indeed that lucky guy."

I can't quite explain the feeling that came over me. Magda used to tell me about Gabe's friend who was in the army. He was a couple years older than her brother, and she had a huge crush on him. She wrote him every week, and he wrote back almost as often. Sometimes, she read me parts of his letters. He had told her that hearing from her made his time overseas bearable. She had freaked out when she heard he'd been shot. She worried about him for days, until his mother let her know that he was okay.

"She wanted to—Jesus Christ that hurts!—marry you."

Chris went still, and I enjoyed the brief reprieve. It hadn't even hurt this bad to get stabbed in the first place. "She deserved better than me. Now, take another breath, sweetheart."

I don't know how long it took him to stitch me up completely. It felt like hours. I'd like to say that I was stoic, and action-movie-cool for the entire thing, but tears leaked from my eyes. I tried to suck it up and accept my consequences, but I was so relieved when he was done I couldn't hold back the tears any longer. He bandaged me up and told me to get some antibiotic cream to make sure I didn't get an infection, otherwise I'd need to go straight to the doctor.

I was going to do all I could to make sure I stayed infection free.

"Give me the knife," Chris said, holding out his hand. "I know you have it." There were traces of powder on his fingers from the latex gloves he'd worn when he stitched me up.

I reached into the pocket of my jeans and pulled out the

knife. I handed it over like a kid being caught with stolen candy.

"I'll dispose of it," he said, and I believed him.

He gave me a T-shirt to wear home. It was just a plain black one, but it looked new. "Keep it," he said. "Think of it as a souvenir." Then he handed me a plastic bag with my coat, shirt and mask in it. I thanked him.

"You be careful." And then he hugged me, wrapping his muscular arms around my shoulders, so as not to hurt me.

"I'll take care of her," Gabe told him. They shook hands. I patted the dog on her silky head. Her tail whacked hard against the floor.

"He was nice," I said in the car on the way back to Gabe's. I'd told my mom I didn't know what time I would be home, and that I might stay at a friend's house, so she wouldn't worry.

"Chris is a good guy. How you feeling?"

"Sore. Thanks for taking care of me."

"I was so fucking scared."

"I know."

"No, you don't." He glanced at me. "You really don't."

I didn't know what to say, so I stayed quiet. My cell phone chirped. I had a new text. It was from Zoe. Where are you? Cops are here. Adam got jumped.

I remembered how the blade had felt cutting through his forehead and my stomach churned. I was going to have to live with that for the rest of my life. Maybe someday I would be able to think of it without wanting to throw up, or being horrified.

I loved Zoe for pretending that I wouldn't know. I texted her back that I was with Gabe and we had snuck off for a little time alone. I apologized and told her I would call her later.

At least I would have something of an alibi if the cops questioned me. I would be more surprised if they didn't. I mean, really. I was the obvious choice. I should have been smarter. I should've planned things better.

All I could do now was hope they didn't catch me before I got to Drew. Because despite all I'd been through that evening, and despite what I'd done, if I didn't make him pay, then none of it mattered.

CHAPTER 19

Gabriel washed my clothes as soon as we got back to his place. My shirt was ruined, my jeans blood- and dirt-stained. He didn't seem so mad at me now that we knew I wasn't seriously injured.

"The cops are going to question you," he told me, as he closed the lid of the washing machine. "You know that, right?"

I nodded. I was wearing Chris's T-shirt and a pair of Gabe's sweatpants. "I know. They'd be stupid not to. I'm the most logical suspect."

"What are you going to tell them?"

I shrugged. "If I have to, I'll tell them the truth."

"You'll go to jail."

"I'm okay with that."

He folded his arms over his chest. "You think I'm okay with that? Do you think my sister would be okay with that?"

I froze. I'd been wrong—he was still plenty angry. "Probably not. Then again, I wasn't okay with her killing herself. Neither were you. That didn't stop her."

His fingers curled into fists. "What Magda did had nothing

to do with us. You're the one who made it all about you, blaming yourself for something you couldn't have known would happen."

"Of course it was all about us!" My voice shook with anger. "We're the ones she fucking left behind! I'm the one she said she yelled for but never came."

One of Gabe's eyebrows rose. "She what?"

My shoulders slumped as I sighed. I ran a hand through the tangle of my hair. I'd never get the knots out. "She yelled for me, called out my name. A couple of people said they heard it. I didn't, because I was off having spiteful sex, leaving my best friend to be gang-raped."

"Did you tell them to rape her?"

I scowled. "Don't be stupid. Of course not."

"Did you tell the people who did hear her not to help her?"

"No."

"Then how in the fuck was it your fault?" He threw his hands in the air in frustration. "Jesus, Hadley, you keep making this about you! You weren't there. You said something stupid. You should have done more. You get to carry around the most guilt, is that it? You want to be the poor, tragic best friend who let Magda down? How about being her older brother who couldn't even avenge her honor? I had to see her fade away, and there wasn't a damn thing I could do because those bastards had restraining orders against me." His dark eyes glittered with anger. "My mother still cries at night because she feels like she let Magda down. She thinks she must have done something wrong. You're not the only person hurt by Magda's death, but don't pretend this whole revenge thing is for her. It's for you, and we both know it. Magda doesn't care anymore."

His words hit like punches right to my sternum. "You're right. It is for me—because I couldn't stand by any longer and watch the four of them get to live while she's in a box in the ground." I wanted to hurt him. I wanted to tell him that if he'd been a better brother, or more of a man, he would have avenged her instead of me, but my mouth refused to say the words—mostly because I knew they weren't true. I only wanted him to hurt as much as I did, but looking at him, I began to realize that my pain was a dull shadow of his.

"I couldn't—" My breath caught. I forced myself to look him in the eye. "I was beginning to think I died with her. I haven't felt anything since she killed herself. And then, I took that photo of Jason and I began to feel something. And then there was you, and I felt even more."

He came to me just as a tear slid down my cheek. He wrapped his arms around me and gathered me close—careful not to put pressure on my injured side.

"I felt the same way," he whispered against my ear. "Until I kissed you."

I shivered at his words and lifted my face so he could kiss me again. Then he took me by the hand and led me upstairs. We sat on the couch in the living room, me snuggled into his side.

"Should we check the news?" he asked.

I nodded. "Better to be prepared." An hour ago I'd been prepared to take whatever punishment I had coming, like jail was no big deal, but at that moment, a sharp surge of fear washed over me. I didn't want to go to jail.

We had to watch the last few moments of *Jaws*, which was on right before the late news. When the anchorwoman's face came on, with footage of police lights in the dark behind her, I knew I was the night's headline.

"A brutal attack at a party held by local teens. Police say the Pink Vigilante has struck again, and this time she's gone too far. That's tonight's top story. But first..."

"Too far?" Gabe turned to me with a worried gaze. "What's 'too far'?"

"After Adam stabbed me, I may have knocked him out and used the knife on him."

His eyes closed. I could almost see him struggle to remain calm. "Yeah, you said you cut him. What did you do?"

"I carved a V into his forehead."

Gabe made a choking sound. For a moment I thought he was crying, but then he threw his head back, laughing so loud and so hard, I thought he might wake the neighbors.

"It's not funny," I insisted. "I want to puke every time I think about it."

Gabe shook his head. "I was afraid you'd cut something off, or maimed him for life."

"Oh." I hadn't even thought of that, but I could understand why he would go there. Cutting Adam's dick off would be the kind of thing a guy would think of. "No. I couldn't do that."

He was serious again. "No, and I'm glad. He'll probably have surgery tomorrow, if his father knows a good plastic surgeon."

"Have you seen Mrs. Weeks?" I asked dryly. "He knows a good plastic surgeon. That woman still looks like she's twenty-nine." Still, it didn't excuse what I'd done.

When the news returned to the Vigilante story, we stopped talking and watched. On the screen, we saw Adam led through the red and blue illuminated night by two police officers. Blood trickled down his face from beneath the cloth he held to his forehead. Shit. Was no one going to see it?

"The young man claims to have been attacked by a young woman in a pink ski mask, who rendered him unconscious before cutting the letter V into his forehead. He says he thinks he might have stabbed her, but police haven't found a knife, or any evidence that there was even another person with the young man."

I snorted. "Yeah, he carved himself up with his fingernails." Gabe squeezed my shoulders.

The news cut to two girls—Megan and Holly from self-defense class. The reporter asked them what they thought of what had happened. My mouth fell open when the two of them suddenly yanked pink ski masks over their heads and yelled, "Rapists are gonna get pinked!"

"Jesus Christ," Gabe whispered. "You've got fans."

Drew's face appeared on screen next. He was flushed, his eyes wild. "The bleeping pink bitch is going to pay for this. She's going to get what's coming to her."

"His father won't be impressed that he swore on TV," I muttered.

"He just threatened you, and you're worried about what his father is going to do to *him*? You should be more worried about yourself—and not just where the Carsons are concerned."

"I know." I also remembered some of the things Mr. Carson said to Mrs. Torres when Magda tried to press charges. He was a disgusting excuse for a human being. I wasn't afraid of him, though. But I was afraid for my mother. Two more faces came on the screen. It was Zoe and Paul. The reporter asked them what they thought of the recent vigilante attacks.

"The Vigilante isn't attacking anyone who doesn't deserve it," Zoe argued. "She's out there, risking her own safety to protect other girls. Tonight is just another example of her trying to get justice where the system failed."

"Not all guys are rapists," Paul said into the microphone. "But those of us who aren't need to step up and start doing something about the guys who are out there taking advantage of girls. It's not cool. I think the Vigilante is stupid brave, and the next time I see something going down, I'm going to stop it."

The reporter faced the camera now. "There you have it, Joan. Is the Pink Vigilante a menace, or is she only making up for a flawed justice system? While many people believe the former, it seems even more believe the latter. Back to you."

The visual cut once more to the anchor desk. "Thank you, Kimberley. I've just been told that there have been three more Vigilante-style attacks since police broke up that party. Two girls in pink ski masks confronted a man who swore at his girlfriend and demeaned her outside a restaurant. The man sustained minor injuries. Another girl, also in a mask, was seen helping a very drunk young woman into a cab after a stranger tried to force her to leave a club with him. The man got a bloody nose and some bruised private parts, and was restrained at the scene until the police showed up. By then, the pink-masked culprit had made her escape. And finally, a man who violated a restraining order set against him by his ex-fiancée was knocked unconscious by at least three young women who left him tied up on his former fiancée's lawn, with a large V on his forehead, written in pink lipstick—a much more temporary punishment than what we heard about earlier. Police chief Warren Keith issued a statement urging women *not* to take the law into their own hands and to call the police if they witness an altercation, or see someone in danger, but Colleen Madison, the woman whose estranged fiancé broke the restraining order, had something to say about that."

A pretty young woman with brown hair and glasses appeared. Obviously, they'd caught up with her at her house. She looked pale, but otherwise unhurt. "This is the second time he's violated the order. Last time the police told me they'd take care of it. They told me he wouldn't be back. Well, he came back, and the police didn't show up until after those girls subdued him. If they hadn't come along, he probably would have killed me before the police got here. I don't know who those girls were, but I want to thank them for saving my life, and possibly the life of my little boy. What does Chief Keith have to say about that?"

Back to the anchor. "We asked the chief that same question by phone just a few minutes ago. He said what happened to Miss Madison is unfortunate, and promised that this time her fiancé will be jailed for violating the order. How nice of those girls to restrain the man so the police didn't have to go looking for him. Tonight, women across town are putting their faith not in the boys in blue to keep them safe, but rather the girls in pink."

Gabe and I turned our heads to stare at each other. He looked as stunned as I felt. "My God," I said. "What the hell have I started?"

The Girls in Pink

It was amazing and stupid at the same time. I mean, it was awesome that we girls were thought of as a cohesive unit, but why did they have to call us anything? And even though I had chosen the pink ski mask for myself, calling us the girls in pink seemed to somehow negate what it was all about.

What had I started? Whatever it was, it wasn't just mine anymore. Getting a little payback on Jason had been a lucky accident, but after that each incident had been premeditated. Cutting that V in Adam's forehead had been too much. I'd lost myself in that moment. It didn't matter that he could probably have it fixed. What mattered was that I had done that to him.

I was no better than he was.

Part of me wanted to walk away from it—what if Adam's knife had punctured something vital? He could've killed me, and here I was wondering how I was going to get at Drew. What was I doing? What would Magda say if she could see me? She would probably tell me to stop taking chances, and to stop putting myself at risk.

Like I kept saying, though, Magda was dead. So what did I care what she would want?

Here was the thing; I felt better on some level. I'd marked her attackers publicly. Even if they were still walking around free, I'd changed public perception of them. What pissed me off was that there were people who saw them as victims—who saw all of these men who were getting their asses kicked by girls across town as victims. That wasn't right. Maybe what I was doing was wrong, but I'd stopped some women from getting hurt, and so had my friends in pink. That had to be worth *something*.

It was just after noon when Zoe arrived at my house with Anna and Caitlin the next day. They hadn't called first, or even texted, so opening the door and seeing the three of them was a complete surprise.

"What's going on?" I asked.

Zoe smiled. "Can we come in?"

I stepped back to let them enter. They followed me into the kitchen. I introduce them to Mom, who looked so happy at the fact that I had made new friends, before leading them upstairs to my room. I shut the door so we could talk privately.

I crossed my arms over my chest. "Okaay, out with it."

"The police are questioning everybody who was at the pit party," Caitlin told me.

My heart skipped a beat. I knew this was going to happen, so there was no use getting anxious over it. "Have they talked to any of you yet?"

"That's why we're here," Zoe explained. "We wanted to tell you that we took the idea you suggested and ran with it."

The idea I'd suggested? Had no idea what the hell she was talking about. I couldn't remember suggesting anything. "Okaaay."

She turned to the other two girls. "Show her."

In unison the three of them lifted the hems of their shirts up to the ribs. Caitlin and Anna had bandages on their left sides, while Zoe had one on her right.

"We passed the word around," Anna added, dropping her shirt. "It was smart of you to think of a way to protect her if the police found her."

It took me a moment to realize that Anna was talking about the Vigilante. She didn't know it was me. Zoe hadn't told her. Part of me wondered if Anna was just naive, or if I was really that good at hiding.

And I was beginning to wonder if Magda had sent Zoe to me.

"So, you and a bunch of other girls have all cut yourselves?" What was I asking for? Duh, I'd just *seen* the bandages.

"Yeah," Zoe replied. "It was your idea, wasn't it?"

"Uh…I got the idea when I saw the two girls on the news wearing pink ski masks. They can't arrest everybody, so if a bunch of us are wounded, they won't know who the real Vigilante is."

"So show us yours." Caitlin was as eager as a twelve-year-old boy about to see his first flash of cleavage.

I pulled up my T-shirt so they could see the bandage on my side. I looked at Zoe. She was a little pale, but her gaze was serious as it met mine.

"It's Detective Davies doing the questioning," she told me. That was something I could've stood to hear up front. Although, I have to admit that I wasn't terribly surprised. What did surprise me was the fact that no one seemed to have blamed her yet. She was the one teaching us how to beat the crap out of somebody. Was she disappointed in us? Or was she secretly impressed?

"She hasn't come by to see me yet."

"She probably will," Anna said. "We told her you had already left by the time Adam got hurt."

"Yeah," Caitlin added. "We didn't tell her about Gabe being with you. We didn't want to get you in trouble."

Didn't want to get me in trouble. She was the sweetest girl. If she had any idea of the trouble I'd been chasing, she'd probably lose her shit. Then again, she had cut herself to protect me, even if she didn't know it was me she was protecting.

"Thanks," I told her. "I'll be up front with Detective Davies.

I don't care if she knows that Gabriel and I were steaming up the windows of his car." My friends "oohed" at me like we were in middle school and I said something naughty.

I turned to Anna, tired of talking about myself. "So, how'd it go with Jenny?"

She blushed. "Good."

"Oh no, you don't get away with just 'good.' I want details." I plopped onto my bed. "Spill."

The three of them joined me, and soon we were talking about things I never talked to another girl about. Even if Magda was alive, I couldn't tell her about me and her brother— it would just be weird.

I let myself tell secrets. I laughed when I was supposed to and offered sympathy when it was needed. I told Anna how pretty she was, and Caitlin that she was smarter than she gave herself credit. And I told Zoe that it was okay that she wanted to go away to college, even though it meant leaving her family behind. And for the rest of that afternoon, I felt like a normal girl.

And then the cops arrived.

CHAPTER 20

Detective Davies wore jeans, a button-down shirt, boots and a black leather jacket. She looked tough and gorgeous at the same time. It was weird, because seeing her made me anxious, but she had a strange calming effect on me, as well. I felt like I could trust her, but I didn't want to disappoint her.

And if she knew the truth about me, she'd be disappointed. I was disappointed.

"Am I interrupting?" she asked with a smile, her gaze settling on the three girls standing behind me.

"Nope," Zoe said. "We were just leaving. See you on Thursday, Detective."

The girls filed out, leaving me to face my interrogator. It was then that my mother appeared. I'd always thought Mom was weak, because of how she was with my father. But when she saw Detective Davies her spine stiffened, and a look came over her face that could only be described as protective. Physically my mother wouldn't stand a chance against Diane Davies, but I wouldn't bet against her in a battle of wills.

"Hello." Mom stepped forward, offering her hand. "I'm Michelle White, Hadley's mother. And you are?"

Detective Davies shook her hand and introduced herself. "I'm sure you heard about the incident at the gravel pit last night. I've been talking to many of the kids who were there about the alleged attack on a young man who was at the party."

Mom pulled her hand back and clasped it in front of her. "You mean that Weeks boy. It sounds as though he got a little of his own."

The detective and I arched an eyebrow at exactly the same time. I'd never heard my mother use that kind of tone, and had always thought she blamed Magda for what happened to her. She'd practically said as much.

"Well," Detective Davies began, "given Hadley's relationship with Magda Torres and what happened to her, I can certainly understand why you would feel that way."

Mom smiled faintly. "That was very diplomatic. Was the boy seriously hurt?"

"Some bruises and a cut." A cut? I'd curved a fucking V into his forehead. That wasn't just a cut.

My mother nodded. "That doesn't sound serious enough to warrant all this police attention. If it had been another boy with whom he'd gotten into a fight, would you be here right now?"

Detective Davies smiled, but there wasn't a lot of humor in it. "Probably not. The fact that it was a girl—a girl who had already assaulted two of his friends—has made this particular incident more than just a fight."

"The fact that his father hopes to become mayor has nothing to do with it?"

Adam Weeks's father wanted to be mayor? How could I have not known that? God, I really was self-absorbed.

"Oh, I'm sure that it does. I'm told that Hadley was at the party, and I would just like to ask her if she heard or saw anything."

"Are you going to ask me to lift my shirt?" I asked. Mom's attitude was contagious. I felt bold and in charge.

The smile changed into something a bit more genuine. She even laughed a little as she shook her head. "No, I am not. I assume that you have a bandage on either your right or left side?"

"Right."

My mother glanced at me. "Hadley, what is she talking about?"

I looked at her. "Adam Weeks said he stabbed the Pink Vigilante when she attacked him." I hoped she'd just fill in the rest herself. I couldn't very well say in front of the cop that the girls were willingly obstructing justice. And I couldn't quite bring myself to lie and say that I was just following the crowd, when *I* was the one actually being followed by the crowd.

Mom grimaced. "He stabs a girl and is still treated like a victim." She shook her head. "If this wasn't your senior year, I'd move so you didn't have to go to that school any longer. Come in, Detective Davies. Would you like anything to drink?"

"Just water, thank you."

"Hadley, show the detective to the living room. I'll be right there." Underneath that polite remark was the unspoken command that I was to keep my mouth shut until Mom joined us.

I gave the detective an apologetic smile as we walked to the living room. "She's not normally like that."

"She's exactly as she should be. Don't apologize, I've seen

worse. *Much* worse. It's amazing how some women distort and defile the title of motherhood."

I didn't want to know. Over the last year I'd vilified men because of the ones who hurt my friend. I was just starting to realize that there were some good ones out there. I didn't need to hear about the rotten women.

Detective Davies sat in an armchair, while I sat on the sofa. Mom came in a few minutes later.

"Thank you," Detective Davies said taking the glass of water. "I won't keep the two of you long."

My mother sat beside me, her hands over her knees as she perched on the edge of the cushion. It was almost as if she was putting herself between me and the detective.

"What do you want to know?" I asked.

She had a notebook in her hand and a pen in the other. "What time did you get to the party?"

"Around nine. We met up with Anna, Zoe and her boyfriend in the parking lot and walked down together."

She smiled at me. "I'm glad you've become such good friends with those girls."

She was being honest, I could tell. All these months since Magda's death I thought I'd been so tough and stoic. I realized at that moment that I hadn't been fooling anyone. In fact, it seemed like everyone around me knew what was going on inside me better than I did.

"Yeah, so am I. Anyway, when we got to the fire, Caitlin and Rick were already there. We hung out with them the whole time."

She scribbled in the notebook and then looked up. "When you say 'we,' you mean yourself and…?"

Heat crept into my face from my neck. "Gabe. Gabriel Tor-res. I went to the party with him." God, I hope she didn't want to question him too, but she probably would.

My mother turned her head toward me—I could see her out of the corner of my eye. "Are you and Gabe dating?" she asked.

I nodded, forcing myself to look at her. "We are."

Mom smiled. There was a lot of relief in that expression. "He's always been such a nice boy."

I smiled too. "Yeah, he is."

"Did you see Adam Weeks arrive?" Detective Davies asked.

"Yes. I always notice when he and his friends show up." There was no harm in admitting that. In fact, it would be weirder if I didn't.

"Were you still at the party when he was attacked?"

Fuck. Okay, so making out with Gabe was a great alibi be-fore I knew my mother would have to hear it. "We weren't at the fire."

"You'd gone for a walk?"

I nodded. "Actually, Gabe and I walked back to his car. We left shortly after and went back to his place. That was proba-bly right around midnight." I'd attacked Adam shortly after twelve, so I wanted to give both Gabe and I a reasonable alibi, but keep the timing close enough in case anyone saw us.

"Was there anyone else at his house when you got there?"

I'd be offended that she was asking if anyone could back me up if I wasn't already up to my eyeballs in lies. "No. His mother and sister are out of town. That's why we went back to his place."

"Oh," my mother said. And then something really weird

happened. I watched in horror as a tear trickled down my mother's cheek.

"Mom, I didn't mean to disappoint you." God, this was awful.

Mom shook her head and wiped at her cheek. "It's not that. You could never disappoint me. After what happened to Magda, I was worried that you would never be able to trust anyone enough to have that kind of relationship."

Wow. I'd really had my head up my ass these last few months. I'd been so caught up in my own grief and anger that I simply hadn't realized what watching me grieve had done to my mother.

I turned back to Detective Davies. "Zoe texted me after Adam was attacked and asked where I was. We were already on our way back to Gabe's."

She closed her notebook. "All right then. I guess we're done." She rose to her feet. "Thank you both for your time, and the water."

Water she hadn't even tasted. I wondered if cops just did that to put people at ease, because even on TV they never seemed to drink anything they were given when they came to somebody's house.

Mom and I walked her out.

"I may be in touch again if I have any further questions." She gave me her business card. "I know you already have my cell phone number, but just in case."

"Thanks." Our gazes met and locked. For a moment I felt like she could see right into my soul, like she knew every last secret in there and was disappointed. She smiled and said goodbye to my mother.

Mom shut the door behind her and leaned against it with a sigh before turning her attention to me. "Well, I'll make a doctor's appointment for you tomorrow, so you can discuss birth control options. I'm going to assume a boy his age knows about condoms and uses them?"

I nodded. My face felt like it was on fire. I could break a man's nose. I could carve a V into his forehead, but talking to my mother about sex made me squirm.

"Good. Do you have any questions?"

I shook my head. "No."

She hesitated, and then said, "He is a nice boy, right? He's good to you?"

Something broke inside me. I think it might have been my heart. I hated that she felt like she had to ask me that.

"Yeah. He's great."

Mom nodded. "Good. You need some kindness in your life." She put her arms around me. "But next time, you use me as your alibi, sweetie."

I hugged her back. "There won't be a next time, Mom."

But there would be, and we both knew it.

Someone organized an after-school program to discuss vigilante justice and how it harmed society. Someone else had hung a poster about a support group for guys who had been the victims of violent crime. Another advertised a group that wanted to discuss the "ramifications of committing violent crimes on the feminine psyche" and how we're "losing our womanly identity" by defying our stronger male counterparts. Someone had drawn a huge pink V on that one—which made me smile.

And then, on pink paper, pinned to the bulletin board was a poster for a group of girls who had been the victims of sexual assault, sexual bullying, or harassment. Take Back What's Ours, it read. It was meeting Wednesday after school. You had to call the phone number to get the location, which I thought was smart—and sad. It was too bad that girls had to be concerned about guys, or even other girls, coming to the meeting just to make trouble, or intimidate them. I took a photo of the poster in case I wanted to attend. I might not have been sexually assaulted, but I'd certainly been affected by it.

And maybe I could talk a few of the girls into joining the self-defense class.

There'd been a big change over the weekend. My jaw almost dropped open as I walked down the corridor and saw all the girls with pink shirts, pink skirts and jeans—even pink hair. They had Vs on their books and bags and on their shirts. Of course, it wasn't everyone. And yeah, there were people—both guys and girls—who made comments about it, but instead of slinking away, the girls being sneered at gave their critics the finger—literally.

And despite the principal's crackdown on vandalism, someone had left a big pink V on Adam's locker. It looked like it had been painted on.

This was surreal. I'd worried about bad things happening because of what I'd done—negative consequences—but I'd never dreamed that anything like this would happen. Sure, I'd hoped some girls might find a little empowerment, but this was crazy. More than I could have ever imagined, or deserved.

Adam wasn't at school, of course. He was probably already

at some swank plastic surgery clinic getting his face fixed. God, I wished I didn't feel so bad about cutting him. Really.

Someone grabbed my shoulder. I whipped around, fists up. "Whoa, tiger!"

I relaxed. It was Zoe. God, I was such an idiot. "Sorry. Tense."

"Did everything go okay with Detective D?"

"Yeah, fine. Hey, thanks."

She knew what I was thanking her for. Her plan hadn't been terribly smart, but getting a bunch of girls to cut themselves so the Vigilante—me—wouldn't get caught was brilliant. "This should brighten your day, check it." She handed me her phone.

On the screen was a webpage. It was for the group Faceless— they were like Anonymous, only they dealt mostly with issues that affected high school or college age people. When I saw the photo, I couldn't believe it. It was Adam. He had blood running down his face from his forehead and his nose. The mark I'd left on him was clearly visible, but that wasn't what was amazing, nor was it the fact that someone at the party had to have taken the picture. What was incredible was the headline:

RAPISTS OUTED. IT'S TIME FOR JUSTICE FOR MAGDA TORRES.

Underneath Adam's photo were the ones I'd posted of Brody and Jason with their own phones. And beneath those, their names were printed in bold font. There was an article as well, publicly outing the three of them, and Drew Carson, as Magda's rapists. It detailed what the four of them had done to her— enough to be enraging, but not enough to demean my friend.

Faceless called for justice, saying that the rapists' identities had been protected by a corrupt system funded by their families' money. They demanded that something be done.

The article had almost ten thousand comments attached to it. And a link to a video that had already had over a million views. It was basically the same as the article, but it featured some photos Drew had posted—and part of the video they'd made of that terrible night. It was all presented with a digitized voice-over demanding justice for Magda.

I pressed my hand to my mouth as tears burned my eyes and scalded my cheeks. Finally, people would know what happened to Magda, and they would know who did it. She wasn't just another victim.

Zoe hugged me as I cried. And afterward, she helped me fix my makeup in the bathroom before the bell for homeroom. As we walked out, I spied Drew on his way to class. He was alone. I don't think I'd ever seen him by himself—there were always little groupies gathered around him. Most people would feel that isolation. They'd shrink back, knowing they'd been ostracized, but Drew was a narcissist, and a psychopath, and his reality was as warped as he was. He still had that sneer on his face, along with that "I'm better than you" walk. He still thought he was untouchable, even after being outed to the entire world.

"What do you have planned for him?" Zoe asked, her voice low so no one else could hear.

"I don't know," I replied. And I honestly didn't. He would never admit that what he'd done had been wrong. There was probably no way to make him sorry.

But I was going to try.

CHAPTER 21

"I'm sorry I haven't been here in a while." I looked down at Magda's headstone. "Things have been crazy, but that's no excuse. I hope you don't feel left out."

It was chilly. Two weeks into October, and it was starting to feel like fall. Brilliant red and orange leaves drifted from the trees above the spot where the box that held what was left of my best friend was buried. I knew there was nothing of Magda in that box—not the parts that mattered—but I came to this place because it was concrete. There was a stone with her name on it, and flowers, but nothing of her. I could have this conversation sitting in my room, but that felt too much like praying, and I had a lot to say.

"Zoe is becoming a really good friend—more than I deserve. You'd like her, I think. And Gabe… Mags, I really like him. Like, I think I love him. I hope you're okay with that. You probably knew I had a thing for him, anyway. You always knew things I thought I'd hidden. I miss that, you know. You always knew when I was upset, and how to pull my head out of my ass."

Speaking of asses...

"My dad's gone. Mom kicked him out. Can you believe it? I couldn't. It's weird. It's like she's changed overnight. She's gone from this dishrag to a mom more like yours. I don't know why she let him keep her down for so many years, or why she decided that now would be a good time to change that, but I think maybe I had something to do with it." I paused. Should I keep ignoring the real reason I was there? Or should I just go for it? It wasn't like she could answer me.

"I know you wouldn't like what I'm doing. You'd tell me not to do it for you. A couple of weeks ago I would have said you were exactly why I was doing this, but it's not true. I'm not even doing it for me, either—well, not completely. I'm doing it so other guys out there will know it's wrong to rape, and that there are consequences. I want girls to know they're not powerless. I want...I want to know that I've done something that makes a difference. You should see how many girls we have in the class now. And at school, girls have banded together against harassment. I feel like I've started something awesome.

"I don't agree with some of what's going on. The other night a couple of girls jumped a guy who hadn't done anything except say hi. Violence without cause is just violence. It's not right. Anyway, I'm going to be done soon. I'm always going to stand up for other girls, and I hope I always get to teach them how to protect themselves, but my Vigilante days are numbered. When Faceless outed Jason, Brody, Adam and Drew as your rapists, it was like something inside me shifted. I thought I could be satisfied with that. All I ever wanted was for people to see them for what they are. But it's not enough. I need to make Drew admit what he did. Once I can do that, then I'll be done. I promise."

I rolled my shoulders and looked up at the trees. A bright red leaf fell straight at me. I reached up and caught it. Magda would have called it a sign, but I didn't believe in that stuff—not anymore. Still, there was a little tingle at the back of my brain as I caught the leaf in my fingers.

My phone buzzed. I reached into my jacket pocket and pulled it out. It was a text from Zoe, asking if I wanted to meet for coffee.

At graveyard. Can you pick me up?

Yep. See you in ten.

"Anyway," I went on, putting my phone away. "I just needed to tell you all of this. I hope, if you're listening, that you'll understand. And I'm sorry I wasn't there to protect you. You told me it was okay, but I've never been able to believe that. Maybe it's just guilt, or maybe it's because sometimes I'd find you looking at me with this strange expression on your face—like you wanted to hurt me. It wasn't my fault you got drunk. It wasn't my fault you went off with Drew. I probably couldn't have stopped you. But it is my fault that I didn't look for you when I noticed you were gone. It's my fault that I got pissed at you and had meaningless sex out of spite. It wasn't my fault they did what they did to you, but if I don't see this through and make each and every last one of them sorry, it *will* be my fault. I went too far with Adam, but honestly? I don't regret it.

I have to live with what I did to him, and I can. I *will* regret not seeing this through. Whatever the consequences, I'll accept them. Anyway, that's it. I hope someday you forgive me."

I turned and walked away. I had only made it to the main road that ran through the graveyard when I noticed two guys walking toward me. Oh, shit, it was Jason and Brody, and they both looked pissed. I whirled around to go in the opposite direction. Two more approached from that direction—Drew and Adam. Adam had a bandage on his forehead. Drew smiled at me—like a psychopath.

Fuck. Gabe had told me I wouldn't be able to take the four of them, and I wouldn't. I pulled my cell phone from my bag and only hesitated a second before I dialed Detective Davies's number.

Then, I ran.

I ran hard and fast, legs and arms pumping, gravel crunching beneath my boots. There was a gate in the west wall of the cemetery. If I could get to the street, I would be safe.

"Hadley?"

I held my phone to my ear. "I'm at the cemetery. West gate." My voice was panicked, choppy as I panted for breath. "Adam, Brody, Jason and Drew are after me."

"I'm on my way." There was a click, and I knew she was gone.

Getting to that gate was the only thought in my head, because I knew if I didn't make it, the seven-foot wall around the cemetery would provide all the privacy the four of them needed to do whatever they wanted to me.

They were gaining on me. Their legs were longer, and Adam took track at school. He'd be able to catch me no problem.

The only advantage I had was the original distance between us, and my sheer determination to survive. I pushed myself harder, to the point where I thought I might actually trip myself my legs were moving so hard and fast.

I could see the gate, black wrought iron set in gray stone. Beyond that was Elm Street, a residential street that was a popular pedestrian route. Safety taunted me. If I could just get to the gate...

A hand grabbed my shoulder. I shrugged it off, stumbling. I veered off the path onto the grass just enough to escape his reach. It was Adam, and he was coming at me again. I wasn't going to reach the gate.

My heart felt like it was going to burst in my chest. The wind—and fear—stung my eyes. My lungs burned. I couldn't run any faster.

About ten feet from the exit, Adam took me down. He tackled me like we were on a football field. I managed to twist my body just enough that when we hit the ground he was the one that hit first. His head thumped hard against the gravel. His friends hadn't quite caught up, and for a second I thought I might actually escape. I staggered to my feet, but before I could run, Adam's fingers curved around my ankle, holding tight. I didn't fall, but the time I took to kick myself free gave Brody, Jason and Drew enough time to catch up.

Drew caught me by the hair, clenching his fist at the roots. I didn't struggle, because I knew he didn't care if he ripped my scalp apart. My heart hammered against my ribs. My throat was dry and my bladder tense with fear. It didn't matter what they did to me, provided I lived through it. And I would live through it. That didn't mean, however, that I wasn't afraid of what they were going to do.

"Hello, bitch," Drew snarled.

"Hello, asshole," I replied through clenched teeth. "What the fuck do you want?"

He smirked. "The Pink *Vagilante*, of course." He pulled me closer. You either know her, or you are her. Either way you're going to give me what I want. I don't mind if you want to fight a little first."

What kind of teenage guy said things like that? A psycho, that was who. A twisted, entitled bastard who thought he could do whatever he wanted to whomever he wanted.

I was just glad he was within striking distance. He said he didn't mind a little fight.

He looked surprised when I grabbed him by the balls. Then his smirk widened, became a little crueler as his fingers tightened in my hair. He pulled harder. I squeezed harder. Pain made short work of that smarmy look on his face. He was pulling so hard on my hair now my eyes watered. I knew he'd ripped some out, but I wasn't going to give up.

"Pull all you want, you son of a bitch." I tightened my grip. "I don't mind wearing a wig, but you might want to consider your balls." To drive my point home, I squeezed as hard as I could. The loose fit of his khakis made it easy to get a good handful and really twist. Now whose eyes were watering? I smiled at him, looking him right in the eye.

That was my first mistake. I let myself get cocky. My reward was a punch in the face that knocked my head back and made stars dance before my eyes. I would've fallen if he hadn't had a hold of my hair and I hadn't had a grip on his crotch. As it was, I stumbled backward, taking him with me. He yelped in pain and hit me again. This time I let go.

The four of them formed a semicircle in front of me. That was good; better to have them where I could see them than have one creeping up behind. Just to be safe, I glanced over my shoulder.

Brody stood on one side of Drew and Adam on the other. Jason hung a step or two back. He wasn't entirely in this, but the other two seemed content to follow Drew's lead. They made no attempt to attack. What were they waiting for, an invitation? Okay, then.

"Nice bandage," I said to Adam. "It's a real fashion statement."

Fists clenched at his sides. "If you're the one who did this to me, I'm going to fuck you up. They won't ever be able to fix what I'll do to you."

A shiver of fear raced down my spine. He meant it. There were a lot of ways four guys could hurt one girl.

I took a step backward, then another, each one taking me closer to the exit.

Adam was the first to break rank. I knew he would be. If Jason was the kindest of the four of them, Adam was the most hotheaded. It made me think that he had to be really insecure about himself. He came at me with his right arm cocked back. Gee, maybe he was going to punch me.

I dodged as his fist flew toward me. As I moved, I grabbed his arm, using his momentum against him as I hiked my knee into his ribs. Then, I gave him a whack to the back of his skull, and pivoted so that I could lift my left leg and kick him hard in the ass, sending him sprawling onto the gravel. The cuts and bruises on my body protested, but I ignored the discomfort. I was too jacked-up on fear to care.

Brody came at me next. I danced around Adam, putting my-self even closer to the exit. Drew just watched with a smirk on his face. That was when I noticed his phone. It was pointed at me. Shit. He was taking video. He was going to try to use this as proof that I was the Pink Vigilante. Beating the snot out of me, or raping me, would just be a bonus. If it looked like I really knew how to fight, the police would definitely suspect me—more than they already did.

So now what did I do? Let Brody pound on me? It would definitely earn me more sympathy than giving him a round-house to the head would. God, but I hated the idea of letting any of them think they'd beaten me.

Brody took a swing, and I braced myself for it. I could tell he didn't know how to throw a good punch, but it was still going to hurt. I tried to angle my head for the least amount of damage. He got me in the side of my nose and upper lip. Shit, it hurt. I knew by the crunch that my nose was broken. I didn't think he loosened any teeth, but I could taste blood as I staggered backward. Then, blood trickled from my nostrils.

Like sharks after the scent, the four of them closed ranks again, this time coming at me as a unit. I tried to wipe away my blood, but it just kept coming.

"Hey, assholes," came a female voice from above. "Four against one isn't really fair."

I recognized that voice. It was Zoe, though she was making herself sound deeper than usual. I glanced over my shoulder and saw her perched on the stone wall, a pink ski mask over her head and face.

The look on Drew's face when he saw her was hilarious.

"What the fuck?" He looked confused and pissed, and a little scared. I knew what he was thinking. At that moment, he doubted himself, and wondered if he and his buddies had just beaten up the wrong girl. It was priceless. I'd never been so happy to see anyone in my entire life.

Zoe made to hop off the wall, but then I saw her glance up, and instead of joining me, she turned and jumped down to the street. Where the hell was she going? I turned my head to look behind Drew and his friends, and that's when I really smiled.

"The four of you put your hands up, *now.*" It was Detective Davies and she had her gun out. "Turn to face me, slowly."

"You still recording this, Drew?" I asked sweetly. He shot me a dirty look as he turned toward Diane, phone in his raised hand. Blood trickled into my mouth, and I didn't care. "I think this just might go viral."

Earlier This Year

She was dead.

I sank onto the sofa as my legs slowly gave out beneath me. We were in the living room. Mrs. Torres and the police were in Magda's bedroom. They hadn't brought her body out yet. "I thought she was getting better."

Gabe sat beside me. "Me too. I guess she just couldn't fight anymore."

I looked at him as tears ran down my cheeks. "What did we do wrong?"

"I don't know," he whispered. He was so pale. In shock. "I don't think we did anything."

"Maybe that was the problem," I said, taking his hand in mine.

* * *

The day of Magda's funeral was bright and sunny. It was a small gathering. I stood with the family, because Mrs. Torres insisted. She had Teresa on one side of her and Gabe on the other. I stood with him, holding his hand as tight as I could as the minister droned on. If I didn't hold on to him, I might lose him too, and then I'd lose my mind. I'd lose everything.

I stared at the shiny box that held the body of my best friend. There wasn't a tear left in my body, which was good, because the sound of Teresa's sobs broke my heart, and if I had tears left, I'd drown in them. Gabe squeezed my hand a little harder. I knew he'd run dry too.

He had a black eye—he'd gone after Drew again. This time Mr. Carson had got a restraining order against him. Apparently he'd knocked out one of Drew's teeth. The gossips said that Gabe would have beaten Drew to death if people hadn't intervened. They were wrong. If Gabe wanted Drew dead, he would have killed him months ago. No, Gabe just wanted to hurt Drew as much as he could, let him heal and then do it again.

No, Gabe wasn't the one who fantasized about killing Drew Carson.

I was.

CHAPTER 22

The bad news was that my nose was broken. The good news was that it wasn't bad, and the doctor thought the swelling would go down in a few days. He gave me some painkillers, told me what to do for the swelling and gave Mom a list of symptoms that would require additional medical attention—like if my brain started to leak out of my nostrils.

There was more good news. Adam, Brody, Jason and Drew had all been arrested. Drew had been nice enough to record the attack. Detective Davies watched the video while some other cops took the four of them away. She looked pissed.

"Let's get you to the hospital," she'd said, her arm around my shoulders as she put Drew's phone in her pocket. "You'll need to call your mom and have her meet us there. Do you have any idea why they came after you?"

I had my head tilted back and held a wad of tissues she had given me to my nose. "It's right there in the video. They thought I was the Pink Vigilante. Or *Vagilante* as Drew so charmingly put it."

"Asshole," she muttered, grimacing. "Watch your head." I ducked as she helped me into the passenger side of her car. She shut the door and came around the front to get into the driver's seat. "Lucky for you the Vigilante showed up."

I wasn't sure if she meant that, or if she was trying to get me to believe she did. "It sure was nice to have some backup." I was going to kiss Zoe when I saw her. Not only did she come to my rescue, but she took some suspicion off me. Drew wasn't so sure anymore, and if Detective Davies had suspected me, she wasn't sure anymore, either.

I fastened my seat belt. "Thank you for getting there when you did. I don't know what they were going to do to me."

She shot me a sideways glance as she pulled the car out onto the street. "Yes, you do."

I closed my eyes, leaning my head back against the seat. "Yeah, I guess I do."

"You're going to press charges."

It wasn't a question, but I answered anyway. "You bet I am, even though their lawyers will probably get them off."

"It won't be so easy, since Drew was stupid enough to film the whole thing. And, don't forget that a police detective also witnessed at least part of the attack. We'll need to get you photographed as evidence of your injuries. Did you get hit anywhere else?"

I shook my head. "No." Even if I had, I wouldn't tell her. I didn't want to risk anybody seeing the bandage on my side, even though my friends had been crazy enough to cut themselves too. If anyone looked too closely, they might see that my wound was the real thing.

"Okay. Call your mom."

Mom met us at the hospital. She took one look at my face and all the color ran from hers. Tears filled her eyes as she came toward me. I let her hug me, making sure her arms wrapped around my shoulders so she didn't hurt my injured side. For all I knew, the wound had opened up again. At least there was no blood on my shirt from that. Yet. There was plenty of blood from my nose.

"Oh my God," Mom whispered. "What did they do to you?"

"I'm okay," I told her. "I think my nose is broken, but that's it."

"Are you sure?" she asked, stepping back to look me in the eye. I knew what she was worried about.

"Yeah, I'm sure. I'm okay, believe me."

My mother's expression hardened as she turned to Detective Davies. "Please tell me you arrested the bastards."

Diane nodded. "They're in police custody. Brody and Jason are only seventeen, so they may be charged as juveniles, but the other two are eighteen, and I promise you I will do everything I can to make sure they are charged accordingly."

I believed her. I looked at Mom. "When I saw them coming at me, I called Detective Davies. She rescued me."

"Thank you," my mother told her. "Thank you for being there when my daughter needed you."

Diane nodded. "I made sure all of the girls in our class have my personal number."

"Why did this happen?" Mom asked. I knew she was going to ask, but I still dreaded having to answer her. I didn't want to lie, but there was no way I could tell the complete truth.

As it was, I didn't have to say anything. The detective said it for me. "The four of them accused Hadley of being the Pink Vigilante."

My mother laughed. "That's impossible. You don't believe them, do you?" She actually looked convincing. I would have believed her if I hadn't told her myself.

The cop smiled slightly. "When I arrived at the graveyard, I saw a girl in a pink ski mask running away." It wasn't a yes, but it wasn't a no, either. It was a careful response.

I smiled—the painkillers the doctor had given me were starting to kick in. "I had two rescuers," I said. "Better than what Magda got."

The two of them exchanged a glance. "I'd better get you home," Mom said. "Detective Davies, is it okay if I take her?"

Diane nodded. When had I started thinking of her as "Diane" rather than "Detective"? Just today—when she proved she was someone I could depend on. "I've taken her statement, photographed her injuries and the doctor has looked at her. I don't see any reason why you can't take her home. If I have any other questions, is it all right if I come by?"

My mother nodded. "Of course. If you could give me a little notice, I can make sure that I'm home and that Hadley is awake. I plan to let her sleep as much as possible the next few days."

"I have school tomorrow," I reminded her. My head was starting to spin a little.

"No," she informed me. "You don't. And you won't have school until I'm certain you're healed enough to attend. And until I'm certain that those boys are not a threat to your safety. I will be paying a visit to your principal tomorrow."

Diane handed my mother one of her business cards. I was

going to have a collection of the damn things. "If you don't mind letting me know when you're going to the school, I would like to meet you there. The principal might take this a bit more seriously if you have police backup."

Mom put the card in her purse. "I will. Thank you." Then she turned to me. "Can you walk, sweetie? Or do you want a wheelchair?"

I was sore and fuzzy. I just wanted to go to bed and wake up in a world where none of this had happened, and Magda was still alive. "A ride would be nice."

Diane found us an orderly who said he would get me a wheelchair. Of course we had to wait what felt like hours for him to return with one, but then he took me straight down to the exit and waited with me while Mom went to get the car.

"What happened?" he asked. "Did you bang into something?"

I glanced up at him—both of him. "Yeah," I slurred. "A fist."

I think he looked horrified. It was hard to tell when his face kept shifting, blurring in and out of focus. He didn't speak again until my mother thanked him for bringing me out to the car.

I slumped into the passenger seat of Mom's car. I was asleep before we even made it out of the parking lot.

God, drugs were *awesome*.

"Oh my God, are you okay?" Zoe's eyes were huge as she looked down at me.

It was Sunday evening. I'd slept until dinnertime, and was now sitting on the sofa covered in a fuzzy blanket and drinking a cup of tea Mom had made. She came from old English stock who believed that tea could fix just about anything.

"Sit down. It hurts to look up."

She sat on the other end of the couch. "They broke your nose?"

I nodded as I lifted my teacup to my mouth. The steam from the tea was apparently good for the fracture. Something about blood boogers, or something equally disgusting.

"They would've broken more than that if you hadn't come along." I reached over and clumsily patted her hand with mine. Shit, these pills were powerful. "Thank you."

She smiled a little. "I have to admit I was almost a little bummed that Detective Davies came when she did. I was hoping to at least land a couple of punches to Drew's face."

"Yes," I said, "but our fabulous detective—and the Rape Squad—saw the Pink Vigilante come to my rescue. I saw the look on Drew's face when he saw you. God, it was fucking perfect. He's not so sure the PV is me anymore. I owe you for that."

Her eyes widened. "Is that why they came after you?"

I nodded. "Drew's smarter than I gave him credit for. To be honest, I can't believe more people didn't figure me out before this. I was being stupid taking chances."

"Are you going to go after Drew?"

I thought about it. Maybe it was the pills again, but I shrugged. "Diane thinks he might actually do jail time. I figure we'll be lucky if he gets a slap on the wrist and probation. At least he's facing some kind of consequences."

Zoe looked at me. "That's it?"

"Dude, I'm stoned out of my head, my nose is broken, and I'm aware of just how fucking lucky I am that's all the damage they did. Do you know how many times I've been hit in the last month? Adam stabbed me. Yeah, that's it for now."

"I'm sorry." She leaned her elbow on the back of the couch. "It's just that you're a symbol for the rest of us."

"I didn't ask for that. All I wanted was justice for my friend."

"I know you didn't ask, but you got it all the same. You're a hero, Had."

Invisible weights tugged at my eyelids. "No, I'm not. I'm a mess, Zoe. An angry, violent mess. When I started this, it was an accident. I found Jason passed out and took advantage of the situation. I didn't care what happened to me, but then I met someone who made me start to feel like a person again."

She smiled. "Gabe."

I met her gaze, forcing my eyes to focus on hers. "I already knew Gabe. I meant you."

Her smile drooped as her eyes went round. "Me?"

I nodded, wincing as the movement made my nose throb. "Magda was my only friend for years. When she left me, I felt so alone. God, I hated her for that. Then, you and Caitlin and Anna walked into class. You kept my secret, and you covered for me. You put yourself at risk for me. You're my best friend, Zoe."

She looked like she was going to cry. If it weren't for the drugs, I might get my bawl on too. "This is the point where you tell me how much you love me," I joked.

Zoe laughed—crisis averted. "You *are* stoned."

I smiled. My lips were like rubber. "Told you."

She chattered on for the next half hour, telling me that Anna and Jenny had gone to the movies earlier. Apparently Jenny texted Anna after the pit party to ask her out.

"Jenny seemed nice. Do you like her?"

"Sure. As long as she's good to her I don't care." An impish gleam lit her eyes. "Speaking of *good*, how's Gabe?"

My eyes flew open. "Oh, *shit!*"

She looked scared. "What? Are you okay? Is it your nose? Should I get your mom?"

"No, my nose is fine." As fine as it could be. "Gabe doesn't know. I haven't talked to him since this morning."

"He won't be mad at you, will he?"

"It's not me I'm worried about. He's going to lose it when he finds out Drew broke my nose..."

Zoe went pale. "Give me your phone. I'll text him and ask him to come over. You don't want him to hear it from someone else."

It was at that exact moment that my mother came into the room. She looked concerned. "Hadley, sweetie, there's someone to see you."

Gabe walked into the room behind her. He looked ready to kill someone. I glanced at Zoe.

"Too late."

CHAPTER 23

Mom had to work on Monday, so Gabe came over to stay with me.

"I don't need to be babysat," I said. I was glad to see him, but it pissed me off that everyone seemed to think I needed to be looked after.

"I know you don't," he replied, bending down to kiss me. "I'm here so I won't go beat the shit out of Drew."

Ah. "Nice to know where I rank in your priorities."

He sat on the couch beside me and took my hand in his. "You're number one, or I wouldn't be here. Now, come here and give me a hug."

I did what he said, because I really needed a hug. "How can you stand to even be in the same room with me? I'm ugly and a bitch."

He laughed. "I think you're beautiful, and I've seen you in a bad mood before."

I lifted my head from his shoulder. "You think I'm beautiful?" God, my voice sounded so deep and nasal.

Gabe smiled. Speaking of beautiful…it was no wonder his mother named him after an angel. "Yeah, I do." Then his smile faded, replaced by something darker. "If Drew Carson doesn't go to jail for this, I'm going to kill him."

A shiver ran down my spine. "Don't say that. Your mother and Teresa need you too much. I need you too much. We can't lose Magda *and* you."

"I feel so useless. Powerless. I hate it."

"I know."

We fell silent. Gabe turned on the TV, and we watched part of an eighties horror movie marathon on one of the movie channels. It was only three weeks till Halloween—one of my favorite times of year. Magda and I used to plan our costumes together. This would be my first year without her. Gabe's too. The three of us always took Teresa out trick or treating before going on to whatever else we had planned for the evening.

"Are we taking Teresa out this year?" I asked, glancing up.

"Yeah," Gabe replied. His gaze was warm as it met mine. "If you want."

I nodded. "I do."

"That will mean a lot to Reesy. And me." He kissed me then. I would have let him kiss me forever if breathing weren't an issue. The swelling in my nose didn't prevent me from breathing, but it felt like I had a cold.

"Is that it?" I asked teasingly when he lifted his head. I was breathing fast, and not just because of my nose. We were totally alone in the house. We could do whatever we wanted…

"Yes," he replied. "For now. I wouldn't feel right, taking advantage of you while you're on painkillers and hurt."

I arched a brow. "Seriously?"

He laughed. My expression must have been hilarious. "Seriously."

Fabulous. My shoulders slumped. "Yeah, I guess it's hard to find this—" I gestured to my face "—sexy."

"Hey." He lifted my chin with his finger. "You're sexy as hell, and trust me—I want you. I just don't want to hurt you, so we're going to wait."

God, he was so *good.* "Okay."

He grinned and kissed me again. Then he asked, "Is Zoe getting your homework?"

"No, I think the office is keeping it for me. Mom was going to pick it up on her way home."

He looked at his watch. "Feel like going to the school?"

I frowned. "Why?"

His eyes darkened to the edge of blackness. "I want everyone to see what he did to you. They won't think he's so awesome when they see your face."

He was right. I'd been so caught up in how much my broken nose affected me that I hadn't thought what it would do for Drew's reputation. If he'd successfully outed me as PV, people wouldn't be half as sympathetic, but my secret identity was still protected, and the bruising did look pretty ugly.

"Let's go," I said, tossing my blanket aside.

"You might want to change," he suggested, gesturing to my pajamas.

I blushed. "You're right."

"Do you need help?"

Tempting. "I thought you didn't want to take my clothes off."

He shrugged. "I'm only human."

I laughed, but inside me a little thrill blossomed. I knew, despite his protests, that if we went to my room we'd never make it to school. There would be time to make out later, but this was probably the worst my nose was going to look, and doing damage to Drew's reputation was more important at that moment than my hormones.

A few minutes later, my hair and teeth brushed, I came downstairs in jeans and a pink lightweight sweater. When I looked at myself in the mirror, I'd been so tempted to at least try to cover some of the bruising with makeup, but there wasn't enough concealer in the world to do the job.

Gabe smiled when he saw me. "I picked out that sweater."

His mother had given it to me for Christmas last year. "Why didn't you tell me it was from you?"

He shrugged. "You were my little sister's best friend, and I didn't know if you liked me the same way I was starting to like you."

You know that thing, where people talk about their insides turning to mush? Getting all melty? That's how I felt at that moment. "It's my favorite sweater."

He looked pleased. "Get a coat. It's cold out."

Once we got to the school, we waited a few minutes in the parking lot before going inside. We timed it so that we would be walking through the hall when classes changed. It was the best way to make sure as many people saw me as possible. This was the one time when I *wanted* to be gossiped about.

We walked through the doors at the opposite end of the school from the office—again to ensure maximum visibility. I wasn't disappointed; the moment the bell rang and the hall began to fill up, I felt the weight of countless curious stares. As I walked, staring straight ahead, Gabe's hand clasped in mine, I heard horrified gasps and whispers. And I don't know how many times I heard someone say, "Oh my God."

We ran into Anna and Caitlin outside the classroom. I stopped long enough to give them both a hug and talk for a few minutes. They hadn't seen me since Saturday night. Poor Anna cried when she saw me. She had such a sweet heart.

And a vicious temper. "I'd like to bash his head in with a brick," she announced.

Gabe gave her a grim smile. "The line starts here."

"Mom's making me stay home a few days," I told them. "I'd love some company if you want to drop by someday after school."

They both promised they would, and after another hug they went on to the next class. Gabe and I continued to the office. By the time I got there, I felt like Lady Godiva sitting naked on her horse—vulnerable, exposed and strangely defiant.

The office administrator looked up as we approached the desk. "Oh, my goodness."

I attempted a smile. "Hi, Mrs. Kent." I wanted to tell her that it looked worse than it felt, but frankly that would be a lie. And the fact that it did look so awful made Drew come off just as bad. "I think you probably have some homework for me?"

The older woman got up from her desk. "Yes, I do. A couple of your teachers haven't handed anything in yet, so you may want to come by again tomorrow, but your morning classes have provided homework as well as a brief syllabus for the rest of the week, just in case." She approached the counter with a thick file folder and handed it to me.

"Did that Carson boy really do this to you?" she asked, her

voice low. It probably wasn't considered proper for the staff to discuss students.

"Yes. It was Drew." By the end of day, I suspected every teacher in the school would know that I'd confirmed the rumor.

Mrs. Kent was a nice woman, and she had this round face that always seemed kind and gentle. At that moment she didn't look kind, and she certainly didn't look gentle. "Monster."

I just smiled. "Thanks. I'll come by again tomorrow for the rest."

I needed to stop by my locker to pick up some textbooks, so this time we walked through the upstairs hall as students hurried to their next class. More stares. More whispers. Every step seemed to vibrate from my feet, up my legs and torso right to my nose until it throbbed with a dull ache. I was tired, and as satisfying as it was to let everyone see what Drew had done to me, I just wanted to go home.

We got to my locker. I opened it, and Gabe made me pass him each book that I would need. I could carry my own books, but I wasn't going to argue with him.

He was looking down the hall when I closed the locker door. "What?" I asked.

He nodded down the line of lockers. "Look."

I turned my head just as he took my hand and led me down the hall. Drew's locker wasn't far from mine on the opposite wall. I stopped dead when I saw it.

The principal had either gotten lax in her crackdown on vandalism, or what we were looking at had all been done this morning. The entire front of the locker was covered in marker, paint, stickers, pictures and paper.

I squeezed Gabe's hand when I saw the photo of Magda. It

was her yearbook photo from last year, the one they used at her memorial. Someone had drawn a big pink heart around her face and wrote "You killed her" underneath it. *Rapist* was the word written most often on the metal. *Monster* was the second. Someone had stuck on a printout of Faceless's article. The entire locker door was one huge collage of just how vile Drew Carson really was. If Drew ever returned to the school, he would find that his status had taken a dramatic fall.

I smiled.

"You're fucking kidding me." That was what I said when Diane came by to tell me that not only was Drew out on bail, but that he claimed he hit me because he believed himself to be in danger from me. He thought that I was the Pink Vigilante, and now that he knew the error of his actions, he was "deeply sorry" for breaking my nose.

My mother didn't even comment on my language. She looked at the detective with a determined expression. "What can we do to keep that boy away from Hadley?"

Diane looked pissed too. We were all pissed. Gabe was going to lose it when I told him. God, if he didn't beat the crap out of Drew, I'd be surprised. Hell, if *I* didn't beat the hell out of Drew it would be a surprise. "I don't believe Drew means Hadley any harm now that he knows she's not the Vigilante."

Maybe I wasn't in danger, but Drew was. I shouldn't be surprised that he had gotten away with it. Sure, he might go to court, but he wasn't going away. His father owned half this town, and had more than enough clout and money to make sure his precious little boy stayed out of jail. I should have known that if his family lawyer could get him out of rape charges, she could get Drew out of an assault case.

"I want an apology," I blurted.

Both women looked at me like I'd started speaking Chinese.

"From Drew," I clarified. "I don't care if he was terrified of big bad me, he broke my damn nose, and I don't want him to tell the court he's sorry, I want him to tell *me* he's sorry for it."

Diane nodded. "I'll see what I can do."

"A public apology." Call me twisted, but I wanted witnesses when he had to admit that he'd done something wrong. It wasn't enough, but it was a start.

She held my gaze—maybe to see if I was joking. "Okay."

"I can't believe this." Mom shook her head. "He hits my daughter and gets away with it. His father was a bully too, you know. Quite a few girls in our senior class said he'd raped them, but nothing ever came of it. The Carsons are a long line of entitled assholes."

"Language," I admonished with a faint smile. "It's all right, Mom. Drew will get what's coming to him."

"How do you know that?" Diane asked, a strange expression on her face.

I looked her in the eye. I couldn't tell her it was because I intended to make sure of it. "The whole school saw what he did to me."

"Mr. Carson has hired security for his son."

Thanks for the tip. "They have to leave him alone sometime."

"And then what?" she asked. There was a sharpness to her gaze that reminded me she was a cop first and my friend second. I shrugged.

And then I'll be ready.

CHAPTER 24

I wanted to go back to school on Thursday, but Mom wouldn't let me. I think she knew I only wanted to go so I could confront Drew, because she did let me go to Diane's class that night.

The swelling in my nose had decreased dramatically, and it was pretty much back to its normal size. I still looked like a raccoon with darkness under both eyes, but the bruising had started to fade, as well. It still hurt some, but was healing, and now that I could breathe normally I wanted my life back.

When I walked into the dojo that night, every girl there cheered at the sight of me. It was awesome. They hugged me and asked about what happened, and if the Pink Vigilante actually came to my rescue. I had to force myself not to smile at Zoe, or even make eye contact.

Apparently Drew had been looking for me earlier that day so he could make his apology. I guess he really wanted to make sure he had an audience, which was weird, because I couldn't imagine him wanting anybody to witness him saying he was sorry for something.

Then again, I guess it was just like when celebrities apologized for doing something stupid, or saying something wrong. They never seemed to mean it—it was just damage control.

After all the girls said hi, Diane approached me. She smiled. "It's good to have you back, but don't think for one minute that I'm letting you spar tonight."

"Yeah, I know." I hadn't been allowed to do anything strenuous since the weekend, and I was starting to feel restless and antsy from lack of exercise. "Maybe I could work with the Wavemaster?"

She considered it. "Sure. Just take it easy."

I nodded. So, no pretending the poor punching bag was Drew.

We were sitting on the mats, listening to Diane speak when the dojo door opened, the bell tingling. We all turned our heads, and a collective "oh" echoed throughout the room.

I stood and everyone else followed me. Drew smiled, but it looked more like a smirk than anything actually friendly. He was on our territory. Invading a space that was close to sacred for all of us.

"Sorry to interrupt, girls," he drawled. My spine stiffened at the mockery in his tone. He looked right at me, and his smile grew. He'd liked seeing what he'd done to me, the asshole.

"What do you want, Mr. Carson?" Diane asked, stepping forward.

Drew's smile wavered a little when he met her gaze. He was intimidated by her, a fact that made me like her all the more. What must it be like to be that confident in your ability to take down a full-grown man? She didn't even have her gun with her, and yet she saw Drew as absolutely no threat. She knew what kind of monster he was, and still he didn't scare her.

He glanced at me. "I went to Hadley's house, but there was no one home. Then I remembered that you girls had this little class every Thursday night. I saw one of the flyers at school."

"Why were you at my house?" I asked. I didn't like the idea of him knocking on my door. I'm just glad that Mom hadn't been home. She would've told him off, and God knows what he might have done in return.

"To apologize, of course." He almost looked sincere, except for the malicious glint in his eye. "Hadley, I just want you to know how much I regret what happened at the cemetery on Sunday. I was wrong to hit you. I have no excuse, except that this Vigilante person has been harassing me and my friends for over a month now. I was paranoid, and I let myself believe that it was you who threatened us. I'm very sorry I hurt you, and I hope you'll forgive me for it."

He was sorry for getting caught, but he wasn't really sorry he'd punched me. I don't think he was capable of the same kind of regret mentally healthy people experienced. In fact, I was pretty sure that Drew had never been sorry for anything in his life. I'd known for a while that he was a psychopath, but realizing this while looking into his eyes was something else. There was nothing redeeming in his gaze, no hint of humanity. He wasn't capable of contrition, and he thought he was better at faking it than he was.

I held his gaze—stared right into those dead eyes of his. "I understand that you were afraid of me, and that's why you lashed out. I didn't mean to intimidate you." His face tightened a little as I verbally poked at him. "Of course you would sus-pect me of being the person frightening you and your friends after what you did to Magda."

He sneered at her name. "She wanted it. All I did was give it to her."

Fists clenched at my sides I took a step toward him. The only thing that stopped me was the fact that every girl in that class took that step with me, backing me up.

It was amazing to see the realization that he was out-numbered in that asshole's face, and that no one in the room was afraid of him.

"Why," I asked, "would you think that any girl would want a slimy douche like you touching her? You can take your apology and shove it up your ass."

Drew's face hardened, his eyes like cold stone. "My lawyer said you wanted an apology."

"I guess I did. I wanted it and you gave it to me." I shoved his words back into his face. "I'm sorry, Drew, but you're just not that good at it."

The girls laughed, and for a second Drew let slip the mon-ster he really was.

"I should have broken your fucking jaw." He took a step to-ward me, and that was when Diane intervened.

"Your father already had to bail you out once this week, Mr. Carson. Do you want me to take you downtown so he can do it again?"

Drew's upper lip curled into a sneer. He barely looked at her, all of his attention was on me. "Maybe you're not the bitch in the ski mask, but one of you is." His gaze traveled across the girls behind me. "Come for me again, and I'll make sure you're reunited with your precious slut, Magda."

Fuck my nose and fuck taking it easy. I pulled my fist back, but just as I was about to knock several teeth down his throat, Diane grabbed my arm.

Drew smirked at me, and I kicked myself for letting him bait me.

"You need to leave," Diane told him. "Or I will arrest you for making death threats."

"It wasn't a threat," he said, backing toward the door. "It was a promise." Then he turned and walked to the exit. "Oh, and Hadley? Tell your boyfriend that includes him too." He opened the door and was gone.

"That's it," Diane seethed. "I'm going to arrest him again." She took a step toward the door.

"Don't," I said. "His father won't miss the bail money, and the charges won't stick. Why put yourself through the hassle?"

She stared at me. "To show him that he can't go around threatening to kill people?"

She wasn't that naive, was she? "Haven't you been paying attention? He does whatever he wants."

Her jaw clenched. "It's time someone put an end to that."

"Yeah," I agreed, staring at the door. "It is."

I went back to school on Friday. When I walked past Drew's locker, I noticed that it was freshly painted without so much as a scuff on it. He still walked around like he owned the place, with Brody, Jason and Adam at his side. Though, it did seem like things weren't as perfect as they had been. Drew's buddies looked at him with resentment. He was the only one of them the Vigilante hadn't cornered yet.

I also noticed, as the days went on, that the crowd that normally gathered around Drew in the cafeteria, or outside, had grown smaller, so I was surprised when he announced that he was having a Halloween party, and that it was open to anyone who wanted to come. It was just like last year.

Last year. That had been the party where they raped Magda. After the attack she'd done all the right things. It didn't matter, though. She'd gone to the police, and they'd conducted an investigation that turned up nothing, despite photos and video showing up online. Drew told everybody Magda had wanted to party with them.

The sad part was that some of what he said was true. Magda'd had a crush on him—obviously we had no idea of his true character back then. She jumped at the chance to hang out with him. Maybe she thought they were going to make out. She might have even hoped for sex, but she had not wanted his buddies to join in.

Afterward she tried to put on a brave face. She tried to ignore the things people said, and did to her. She knew she hadn't done anything wrong. She went to therapy, and she did the work. She wanted to be whole again. She wanted to be okay, but almost every day Drew, or somebody else, did something to humiliate her. Eventually, it just became too much. She had survived for months—to the point where I thought she was actually getting better. I was wrong—she was only getting better at hiding how bad things really were.

There hadn't been any warning. People always say that there were warning signs before someone committed suicide, but that's not always true. Believe me, I tried to find them. I went back over the weeks and months looking for any clue. I tortured myself with it, thinking I had somehow missed the signs that I hadn't been a good enough friend. I hadn't been a good enough friend at times. Sometimes I was an awful friend, but lately…well, I was beginning to realize Magda hadn't killed herself over something I said. I didn't have that kind of power, and it wasn't all about me. I'd made what happened to her about me—me not being there for her, me not being a good friend, me, me, me.

And this revenge thing? That wasn't all for Magda. It was for me too. For both of us—and all the girls who had been abused before, and those whose abuse I might be able to prevent. Maybe I had some kind of hero or martyr complex. I was okay with it.

I was going to go to Drew's party. Pretty much every girl from self-defense class was going to go. Gabe tried to talk me out of it, but only because he'd violated the restraining order Drew had against him by punching him at the dance, and if he showed up at the party he would be in big trouble.

"You're going to get yourself killed," he said, raking a hand through his long hair. "He said he wanted to kill the Pink Vigilante, and you're basically going to go there and offer yourself up."

"I know it sounds insane. If I were you, I would think I was totally nuts. But you weren't there at the class that night he showed up. The things he said about Magda…"

Mentioning his sister was not a good idea. Gabe's face hardened, and his eyes took on an angry glint. "I should be the one to go after him. Am I supposed to just sit back and let you be the one to avenge my sister?"

My eyes widened. "I'm not trying to take anything away from you."

"No? Because so far you've been taking revenge that ought to have been mine. I should be the one to give them payback."

"Gabe, Drew's father would make sure you were tried as an adult and sent to prison for a long time. Your mom and Teresa can't lose you. We've been through this before." Several times, it felt like.

He nodded, his gaze averted. "I know. I don't fucking like it, but I know. I just...I just wish I could've done more for her. I didn't even see how depressed she was."

"Neither did I, and I saw her every day." Well, not quite every day. Toward the end—just before she killed herself—she started to spend more time alone. She told me she was studying, but now I realize she was just putting distance between us so doing what she thought she had to do would be easier for her. And maybe for me.

"Is any of this actually making you feel better?" he asked.

"Yes." And it was true—to an extent. At least I felt like I was able to *do* something. I understood Gabe's frustration and how helpless he felt. He'd gotten into fights with all four of the guys after the attack. He'd done his part for Magda then. And he had done everything he could to make those bastards pay. He fought them. He went to court and testified. He spoke out to the news outlets, and on TV. Even when Drew's lawyer threatened him with harassment, he still tried to get justice. It hadn't worked. It took a pink ski mask and video to make people wake up. It was because a girl was behind it that people noticed. By definition we were weaker. Usually girls were the victims of such degradation, or guys did it to other guys. Occasionally girls did it to other girls, but hardly ever did girls do it to guys. I'd broken some kind of unspoken rule, and that's what got me noticed. That's what got Faceless involved. I was supposed to be the weak one, and so far my record was three for three.

What was I going to do to Drew? No idea. Oh, I'd had all kinds of fantasies about what I'd like to do, but nothing that struck me as perfect. Hopefully it wouldn't involve him punching me in the face, because a couple weeks had passed since he broke my nose and it was pretty much healed. I really didn't care to get it broken again. He would probably get drunk—he usually did. That would make it easier.

I tried not to think about the fact that regardless of what I did to him, it probably wouldn't make a difference. I was never going to make him sorry, not really. I could humiliate him, get some payback, but no matter what I did he would never be sorry for what he'd done to my friend. He wasn't capable of it.

Maybe that was why I didn't know what to do to him. You couldn't make somebody who was incapable of feeling, feel sorry for anything.

I agreed to call Gabe if anything happened. He insisted on parking not far from Drew's house so that he would be close. I was going to the party with Zoe, Anna and Caitlin and their boyfriends. I had backup. The three girls—especially Zoe—had learned a lot in class. All of the girls had.

My costume was simple—I was Harley Quinn. I'd considered going as the Pink Vigilante, but that might be seen as me baiting Drew, and I didn't want to invite more trouble than

I had to. The costume was snug, and revealed a little more skin than I liked, but it was extremely flexible. So, if I had to fight, my movements wouldn't be restricted. It wasn't like my costume was the skimpiest one there, either. There was a naughty nurse at the party, along with a slave Princess Leia and a sexy policewoman. There were other superheroes too. Zoe was Catwoman, and Anna was Black Widow. Caitlin was a vampire, but she was wearing leggings and sturdy boots. We looked pretty kick-ass.

The problem with wearing snug clothing was that some guys took it as an invitation. Now, if a guy walked in dressed like Captain America, and he looked good in the suit, I would stare at him. I'm pretty sure I would admire his muscles and other...attributes. I couldn't blame teenage guys for looking at my chest. However, I didn't feel the least bit bad about jabbing hard in the throat the one who actually tried to touch me.

Zoe stood beside me, drinking water from a bottle she brought herself. The four of us had made an agreement not to drink anything that was given to us. That was how Drew had gotten Magda. Soda that was still in the can was okay, and I helped myself to a Diet Coke. Thank God for the pop top—it was pretty much tamper proof.

"Ugh," Zoe said. "He's dressed like a gangster."

I followed her gaze. There, surrounded by a crowd, was Drew. He wore a pinstriped suit and a fedora, and had a cigar clenched between his teeth. Obviously he'd gotten some of his fans back, because the crowd around him was bigger than it had been lately.

At that moment Drew looked up, his gaze meeting mine. He smirked. I smirked back. The expression on his face was almost comical. He hadn't expected that. Then I looked to his left and laughed. He turned his head, and I laughed a little harder.

Two guys—and I could tell they were guys because the skin below the hem of their crop tops had hair on it—stood not far from Drew. They were dressed in drag—bad drag—but that wasn't what made me laugh. It was the pink ski masks they wore beneath their Halloween-store wigs that made me incredibly happy. I pulled out my camera and took a picture just as Drew shoved one of them, his face flushed with rage.

Everyone laughed at the guys—well, almost everyone. People were still laughing when Drew and his friends forcibly kicked them out. One grabbed at the door frame as they lifted him off his feet. His wig was only half-perched on his head as he shouted, "No man is a match for the Pink Vigilante!" Then his wig fell to the floor. Brody picked it up and threw it out the door.

"Oh my God!" Zoe grabbed my arm. She was laughing so hard, tears threatened to ruin her makeup. "That was awesome."

"It was," I agreed with a grin.

Caitlin and Anna ran up to us. "What the hell was that?" Caitlin asked, laughing.

"I think it was Corey Smart and Andrew Lawson," Anna informed us.

"They're probably going to get the snot kicked out of them later," I said, my smile fading.

Paul put his arm around Zoe's shoulders. "Anybody messes with them, they're messing with the rest of us."

Zoe smiled up at him. They were nuts about each other. God, I wished Gabe had been there to see Corey and Andrew.

I sent him one of the photos I'd taken. Thought you might get a laugh out of this.

A few seconds later he replied, LOL. Just saw them walking down the street. How's it going?

All right. I'm going to stay till midnight. Want to pick me up?

Just call.

I slipped my phone back into my bag—no pockets on a Harley Quinn costume. If I hadn't gotten the chance to get to Drew by midnight, I'd just leave. It wasn't like I was in the party mood—not really. I just kept thinking about the year before, and Magda.

I could almost see her, standing there in her Cleopatra costume. She'd looked awesome. "Do you think Drew will like it?" she had asked me.

"He'd be dead not to," I'd replied. God, I'd been so indifferent about him then. I seriously hadn't thought he was a threat to her, even though we'd both heard rumors about him over the years. Magda assumed it was gossip and nothing more.

Were any of the girls there previous victims of his? Had they come just so they could stand up to him—face him unafraid? Did they wonder if anyone would ever stop him? Did they wish they'd reached out to Magda?

I shook my head. If I kept thinking about it, I'd get even angrier than I already was, and then I'd pick a fight with him, and that wouldn't do anything but get me slapped with a restraining order too. No, I'd stay till midnight, and then I'd leave. If I couldn't get payback for Magda, I'd rather spend the night with her brother, feeling loved rather than the hatred I felt for Drew.

Yeah, I was tired. Tired of all the violence and the fighting and the scheming and trying to keep from getting caught. And all the while, I kept wondering why I hadn't gotten caught. I'd been questioned and that was it. I wasn't a criminal mastermind, so what if the police were just waiting for me to make a move on Drew and then were going to arrest me?

At ten to midnight I decided to call it a night. I had just come out of the bathroom down the hall from the party, and was about to text Gabe to pick me up at the bottom of the driveway when I spotted Drew climbing the winding staircase. He had a girl with him—a very drunk, very young girl.

I had to stop it.

I put my phone back into my bag. I waited a few moments, trying to keep my heart rate calm. Then I made sure no one was looking and I followed them.

CHAPTER 25

Drew took the girl to his room. I could see them from where I crouched in the shadows near the top of the stairs. The girl staggered on her high heels, falling against him. He grinned down at her and ran his hand over her ass.

"I just need to lay down," the girl mumbled.

Drew steered her into the room. "Yeah, you'll be on your back real soon. Just a couple of minutes and you can sleep."

I wish I could say it was anger that filled my veins, but it wasn't—not completely. My heart hammered hard against my ribs, adrenaline pumping in my blood. I should have jumped him right then, but I couldn't make my legs move.

Mad as I was, I was afraid. Scared of Drew. He wasn't right in the head. I didn't know how he'd react when I came after him, but I believed that he meant to kill the Pink Vigilante if he could. He was the person who had planned everything he and his friends had done to Magda. I'd be stupid not to be at least a little apprehensive about going after him.

He closed the door behind them. I waited a couple of minutes to see if any of his friends were going to join him, but no one came. They might already be in the room. I could be walking into a trap. The four of them could be waiting for me. To kill me. That's if I was lucky. They might decide to have a little fun with me first.

I had no weapons except for my feet, fists and head. For all I knew, Drew could have a gun. What was I doing?

A girl cried out. My head jerked up, gaze snapping to that closed door. My fear evaporated, replaced with cold determination. Yes, Drew might have a gun. He might have a knife, or something else. He also had a drunk, and probably drugged, girl in that room with him who he planned to violate. He'd probably film or photograph her like he had Magda. Maybe he'd post the video for the whole world to see, as well.

Danger or not, there was no way I could just sit there, and I couldn't walk away. I rose to my feet, climbed the last few steps to the hallway and moved quietly to Drew's door. I hadn't planned this properly. I hadn't planned anything at all. Drew would know it was me for sure if I stormed in with my Harley costume on. Pulling the ski mask over her head wouldn't do anything, either. Really, what had I been thinking? I hadn't.

I looked at the door. I heard another soft cry from behind it. I was going to have to do this one without the mask. I had to save the girl from that bastard, and I was going to have to do it as myself.

I dug out my phone. If I could get photos of Drew attempting to rape the girl, it might help make charges stick. Video would be even better. I swiped and tapped the screen until the movie icon came up. I selected it and then slipped the phone into the belt of my costume, the lens pointing out.

I sucked a deep breath into my lungs, then reached out and turned the doorknob. He hadn't even bothered to lock it. I guess he figured anyone who dared walk in would want to join in his sick fun. I pushed...

The door opened. I expected it to be dark inside the room, but it wasn't. Of course it wasn't. Drew liked to be able to see what he did to his victims, and he needed good light to record his crime.

He was on the bed, shirtless and straddling the girl. He'd removed her top and bra, and was running his hands over her skin. He pinched her, laughing when she whimpered in protest.

"That's it, baby," he said. "I like when my girls make a little noise."

God, he was gross. There was a camera mounted on the headboard of his bed. How many girls had he recorded with or without their consent?

"'m gonnabesick." The girl tried to sit up, roll to the side of the bed. Drew grabbed her and shoved her back, his hand over her mouth.

"Swallow it," he commanded. "You fucking puke on my bed, you'll regret it. Swallow it, bitch."

The girl made a sobbing sound. Her body convulsed, but he kept his hand over her mouth. She was vomiting, and he wouldn't let her spit it out. He was going to choke her.

"Get off her."

Drew went still. Slowly, he turned his torso to face me. I watched his muscles shift beneath his skin, trying to gauge his physical strength beyond the ability to break a nose—anyone could do that. The girl broke free of his hold and wretched over the side of the bed onto the carpet.

"What the fuck?" Drew swore, grabbing the girl by the hair. "You're cleaning that up."

"No," I said. "She's not." I walked farther into the room.

Drew smirked at me. "Volunteering to take her place?"

I glared at him. "Are you high?"

"Maybe. Come on, Hadley, get on the bed. We can have a threesome."

"Let her go, Drew."

"No. I went through a lot of work to get her like this, and I plan to enjoy it."

"Not going to happen."

"Do I need to break more than your nose?" he asked, climbing off the girl—who had passed out with her head hanging over the side of the mattress—and the bed. He walked toward me, slowing removing his belt. I swallowed. I should have brought a weapon—my brass knuckles or something.

"What's she to you?" he asked.

I glanced at the girl. "I don't even know her."

"So you saw me with her and decided you'd come running to her rescue?"

"Something like that."

"What a Vagilante thing to do." He coiled the leather around his knuckles. "I was right, wasn't I? It is you."

I didn't know what other recording devices he might have in the room, so I couldn't afford honesty or even half-assed lies. "You saw her that day at the cemetery."

"That wasn't really her. You and that boyfriend of yours are the only ones who'd come after all four of us."

"I doubt we're the only two. How many other girls have you

raped, Drew? They must have people who love them, or want revenge all on their own."

He actually paused for a moment, as though thinking about it. How many girls had he hurt? "You bastard."

He swung at me, and I easily dodged it. "Not such a tough guy without your friends to hold me still," I taunted. "You can do better than that, can't you? I'm just a girl." And then, to insult him further, I punched him in the sternum.

"Bitch," he gasped, taking another swing. I wasn't fast enough this time, and his leather-wrapped fist connected hard with the side of my head.

I shook it off and kicked him in the knee. I thought it would take him to the floor. What I didn't anticipate was that he'd grab me and take me down with him.

I hit the floor on my back. Carpet softened the fall, but my head still bounced, messing up my vision for a second. I'd smashed my hip on the side of the bed on the way down. God, it hurt.

Drew was on top of me. He pinned my arms above my head. With strength and gravity on his side, I couldn't move. He pressed himself against me. He got off on overpowering me—the evidence was hard against my thigh. I swallowed the urge to puke.

"It was you I really wanted that night," he told me. "But your little friend was just so pathetic, batting her eyelashes at me."

I whipped my knee up, but he snapped his legs shut, angling himself across me so I couldn't slam him in the junk.

"Do that again," he warned, "and I'll head butt you in the nose."

I went still. My nose was barely healed, and I did not want it broken again.

"Good girl." He grinned. "So, here's how this is going to go. I'm going to fuck you, and if you're good, I'll let you live."

"And if I'm not good?"

Suddenly, there was a gun in my face. I hadn't even felt him reach for it. Where had it come from? I went completely still as Drew smirked at me. "You've really pissed me off these last couple of months."

"You're not going to shoot me. Even you can't get away with murder."

"I can if I tell them I took the gun from you when you barged in here and tried to kill me."

"If I was the Vigilante, no one would believe that I tried to shoot you. She only uses her fists and feet."

"But I broke your nose. And we both know I'm the one you really want. Aren't I?"

He made it sound sexual. It was sick. My stomach roiled as he ground his hips against me. Then, he came up on his knees, straddling me. "Take off your shirt."

"No."

He pointed the gun at me. "Do it."

Where there had been fear before, now there was only calm. My arms were free, and I used my left to shove his gun arm away, while I lunged up and punched him hard with my right fist. He didn't drop the gun, but he fell backward. I tried to crawl away, but he punched me in the kidney and then grabbed me by the hair, hauling me back. My eyes watered. I kicked at him, but he managed to avoid my feet. He punched me in the jaw and then higher up on my cheek. He punched me two more times before I got another jab in at him. His fingers ripped free of my hair. God, that hurt!

I got to my knees and lunged at the door. Drew grabbed the top of my costume. I heard the loud rip as the shoulder seam gave—he tore the sleeve so that it hung down my arm. Then he bounced my head off the door frame. Stars burst in the darkness before my eyes. He dragged me away from the door, slammed me down onto my back. He forced my mouth open, and something hit my teeth, forcing itself between. I tasted metal.

He'd put the gun in my mouth.

I froze. As my vision cleared, I found myself staring up into his glittering eyes. He grinned down at me.

Drew shoved his hand down the top of my costume, his cruel fingers biting into my flesh. He grabbed my breast and pinched it. He kept pinching—harder and harder—until I cried out. He laughed.

Then he shoved his hand down my pants. I was going to be sick when he tried to cram his fingers between my legs. "Open them," he commanded.

I did. Tears leaked from my eyes as he violated me. "Lick the gun," he commanded, easing the barrel out of my mouth. "Lick it like you want it."

I hated him. And that hate blossomed inside me like a mushroom cloud. I was not going to be another one of his victims. I ran my tongue along the barrel of the gun, staring into his eyes as I did so. I could tell he got off on it from the way his gaze changed. I knew the exact moment he stopped paying attention to what the rest of me was doing. His focus was just on my mouth. "That's it," he murmured. "Take it."

I moved fast, swiping the gun hand aside as my other fist

struck him in the balls. He fell to the side, and again, I lunged for the door. I almost made it before he threw himself on me.

"You fucking bitch!" he shouted. "I'm going to kill you!"

This time I was ready for him, and I managed to use his own momentum against him to put myself on top. I felt the gun pressed against my ribs. I wrapped my fingers around it, nails digging into his hand as I tried to wrestle it away. Our fingers tangled around the trigger as I pushed with all my strength.

The gun went off.

Drew stared up at me. I stared down at him. We were both perfectly still. Then, his hands fell away, leaving me holding the gun. Blood soaked the front of his shirt.

Drew was already dead by the time the police arrived.

I just sat there and watched the life leave his eyes. That's how Zoe, Anna and Caitlin—and everyone else who heard the shot—found me. I was sitting between his body and the bed, the unconscious girl's hand resting on my shoulder. Apparently I told Zoe to call Diane, but I didn't remember saying anything.

It was like a dream. Everything seemed fuzzy and far off, even though I could see it all happening around me. Diane got there just before the uniformed police did. She asked me what happened, and I told her. I even told her about Drew shoving his fingers inside me, and how he'd put the gun in my mouth. She hugged me.

"The girl," I said. "Is she okay? He drugged her."

Diane nodded. "She's gone to the hospital. She'll be fine. You saved her."

I looked into her concerned eyes. "He said he'd wanted me,

not Magda. I couldn't save her. The Vigilante couldn't save her." I looked down at my bloody hands. I needed to wash. Wash off his blood, wash off his touch.

Diane shushed me and wrapped a blanket around my shoulders.

When they led me out of the house, my friends were behind me. The party had been brought to a stop, and I felt the stares of dozens of my peers. They stared at me, their masks and makeup lending an absurd touch to their shocked stares. When I walked past a girl dressed as the Pink Vigilante, I took one look at her pink ski mask and burst into tears.

Gabe was outside. I didn't know who called him, but I ran to him the second I saw him. Diane came after me, but I didn't care. I threw myself into his arms. He held me tightly, his warmth fighting off the chill that seemed to have me right down to the bone.

"Can I come with her?" he asked.

Diane nodded. "I'm taking her to the hospital to get checked out."

My head was on his shoulder. "Did he hurt her?"

"I'm not sure," Diane replied. Gabe's arms tightened around me.

Next thing I knew I was in the backseat of Diane's car. Gabe held me all the way to the hospital, but they made him wait in another room at the hospital. They did a rape kit, even though I told them Drew hadn't raped me. I heard the doctor tell Diane that I had "abrasions that suggest sexual assault."

"It was just his fingers," I said, like it was nothing.

Diane looked like she wanted to cry.

"I'm okay," I told her. "I'm going to be okay."

She nodded. "I know you are. You're tough."

I held up my hands. "I just need to get him off me. *Now.*" Suddenly, I knew that if I didn't get clean at that moment, I never would. *"Now!"* I heard screaming echoing in my head. It was my own voice.

Something sharp poked my arm, followed by a rush of calm that sucked me out of my body, up into a corner of the ceiling. I felt light and free. Safe. My eyelids drooped, obliterating the offensive brightness of the hospital and shoving all the noise far, far away.

CHAPTER 26

"Did you go into that room planning to kill Drew Carson?"

"Are you the Pink Vigilante?"

"Did you attack Jason Bentley in his home?"

"Did you attack Brody Henry?"

"Did you physically assault Adam Weeks?"

No. No. No. No. No. I kept repeating the word—in my head and out loud. My mother was with me as the police questioned me, and so was our lawyer. I didn't even know we had a lawyer. Apparently my father did. The one thing I would remember my father doing for me was getting me a lawyer while the police tried to decide if I'd murdered Drew Carson, or it was self-defense. Or an accident.

I didn't care what they decided; I just wanted it over.

They got a warrant to search our house. I waited for them to find the ski mask in my room, but they didn't. The thing was, when I went looking for it later, I couldn't find it, either. It wasn't where I'd left it.

They talked about Drew's funeral on the news. They showed

his mother bowed over his casket, but her makeup stayed perfect. His father was as red-faced as usual. "My son was a good boy. He was an honors student, popular and well-liked. For him to have been taken from us so soon is a crime. I have faith that justice will be done."

I stared at the screen. That was almost exactly what Mrs. Torres had said about Magda. Now, here it was Drew who was gone, and I was the one with the video that made him look bad. I was the one lying to police. Someday, was someone going to come after me to avenge Drew?

I called Diane. Asked her to come over when my mother was at work. When she arrived, she hugged me. "What do you want to talk about?" she asked as she sat on the couch.

"I'm the Pink Vigilante," I told her. "Me."

She didn't look surprised. In fact, she looked like I'd just told her a stupid joke. "Are you?"

"Yes. It's me."

"So, you broke up a domestic dispute outside Hurley's bar last night?"

I stared at her. "No."

"Did you show up at a college party the night before and drive drunk girls home?"

"No."

She leaned forward, resting her forearms on the thighs of her jeans. "Since that night at Drew's, two other people have confessed to being the Pink Vigilante. One was a guy, and the other was someone you know."

Zoe, I was willing to bet. "You didn't believe them?"

"No, I believe them. I believe you, too. The thing is, Hadley, that the Vigilante is no longer one person. It's bigger than that."

"But I was the first. I started it."

"Can you prove it?"

"What?" This was too surreal. "That's your job, isn't it?"

She shrugged. "When this first started, I thought it was you, but I couldn't find anything but circumstantial evidence. The blood we found at the pit party was contaminated, so we couldn't get a DNA sample. That day at the cemetery, I saw someone else wearing a pink ski mask fleeing the scene as I arrived. Jason, Brody and Adam weren't able to identify you as the Vigilante—or anyone else for that matter. If you want to confess, go ahead, but at this point, unless you can back it up, you're just going to be another attention seeker."

Was she high? "You're joking."

"You don't even have a ski mask. At least the other people have had masks. We didn't find one when we searched the house."

"So what you're telling me is that you wouldn't arrest me even if I asked you to."

"Do you want me to arrest you?"

"I should pay for what I've done, shouldn't I?"

Her expression turned sympathetic. "Oh, honey. You don't need to be arrested for that. I look at you and it breaks my heart. I can't imagine what it was like for you in that room with Drew, or what it was like to watch him die. I know your mom is arranging for you to see a therapist, and I think that's a good idea. I hope your doctor will be able to help you come to terms with things."

"Come to terms?"

She nodded. "Two years ago, I shot and killed a man who had broken into his old house to kill his former girlfriend. It was a good shooting, but I still dream about it. It still keeps me up at night wondering if I did the right thing, thinking about the fact that I took a life that I truly don't believe was mine to take."

I swallowed. There was a lump in my throat that felt like my heart. "You mean I have to find a way to live with it."

"Can you?"

"Yes." It came out as a whisper. "I think I can."

Diane gave a sharp nod. "I think you can, too. I'm always here for you, if you want me. I hope you'll continue to help with the class."

I nodded. What was this feeling inside me? Confusion? I felt...lost. Like I didn't know which end was up. I'd just confessed and it meant nothing. No more than Drew's apology. No more than Magda's reputation.

"Good." She stood. "I wish I could stay, but I'm on duty and have to get back. Are you going to be okay here alone?"

I nodded. "Yeah." I had homework, and Gabe was coming by later.

She smiled and put her hand on my shoulder. "You're going to be okay, Hadley. I know it."

"Thanks."

"Just tell me your vigilante days are done."

I met her gaze. "You know they are." I'd already confessed, so more honesty didn't matter.

"Yeah," she said, her expression softening. "I guess they are. I'll see you later."

I rose to my feet and watched her leave, her shoulders

straight beneath her leather jacket. "Hey." She turned. "My mask. What happened to it?"

Diane's lips lifted on one side. "What mask?" And then she was gone.

"It feels like snow."

Gabe placed the flowers we'd brought with us at the base of Magda's headstone. "She loved snow." He straightened and put his arm around my shoulders. "Maybe we can take Teresa sledding."

I smiled. "I'd like that." We used to go all the time, the four of us. Me, Magda, Gabe and Teresa. It was the only part of winter I found even remotely enjoyable. We hadn't gone much the year before; Magda hadn't wanted to do it.

It was late November. Thanksgiving was tomorrow. My mom and I had been invited to dinner at the Torres house. It was our first holiday without my father, and the first Thanksgiving since Magda's death. It felt right that we should all spend it together.

I had a lot to be thankful for, I knew that. I just didn't completely believe it. I was alive. Drew hadn't raped me, hadn't killed me. He was gone, and would never hurt anyone ever again.

But I had killed him. I hadn't planned that, and for all my talk of revenge, I hadn't wanted to kill him, even if I'd wished him dead. I had to live with that. I understood what Diane had said to me a couple of weeks ago at my house. I think what made me feel the guiltiest was that I *could* live with having killed him. Sure, sometimes I dreamed about that night, and

I woke up sweating, my heart racing. But I always went back to sleep. It wasn't Drew's death that weighed on my soul.

It was Magda's.

My revenge hadn't brought her back. Hadn't changed anything that happened to her. The only thing that had been changed was me. I still mourned her, but the anger was gone. I almost missed it. Anger felt like purpose, but sadness…well, it was just sad.

Drew Carson's father had wanted to hang me for killing his kid, until the police found Drew's library of "conquests." He'd recorded himself raping five additional girls—all of whom had been too drugged to fight him. One of the girls was Zoe. She hadn't told anybody when it happened, but she told me after the video had been found. We talked a lot about what had happened to her, and Magda.

And me.

It was hard to talk because Zoe's mother didn't want her talking to me. We had to be sneaky. I hadn't seen Anna and Caitlin since Halloween. Their parents had completely forbidden them from coming near me. Apparently they'd pulled both of them from the self-defense class too. I sent them both emails to apologize, but they never responded.

I was also not welcome back at Carter. The school board decided that it would be "best" for me and the rest of the student body if I finished my year online rather than cause upset with my presence. I'd managed to keep my grades up, so I was still going to be able to go to college next year. Maybe I'd go away, where they didn't know who I was or what I'd done. Gabe and I talked about taking off together. I didn't know if it would ever happen, but it was nice to talk about. I was thinking about becoming a therapist. The one I'd been seeing—Dr. Anders—was good. She didn't make me feel like she judged me, and she told me she often worked with victims of assault.

I didn't kid myself that I wasn't one of them.

The law had decided that what I'd done was an accident. Drew's previous attack on me helped back that up. Plus, Drew had been obsessed with the Pink Vigilante and told several people he'd kill her if he ever found her. He'd recorded attacking me that night, and everyone who watched the video heard him accuse me of being the Vigilante. Everyone agreed that he had been a sexual predator and that I, as his last victim, would have been raped and quite possibly killed.

His *victim*. God, I hated thinking of myself that way, but Zoe had been right that day at school when she said that Drew and his friends hadn't needed to *physically* rape me. They'd still hurt me. So, people could call me a victim if they wanted. That didn't mean I had to think of myself as one—or act like one.

The self-defense class continued. We had to start a second one we had so many girls. I still helped Diane teach it. My mom wanted to learn too, so Diane started an adult course, as well. It kept me really busy, but I liked it. It gave me the social connection that had been taken away from me when the school kicked me to the curb.

I asked my mom about the ski mask. At first I thought she was going to deny it, then she told me she burned it in the kitchen sink and put it through the disposal. I cried, because I knew how much trouble she could get into because of me. How much trouble Diane, Gabe and Zoe could get into because of me. How much trouble girls who didn't even know me had risked to protect me—and protect other girls. It was humbling.

Gabe squeezed me close and kissed me. His lips were warm, despite the chill in the air. "Ready?" he asked. We had plans to go to a movie and then grab some Thai. I was staying over at his place that night—Mom and Mrs. Torres were okay with it. I think Mom was just glad I felt like being with a guy after all that had happened. Her dragging me to the doctor for birth control had been embarrassing, but I knew she trusted me to make the right decisions where my body was concerned.

"Almost," I said, giving him another peck. I stepped away so I could open my bag. I took out the brand-new pink ski mask that was folded up inside. I unfolded the mask and draped it over the top of Magda's headstone, like an offering. Or a goodbye.

There were still reports of the Pink Vigilante in the area, stepping in to help girls and women when needed, but it wasn't me anymore. I might have started something, but my part in it was finished. Diane had been right when she said it was bigger than me now. When I first put on that mask, I hadn't meant for it to stand for something, or for it to become a symbol. I just wanted to hide my face. I was fine letting other girls pick up the mantle and carry on. I didn't need the Pink Vigilante anymore, and if I wanted to help someone, I didn't need to use my fists.

"Now, I'm ready."

He smiled and held out his gloved hand. I placed my own in it, and we walked away. The sun peeked out from between the clouds, chasing some of the chill out of the day. Gabe and I had lives to live, and we were going to live them together for as long as we could. I was going to look forward from now on, not back. I didn't even glance over my shoulder at Magda's grave. She wasn't there, and nothing could bring her back. I had finally started to accept that.

She would be with me. And so, I realized, would Drew Carson. I was going to carry his memory with me for the rest of my life. I would have to live with the fact that I ended his life. Could I live with that?

Yeah. I could live with that.

* * * * *